# Forbidden Night

# Book Two of the Forbidden Trilogy

by

Joanne Lewis

Cover designed by Johnny Breeze

Cover art Copyright © iStockphotos:

iStock_000008168936_Large

iStock_000033889696_Large

iStock_000051920388_XXXLarge

Published by Soul Attitude Press, Pinellas Park, FL
https://www.soulattitudepress.com


Visit the author website: http://www.joannelewiswrites.com

ISBN: 978-1-939181-73-2 (eBook)

ISBN: 978-1-939181-75-6 (Paperback)

First Edition

For my mother
I love you more

# Michael's Paternal Family Tree

Dimitriy "Dedushka" Turgenev/Tucker    Gertrude "Gram" Pishkin
Grandfather                        Grandmother

Dedushka and Gram's child: Abram Tucker

Abram Tucker  (m)  Mariya Melikov
Father               Mother

# Sara and Soldier Boy's Paternal Family Tree

Jacob Krochmal    Amalie Krochmal    Ruby Friedman
Great Grandfather  Great Grandmother    Great Uncle

Jacob and Amalie's children: Siegfried, Renate, and Liana

Liana Krochmal  (m)  Wilhelm Goldstein nee Goldenstein
Grandmother                Grandfather

Liana and Wilhelm's child: Stephen Goldstein

Liana's child with unknown father: Claire Goldstein


Stephen Goldstein  (m)  Cassandra Carrara
Father               Mother

Claire Goldstein  (m)  Eddie Harpon
Aunt              Uncle

# Sara and Soldier Boy's Maternal Family Tree

Charles Carrara    Alfonso Carrera    Sophia Milano
Great Uncle        Grandfather      Grandmother

Alfonso and Sophia's child: Cassandra Carrara

Cassandra Carrara  (m)  Stephen Goldstein
Mother              Father

# CHAPTER ONE
## MICHAEL TUCKER

I REPRESENT INNOCENT people. Michael's Rule, I called it, an edict I thought would be simple to follow.

I'm dressed down from my usual monkey suit, instead wearing a pair of jeans, an Abercrombie and Fitch green polo, and the latest addition to my beloved sneaker collection, a pair of Givenchy high-top Tysons. I'm not wearing a suit and tie because as I enter Erica Stark's law office, I don't do so as a lawyer, but as the client.

Four years ago riding the Long Island Railroad into Manhattan I stumbled upon Sara Goldstein, the Long Island heiress accused of murdering her Uncle Charlie to get the family fortune. One look, and I believed she hadn't done it. Maybe it wasn't a signal from my brain, no one could deny her beauty. I agreed to represent her, a decision I wish I could say I regret today.

"Michael." Erica greeted me in the waiting room with a warm hug. "I'm surprised you called."

"I'm surprised you're willing to represent me." I tightened my grip on the thick folder squeezed between my fingers.

"I prosecuted Sara, you were her defense attorney, and now you want me to defend you against her, that's unusual."

Erica was my babysitter when I was growing up, yet as I followed her it was as if I walked into the principal's office.

The small, dark waiting room occupied by an empty desk led to a moderate-sized rectangular space. Her interior office appeared similar to what mine looked like when I first started in private practice five years earlier, a hand-me-down couch and two chairs angled around a scuffed coffee table set on a throw rug. She splurged on her desk, a handsome solid-oak table with ornate legs. She had no bookshelves, since lawyers no longer carried or kept statutes or tomes on evidence and civil procedure. Now all of that information was digested in smart phones and tablets. Bookbinding was out. Hyperlinks were in.

"Nice." I smirked at a rip in the cloth couch.

"Still a smart aleck?" She threw a scarf over the tear.

"At least your desk is new. I bought all of my furniture at the Salvation Army."

"You don't need to do that anymore."

She referred to the inheritance I received from Gertrude Tucker, my grandmother, and the uptick in my practice since I represented Sara. I didn't mind the ribbing but the thought of Gram brought a profound sadness. Two days before Sara's murder trial, Gram died. That was three years ago, not only had I lost my grandmother, but also my best friend, mentor, and idol.

I assessed Erica's suit, probably purchased off a sale rack at Macy's. "You look like a lawyer who's been in public service way too long."

"Lawyers who grow old in the D.A.'s office die in case filing." She sat in a chair across from the couch. "I was offered a job at the Statewide Prosecutor's office, but thought I'd see if I could hit it big like you. I figured if I could beat you in court as a prosecutor, maybe I'd make a decent living in the real world."

Erica had been an assistant district attorney for twelve years. One year after getting a conviction for murder one in People of New York vs. Sara Goldstein, and whipping my butt, she hung up her reputation as a legal do-gooder. She had been in private practice two years now and hoped to add another digit to her income.

I sat on the couch. "Feels odd."

"I had it cleaned."

"Not the couch. Being the client."

"You know the saying, a lawyer who represents himself has a fool for a client."

"I'm done playing the fool."

She folded one leg over the other. "I did research, asked some colleagues, and called the New York Bar. I'm comfortable there's no conflict for me to represent you."

"Great. You're hired."

"I accept." She laughed a girlish giggle that belied the toughness I knew festered within her. "I'm looking forward to going up against Glen Trautman."

"His son Trace is the lead attorney. Glen will do nothing and take all the credit."

"Makes sense. Trace is the head of litigation. Guy's a real jerk. I swear he coaches his clients to lie."

"He's going to be more of an asshole because of Sara's money. He'll file a ton of motions and build up billable hours. Make daddy proud."

She motioned toward the file. "Let me see it."

I looked down at my fingers, white from clutching the manila folder, reached across the coffee table, and handed it to her as if giving away my life savings. She rummaged through the documents, and I explained almost all of the events since Sara's conviction for murder. I left out how I still mourned the end of our romance. I also didn't tell Erica during my second and final visit to Rikers Island, I believed Sara confessed to what really happened the night Charlie was murdered.

A paperclip hit me in the cheek.

"Hey," I protested.

"Where'd you go?" Erica asked. "You were telling me about Sara's lawsuit against you, and you spaced out."

"Right. Sorry. Well, as you can see from the pleadings, she's not only claiming ineffective assistance of counsel as a way to overturn the guilty verdict and get a new trial, but she's also suing me personally."

Erica's ruby lips clamped straight. Blond hair fell around her green eyes. She was an attractive woman and my first crush, which hadn't waned when she confided in me on my sixteenth birthday she dated women. Erica and Tisha have been life partners since they were first years at Columbia Law, and recently married.

"Suing a lawyer personally is a novel approach." Erica read the complaint. "Respondent entered into a romantic relationship with Petitioner in violation of New York Bar Disciplinary Rule section one dash one-zero-two, sub-section seven, which forbids an attorney in a domestic relations case to begin a sexual relationship with a client during that representation." She looked up at me.

"I didn't represent her in a domestic relations case."

"I know, Michael, I was there, remember? The rule doesn't specifically address entering into a sexual relationship with a client in a non-domestic relations case, but case law is clear. Any sexual relationship between an attorney and his client may violate the code of conduct."

I jumped up and paced. "Gram warned me about falling in love with her."

"Sit down. Please."

Petulant, I sat.

"One of the purposes of the rule," Erica continued, "is to protect the client from having an attorney use his position to gain financially from the relationship."

"Doesn't bode well. Sara's worth a gazillion times more than me."

"But if she had something to gain—"

"You mean she courted me for personal reasons?"

"It's worth exploring. The rule assumes the attorney has the upper hand over the client. The client idolizes the attorney and is vulnerable to being taken advantage of. But what if the upper hand belonged to the client?"

It was an interesting theory. *Why hadn't you thought of that, Tucker?* I leaned toward her.

"I mean," she persisted, "Sara is super rich, right? Why didn't she hire Roy Black or Mark Geragos over inexperienced and unknown Michael Tucker? She could have even hired Glen Trautman back then. Everyone knows he was her family's attorney and he had the cellphone number of every state legislator."

Feeling defensive, I sat back. Even with my baby face, I'm sure I looked older than my thirty-two years. *Why wouldn't Sara have hired me?* Sure, as a new attorney at the time, I never tried a case more complicated than leaving the scene of an accident, but I graduated from NYU Law School, and Gertrude Tucker and I shared the same genetics. Wasn't that qualification enough?

"Think about it," Erica urged. "If you were in my chair, what would you be wondering?"

I hesitated.

"Say it," Erica ordered.

"Fine. Why *had* Sara hired me?" I blurted.

"Right, it's a logical question under these circumstances. Take me through how you met."

"A couple of weeks after kids found Uncle Charlie's body in the woods behind Sara's house, I saw her on the Long Island Railroad traveling into the city. I don't recall if she noticed me too. Then we came into contact on a street corner. Her high heels were hurting her feet and I gave her my Air Jordan Nine Cool Gray sneakers to wear. We went our separate ways and met again in my office building."

"You walked barefoot?"

"I had socks on."

"Go on," Erica encouraged.

"At the time, my law practice was so pathetic I had to work at my cousin's talent agency to bring in extra cash, and I saw her again when she auditioned for a part."

"A part for what?"

"A low end sci-fi movie they were casting."

"Do you think her auditioning was a coincidence?"

Had Sara been calculated in her actions? The train, the street corner, my office building, and then the talent agency? Why hadn't I considered this before?

I shook my head. "It's a thought-provoking theory, Counselor. The worldly and wealthy client manipulated the baby lawyer, but that'll make me appear like an idiot."

"It's not about your ego, that's what gets most lawyers in trouble. Think about it. Your first murder case falls into your lap. If I remember, right before you met Sara you handled only traffic tickets, and mostly for friends."

"I don't want to be made out to be the victim."

"I understand, and I respect that, but have you considered maybe you are?"

# CHAPTER TWO
## MICHAEL

ERICA BALANCED THE folder on her short, dark skirt. "There's an affidavit here from Ronald McGuiniss."

I was glad to talk about something other than me. "He's Sara's ex, a real nitwit."

"I don't remember him testifying at trial."

"Sara wouldn't let me call him."

She scanned his affidavit. I tried not to look at her legs.

"McGuiniss swore under oath you asked him detailed questions about her financial worth, her bank accounts, if he knew any of her passwords. You even offered him a cut if he would help you, quote, hack into her accounts online and transfer funds to a yet-to-be-identified overseas account, unquote."

"The guy's a psychopath."

Erica perused another document. "Sara's not only seeking a new trial but also punitive damages, and she's trying to get you disbarred."

I needed Gram. Procedurally she would kick Trace Trautman's ass and anyone else who dared to duel with us. While no one could beat Gertrude Tucker in the courtroom, if she were actually here I would be mortified to face her. What would she think of me allowing myself to get into this position? Especially when she had warned me. The thought of her disappointment devastated me.

"Here's another statement," Erica said. "It's in Spanish."

"That's Blanca, Sara's housekeeper. The English translation is behind it."

"Give me a moment." She shuffled past the two pages and then silently read.

While Sara's attorney I interviewed Blanca, whose claims of not knowing what happened the night of Uncle Charlie's murder were as porous as pumice. Each time I approached Blanca to discuss Uncle's Charlie's murder, sudden memory lapses overcame her, not only as to what happened that night, but also as to her understanding of the English language. As Sara's defense attorney and then-boyfriend, I hadn't pushed the issue, not knowing if Blanca would be helpful or hurtful to our defense.

Now, as Sara's target, I mentally replayed my conversations with Blanca, recalling nothing new. She claimed to have been at her sister's house the night Uncle Charlie was killed. I knew it wasn't true, but I had no evidence suitable for a court of law. Blanca's sister and extended family had sworn they were together that night. Even the family dog, if he could swear on a Bible, would have said the same. Regardless, what would it matter now? I couldn't retry Sara's murder case.

Erica looked up from the affidavit. "Blanca swears she found you one day in a closed-off room upstairs in Sara's house."

"The Forbidden Room."

"Seriously? That's what it's called? Sounds dramatic. Forbidden from what? From whom?"

"Well, see…" I faltered. How could I explain?

Her eyes narrowed. "Let me help you."

About to be cross-examined, I shifted.

"Did you enter a room in Sara's home called the Forbidden Room?"

"Yes."

"How many times?"

"Twice."

"How come?"

"Once to look at the scene."

"The scene?"

"Uncle Charlie was murdered there."

"That's the same room? How come the name of the room was never mentioned at trial?"

I shrugged. Any explanation felt complicated, and I knew where it would lead. I'd have to talk about Soldier Boy. Even though he was the only person I could think of who could help me against Sara, I wanted to keep him out of the picture. I figured it was because of some weird loyalty I felt toward Sara, not an attorney-client relationship I hesitated to break even under the weight of her false accusations, but something more deep-rooted and intimate.

Another paper clip hit me.

"Hey." I rubbed my cheek. "You know that hurts."

"Good. What was the other time you were in the room?" Erica demanded. "Don't lie, and no half-truths either."

I spoke quickly. It was the only way to say it, all at once or not at all. "I was in the Forbidden Room the second time to ride the carousel horses."

"Real carousel horses?"

"Yes." I fidgeted. "I mean, no."

She closed the folder and pushed a stray hair from her forehead. Her gaze bore into me. I knew that look, especially when it was accompanied by the pursing of her lips, the same look she gave when as a child I claimed I didn't eat all the cookie dough or if I lied about brushing my teeth before bed.

I swallowed hard. "The carousel horses were about twelve inches high and made of glass."

"So not real."

"They were real to me."

"Michael. Come on."

I didn't know how to explain. A person had to experience the horses. The experience couldn't be expressed through words.

She put the folder on the coffee table and sat back, exasperated. "I understand you went into that room the first time to see the murder scene. As Sara's attorney, that was your responsibility. But why go in a second time?"

"This is starting to feel like a therapy session."

"We're called counselors at law for a reason, and stop stalling. By the way, it wouldn't hurt for you to see a therapist. You've been through a lot, and not just losing Gram."

"Whatever."

"Look." She leaned forward. "Maybe I'm not the right lawyer for you. Maybe we're too close."

I sighed. I needed Erica to be my attorney. I would trust no other.

"I'll behave. I promise."

"Good. Now, why did you go into the room a second time?"

"Sara and I made love."

"Where the murder took place?"

I nodded.

"And is that when…" she hesitated.

"That's when I rode the carousel horses." I coughed, my throat unnaturally dry.

"You rode twelve-inch-high horses made of glass?"

"I know it sounds crazy."

"You were fantasizing." She dismissed the greatest moment of my life with a flick of her wrist.

"It felt real."

"No. She was your first love and your first serious client. It wouldn't be unusual to romanticize your relationship."

I corrected her. "She wasn't my first love."

While Erica had been my first crush, Elaine Weitzman, my law school professor, was my first love.

"It's understandable you'd have your love goggles on," she said.

"Love goggles?"

"Like beer goggles except you see things through eyes that are in love."

"Is this the counselor-at-law part again?"

"I'm saying you couldn't have ridden the carousel horses."

"Fine." There was no point in arguing. To the sane, Erica was correct, but even now the carousel horses felt real.

# CHAPTER THREE
## SARA GOLDSTEIN

I KEPT TWO diaries when I was small. The one with Batman on the cover was reserved for my personal observations and secret desires. The other was a blue notebook adorned by Wonder Woman springing through the air in her red, white, blue, and gold outfit, her red boots propelling her like bursts of flames, and her gold indestructible bracelets ready to defend. That's where I'd write the stories my father, Steven Goldstein, shared with Soldier Boy and me of our family history.

I wrote about my paternal grandmother, Liana Krochmal, a Viennese Jew who survived the Holocaust and who had been given carousel horses as a gift from her father. I jotted notes about my Great-Great Uncle Ruby on my Dad's side who migrated to America before World War II to succeed in Vaudeville. I penned verses about my maternal grandfather, Alfonso Carrara, and how he and Ruby became friends near the end of the Depression. Ruby helped Alfonso run his first hotel and start the Rest Well Inc. empire, which Soldier Boy and I inherited. I wrote of how through Ruby and Alfonso's friendship Mom and Dad met. I even scribbled notes on Uncle Charlie who was Alfonso's younger half-brother by thirty years and the offspring of my seventy-year-old great grandfather and a twenty-year-old showgirl.

Now, on a prison-issued yellow pad one thousand and eighty-six days after my life sentence for Uncle Charlie's murder I write about

Rikers Island, where I have been housed for the past three months. Prior to that, I languished at Bedford Hills Correctional Facility.

At New York City's main jail, inmates dress in white or gray with no metal or strings on their clothes. With drab complexions from lack of sun and vitamins, we look like angry, waxen figures. My blond highlights have long grown out leaving me a natural brunette. My hair that grew down my back cut short. Glasses replaced contact lenses. The lesbians and prison guards still tell me I'm hot.

Rikers is better than the prison at Bedford Hills. My attorney, Trace Trautman, obtained a court order requiring that I remain here until my appeal is finished. One of the advantages of hiring a large and established law firm, even if Glen Trautman passed my case to his son and pretends to be significantly involved, is they have judges and congressmen in their pockets. Money talks, even inside Bedford Hills and Rikers Island. Since day one of my incarceration, I have bribed guards, kept the commissary accounts of bullies and gang leaders fat, and even obtained a few favors courtesy of the warden. While incarceration hasn't been easy, it hasn't been Alcatraz either. Still, I want to go home.

I am housed in Women's Pod 16B which consists of eight one-room, seven-by-seven-foot cells that branch into a common area with four metal picnic tables, benches, and chairs. In the main area inmates talked, joked, and quietly quarreled, so as not to get in trouble. Some played cards. A few paced and spoke to no one I could see. Others stared into space. Surrounded by bulletproof glass and overseen by guards, inmates were permitted in and out of their cells from eight a.m. until eight p.m. This was no problem for me. I spent most of my time in my room or at the library, writing and thinking of the trial, Soldier Boy, my family, the Forbidden Room, the carousel horses, and Michael.

Did he know I was in love with him? Too bad money can't reverse time. I'd buy a do-over.

I told Michael he did all he could to defend me. I continue to feel this way, but Glen Trautman and Trace put it to me succinctly when they explained my appellate options. *Blame your lawyer, Sara. Attack him professionally and personally. It's your best chance at a new trial.* They explained the court record from the trial, which consisted of more than 2,500 pages, was clean. They could attempt to get a review in a few areas that the appellate court might consider prejudicial to our defense or reversible error, but thought it would not be successful.

"Our greatest shot," Trace said, "is a claim of ineffective assistance of counsel, failure to call witnesses, to admit evidence, and to properly cross-examine state witnesses."

I knew that was the way of attorneys. Throw stuff against a wall and see what sticks.

Without a new trial and a not guilty verdict, or a plea deal, I looked at life with no parole. What else could I do? I gave Trautman, Lewis, Simmons & Leigh, P.A. half a million dollars and permission to file everything and do anything they could to get me out of my predicament.

Erica Stark, my prosecutor, had gloated to the press over my conviction and then skipped out of the D.A.'s office to pursue legal fame and fortune, riding on my infamous coattails. While she may have put a murderer behind bars, she had done so for the wrong murder.

I cannot say exactly why I hired Michael, a new attorney at the time. Best I can come up with, I never imagined being convicted. He was cute and gallant, giving me his sneakers to wear when my shoes were pinching my feet. Plus, along with Michael came Gertrude Tucker. Who wouldn't want her on your legal team? I felt good about Michael from the moment I saw him watching me on the Long Island Railroad. Different from the Glen Trautmans of the world and all the attorneys I've had to deal with over the years, Michael cared and would make me a priority since I was his only case of significance. I knew I could control him. He wouldn't drive my defense, I would, which meant I could keep Soldier Boy out of it, and that's where my brother needed to be, as far from the madness as possible.

Michael was right and wrong at the same time, the right man but the wrong lawyer.

# CHAPTER FOUR
# MICHAEL

"YOU HAVEN'T ANSWERED my question," Erica said.

We were still in her office at our first meeting for her to represent me against Sara's crazy accusations.

"Which question?" I asked.

"What was forbidden about the room?"

"A murder was committed there?"

She frowned. "It was called the Forbidden Room before the murder, right?"

"Yes."

"How long before?"

"For as long as Sara could remember."

"So I'll ask again. What was forbidden about the room?"

I hesitated. "The carousel horses?"

Her exhale was arctic. She was dissatisfied with my response. "Was there anything else in the room?"

"Train tracks and toy trains."

"This is getting weirder."

Normally the ever-present kid in me would enjoy the mystique that surrounded this conversation and Erica's confusion, but even I felt uncomfortable.

She picked up the file and put it down again. "Do you know of anyone who might be able to explain about that room?"

I squirmed. Of course I did, but it didn't mean I was willing to tell.

I hedged. "Will that help me against Sara?"

Erica was exasperated. "This calls for a yes or no answer. Do you or don't you know anyone who might know the truth about that room, other than Sara?"

I grinned. I would have done the same thing with a reluctant client. "No."

Erica knew I lied. "You're looking at having your reputation as a criminal defense attorney tainted, as well as having financial repercussions. You could lose your license to practice law. Sara is going after you personally too."

My eyes widened. I hated to be reminded. "Gram's money."

"Precisely."

Moths rattled my stomach. Not only had I disappointed Gram while she was alive, but my actions could also lead to her hard-earned and well-deserved fortune going to Sara and her legal team, more to her lawyers than to Sara herself.

What if my scarlet letter tainted Gram's posthumous reputation? The moths in my stomach became vultures. I wanted to throw up.

"That person might be able to help with your defense too," Erica prodded. "How about telling me the truth? Do you know anyone who can explain about the Forbidden Room?"

I fidgeted and breathed through my mouth to relieve the queasiness. I recalled Gram on her deathbed, telling me with raspy breaths about meeting Soldier Boy. I hadn't paid much attention to it then, even though I had seen him leaving her hospital room as I arrived, minutes before Gram released her last breath.

"I know someone," I said. "He's loyal to Sara. He won't help me."

"Who?"

"Her brother."

She picked up a pad of paper and waited with a pen paused over it. She wanted his name.

"Soldier Boy," I said.

"Is he a child?"

I shook my head. "His real name is David Goldstein."

"Oh, yes. I read about him in the police reports when their parents were killed. Was he at Sara's trial?"

"Only at the end."

"You think David can explain the mystery around the Forbidden Room and the carousel horses?"

"I know of two living people who can explain. One of them blames me for being found guilty at trial, wants me stripped of my license to practice law, and wants to take Gram's money. The other, I'm sure, wants me dead."

She ignored my dramatics. "I need to question Soldier Boy. Can you find him?"

Finding Soldier Boy wasn't the first question I had to answer, the first inquiry was: did I want to be the one to find him? The guy scared me.

# CHAPTER FIVE
## SARA

My father never kept the Forbidden Room locked, figuring, I imagined, his repeated warnings enough to keep us out. He had been correct that we wouldn't venture into the room, until the day Mom flung a tumbler at the mirror over the piano. It wasn't the first time she threw something in drunken defiance, but that day in 1992 was different from the numerous other times her drinking led to violence. I was nine years old, my brother four. We huddled in a linen closet on the second floor, our typical hiding place when the fighting began. Before long, we became deathly afraid.

Glass shattered on the tiled floor. Soldier Boy wailed.

"If you take one more drink…" Dad's voice ascended from the floor below.

"Shut that kid up or else," my mother slurred.

"Don't go up those stairs," Dad yelled.

Not waiting to see our mother's intentions, we sprinted out of the linen closet and to the first door on the left at the top of the stairs, the Forbidden Room.

That night was the first time we rode the carousel horses. Soldier Boy sat atop a white Arabian with a bronze mane and tail. I hopped on a palomino. A chocolate bay nudged the window open, and along with a spotted appaloosa, we flew into the spring air. Soldier Boy laughed like the little boy he deserved to be, while I immersed in a perfect moment I spent my entire life trying to recreate.

Six years later, Mom and Dad were dead. I won't go into the details while my appeal is pending, but I will say this: you know how when a parent or grandparent dies and you wish you asked more questions about the past? Naturally inquisitive, I didn't know I chronicled family history in my Wonder Woman journal, but am now glad I did. Over the years, while Dad collected and played with his beloved Lionel trains, I asked hundreds of questions about our family, about the Forbidden Room, and about the carousel horses. Patiently he answered with remarkable detail, about his side of the family, and about Mom's too. This information filled my notebook.

Soldier Boy listened, never asked questions or took notes as the gears in his brain recorded and interpreted history in a way only he could do.

I sat on an orange plastic chair in the visitor's lounge at Rikers, glad for the scratched and scarred table between Billy O'Brien and me. Even with the armed guards, he scared me.

Calling it a visitor's lounge was peculiar, as if we reclined on couches and drank tea. At nearby tables, other inmates chatted with their guests. Time was regulated, and the amount of inmates permitted to talk with loved ones limited to five at a time. Guards roved a few breaths and a bullet away.

Billy's long dark hair was greased back. Sideburns framed his horse-like face. He wore a white tank top and his arms were sleeved with tattoos. A fire-breathing dragon slithered along his shoulder and roared up his neck.

"How you doing, Sara Goldstein?" He accent thick like a New York gangster from a movie, James Caan's Sonny in "The Godfather", or Ray Liotta's Henry Hill in "Goodfellas".

My heart pounded. Always unpolished, rough inside and out, I heard Billy hardened from his time in prison.

"What are you doing here? You're not on my visitor's list."

He stared, his eyes dark blue and murky like a sea of unknown depths. "David Aaron Goldstein is," he said. "Or as you call him, Soldier Boy."

Soldier Boy and Billy had been friends growing up. They met after our parents' deaths when we resided with Aunt Claire and Uncle Eddie. Billy had been riding his bike and saw Soldier Boy fixing a lawn mower. Fascinated with my brother's mechanical abilities, Billy became obsessed with him. Throughout elementary, junior high, and much of high school, they remained friends. As far as I knew, Soldier Boy cut off contact when Billy got in with a bad crowd and was the driver of the getaway car of a robbery in which a storeowner was killed. Billy did time for being an accessory to murder. He's been out three years after serving a nickel.

"Wasn't hard to make a fake ID with David's name. Told the guard I shaved my head. We look enough alike and the guard was an idiot, so here I am." His smirk showed a gold grill along his top teeth. "How's prison?"

"What do you want?"

"Prison sucked for me, thank you very much. Got treated worse than an animal, like I was a piece of shit that didn't deserve to be stepped in. It's even worse when you're in for something you didn't do."

I tried to gauge why he was here. "Are you saying you weren't driving that car?"

"I'm saying I didn't kill nobody. Driving a car is a traffic offense at the worst. It's like going to prison for speeding or having a tail light out."

"The law doesn't see it like that."

"Fuck the law and the cops and all this bullshit," he shouted.

A female guard walked near us. "Hey, keep it down."

Billy sneered and lowered his voice. "I'm pissed as hell, but I'm making amends. I got a wife and a baby now. Alls I need is a job."

I sat back and relaxed. This was going to be easy. Billy wanted a job.

"What are you looking for?"

His dark eyes lightened and he laughed. "You think I'm here to ask you for work? What kind of fucking job could you give me anyway? You're like me now, a convict. Can't vote, can't own a gun. Shit, can't even be on a jury."

"What do you want, Billy?"

"You think I don't read? You've filed an appeal, and you're suing Michael."

"What'd you think? I'd rot in prison for something I didn't do?"

He folded one arm over the other and leaned like he was under a sun lamp. "Actually, yeah, I did."

"I'm not."

"Might want to rethink that." His eyes gray steel. "Serve your time, Sara Goldstein."

A squeal startled me, and I jumped. A twenty-year-old woman doing seventeen for an armed burglary screamed with joy and hugged her baby girl. At the table next to her, a fifty-something inmate grasped hands with her grown son. Across the room, a pockmark-faced girl cried as she prayed with her pastor.

When the room quieted, I became fortified with a burst of courage. "Go home."

"Drop your appeal."

"Are you protecting Michael?"

"Fuck no. True, he was good to me when we were kids, like a big brother, but I don't have no love for no lawyer. In fact, I fucking hate him and want to see him dead. If he had any competence you'd have been found not guilty and I wouldn't have to worry about this shit."

"What do you have to worry about?"

He sprung forward, and I thought he was going to grab me. He stopped short, his elbows on the table and his hands inches from mine. I looked at the guards, who didn't notice or didn't care.

"Ask David what happened the night your uncle was killed."

"I know what happened." At least I thought I did, but I wasn't going to let Billy see my doubts. I needed to make a move, to get this clown out of here. I hedged. "All I have to do is make one phone call, and you'll go back to prison."

His retort was quick. "Keep this appeal going, and you're opening a can of worms. It's enough you're already in the can." He laughed. "I'm sure you don't want your precious brother to end up here too."

I flinched. I hadn't come this far protecting Soldier Boy to have him incarcerated too.

Billy read the reluctance on my face. "As I thought. Drop the appeal, Sara Goldstein. Do your time like a good girl."

# CHAPTER SIX
## BILLY O'BRIEN

HERE'S WHAT I know about Charles's murder. No bullshit, okay? My whole life has been one mound of crap piled on top of another and stinking up everything I cared about and every person who ever thought twice about me. Maybe telling the truth will be penance like saying a million Hail Marys and then I won't spend eternity frying in hell. I want to do right for my wife and two-month-old daughter, Gracie. I can't support them and they live on welfare like dogs. What kind of a man am I?

I'm being set up, I know it, and even with my move to force Sara to keep her mouth shut and take her punishment like she deserved, I know I'm doomed. I never stood a chance. I should have known it when I agreed to help. Aiding and abetting, the *popo* call it, like when I had to do time for murder because I was driving a car. How absurd is that, getting tagged with murder for driving? I didn't even have any traffic tickets at the time, and now I'm going to do life in prison when again I didn't pull the trigger.

So what if Sara didn't kill her uncle? She's doing the time for taking out her own mother. Isn't that worthy of life in prison? Isn't that what karma is all about?

At least I never killed anyone I knew, that way if they looked me in the eyes right before I fired the pistol, I didn't feel nothing. Ruby bragged he ran with Meyer Lansky, Bugsy Siegel, and Alfonso Carrara back in the day. Those guys showed no hesitation and had no regrets, that's the kind of gangster I want to be.

Ruby is a lot like Meyer, all brainy and stuff. I know because I read all about the mafia's accountant. He worked his way up the ranks using his brains and not his muscle. I have to say I admire that about the Meyer Lansky, and about Ruby too.

Me, I'm more of an Al Capone kind of guy. Shoot first and ask questions later. I wasn't always like that, but prison does that to a man.

I took the job when David asked. Since that family is loaded with dead presidents, I figured my association with them would get me some significant dough, prestige and power, and maybe I'd be able to bring in some of my own guys, you know, form my own mafia-like organization. We'd run numbers, shake down drug dealers, and get payments for protection like in the old days. Maybe then Gracie would be proud of me and my wife would stop fucking the superintendent of our roach-infested building so she could slide on paying rent. I should have taken the guy out, but the free rent took pressure off me.

If you haven't figured it out yet, I'm a student of the mafia. I love those guys. I've seen all their films like *The Godfather* movies, *Scarface, Mean Streets*, and *Goodfellas*. I have a whole Blu Ray library at home that's fly.

While I can't say I don't deserve the same fate as Sara, which is to do time for a crime I didn't commit as fate for the ones I did do, this time I am innocent. I didn't kill Uncle Charlie, but I know how those rich people connive and manipulate. They'll try the legal route first, the appeal and all, and if that doesn't work, they're going to frame me and make it look like I murdered Uncle Charlie. They didn't frame me when Sara was on trial because they never thought she'd get convicted. Pompous assholes, guess that's what happens to people when they're born super fucking rich.

It's not that I had this bad childhood that made me into the gangster I am today. I grew up on Long Island in a middle-class family with an okay mom and dad. They could have kept better tabs on me, but those days weren't like today where kids shoot up schools and run away to join ISIS. Michael tried to watch over me but he was always too kindhearted and naive to understand what I needed: military school, maybe that would have saved me.

I guess that's what attracted me to David. We met by chance after his parents died and he and Sara lived with their aunt and uncle. I saw him working on his bike or a lawn mower or something in his driveway and struck up a conversation. He was dressed in fatigues, my kind of guy, and a real brainiac. We talked about weapons, how to make bombs, and yes, how to blow up our school. We never were serious about doing it, but I sure loved those talks. If we were high school kids now, we'd be in juvenile detention because today the whole world knows what you're thinking before you do.

David had always been there for me. I tried to be a good friend too, so when he came to me a few years ago one August and asked for guidance I said, "hell yeah". He handed me a ton of chedda, that's money in hip-hop. I was moving up into the consulting business, climbing the corporate ladder.

I met with Sara and David and told them how it should go down, how to get Charles to come over without raising suspicion, what weapon to use, where to shoot him on his body so one bullet would do the job, the best location for the murder, where to dispose of the body, and so forth. After Charles's body was found in the woods and the stuff came out in the newspapers and on the Internet, I knew they hadn't followed my instructions. I had told them to kill him in the woods, to use a silencer, and to chop up the body and dump the parts at a landfill in Jersey. They didn't listen to a fucking thing I said. No silencer, shot him in their house, and dumped the body in the woods behind the home. What the fuck were they thinking? Anyway, I ended up following the story of Sara's trial like every rubbernecker. I never thought it would come back to me, but I should have known. True to the ways of the mafia, family comes first.

# CHAPTER SEVEN
## LIANA KROCHMAL
## VIENNA, AUSTRIA
## NOVEMBER 9, 1938
## KRISTALLNACHT DAY ONE

HALF PAST SIX in the morning, cuddled with my stuffed bear Bruno, I dreamed of America. I played at a street fair on the lower east side of Manhattan and rode a beautiful carousel of glass horses. The air smelled of freshly baked goods and sweat, not the body odor of dread brought on by fear, but the scent of freedom.

As the carousel horses circled, the palomino I sat atop whinnied and leapt into the air. Its long white mane flowed. I laughed from my gut and gripped his gold and red bridle. From the vast blue sky, I viewed the Statue of Liberty below.

Flying across the Atlantic Ocean, we soared over Vienna. I looked down on my family's second-floor apartment, baroque castles, the Schönbrunn Palace, the Great Parterre, lush lawns, a tiergarten, and a maze of finely landscaped shrubs. Mozart's *Requiem Mass in D Minor* played. The same requiem sounded when I pulled the lever on the thirty-centimeters-high glass carousel, which was the same height as my brother's size-twelve foot and which Papa gave me for my thirteenth birthday last August.

In New York City, the palomino gently knelt; I slid off and landed in front of a row of food stands. Chocolate icing dripped over the sides of sweet cakes. Steamed frankfurters and bratwursts awaited mustard, buns, and eager stomachs. Fresh apples, pears, and oranges glistened in the sun.

Sticky cotton candy and rich chocolates mingled on my tongue when something hit me in the head. "Owww." I shot up.

Cold stung my face. Broken glass sprayed against my skin. Shouts came from the street outside our bedroom windows. Outlines of my brother and sister, Siegfried and Renate, came into view, also sitting up in their beds. Were they okay?

Wind rustled the newspapers that covered our windows. Tabloid tails fluttered. Glass showered my face. I picked shards out of my cheeks.

Mama used the curtains in our bedroom to make clothes. When she took the hangings down, she covered the windows with newspapers. I studied the headlines many times, dated March 11, 1938, eight months ago and the day before the Eighth army of the German *Wehrmacht* walked into Austria unopposed.

The headlines read:

*Nazi Troops Mass on Austrian Border*

*French Seek United Stand for Austria*

*Vienna Calls 130,000 as War Fear Grows*

That was the last newspaper we received.

My head throbbed. I touched my forehead and examined the blood on my fingertips. A brick landed on my pillow, inches from my face.

"Hey! Stop it," I yelled.

I had not imagined my big day starting this way.

One month after the Nazis entered Austria without resistance, my beloved country became a province of Germany. Since then, some of my classmates and their families abandoned their possessions and paid the Nazis so they could move to Switzerland and Hungary. My synagogue vandalized. Jewish graves dug up. Mr. and Mrs. Goldhaber on the third floor ate rat poison.

Mama and Papa made no effort to hide that Hitler limited the rights of Jews in Vienna, including our ability to work, travel, and obtain medical care. They couldn't conceal it anyway, it was all we Jews talked about. Between stickball games, my friends and I tried to understand the confusing changes, the older kids concluded that the Nazis would leave Austria soon and everything would return to the way it was. Increasingly, I feared it would not happen, although I didn't want to believe it.

Seated on our living room rug, I had listened intently to conversations between Rabbi Solomon Ehrenfeld, Papa, and Mama. I ached to know everything.

"There are over 170,000 Jews in Vienna," the Rabbi said. "There is no way Hitler and his *sturmtruppen* can restrain us all."

"We have to fight," Papa said.

"Too risky," Mama replied. "We have to get out. No matter the cost. We have to protect the children."

Mama convinced Papa the three of us *kinder* would be safe in America. With the large red "J" on our expired passports, and Papa and Siegfried's refusals to cut their long side curls, where else could we go? Switzerland, Hungary and Czechoslovakia hesitated to admit more Jews and would surely reject my family, even if we could make it to those countries.

So on this day, Madame Juliette was going to escort my two siblings and me to Paris and eventually to New York City to live with Uncle Ruby.

Even though our parents wouldn't join us right away, we were eager to go. We believed there were no bread lines in America. We were positive in America we would be treated as people and not as Jews.

Uncle Ruby was a famous actor who lived in an expensive brownstone on the Upper East Side of New York City. Mama and Papa gave their savings to Madame Juliette, a French actress and Uncle Ruby's friend, to aid our escape. Later in the day we were scheduled to leave with Madame Juliette on the Orient Express to Paris. She would then arrange our transport to America, where we would live with Uncle Ruby until Mama and Papa joined us. I didn't understand why our parents planned to stay behind, but they grew irritated at my incessant questioning on the subject so I stopped asking. I wished they intended to leave with us, hoping they played a joke.

We were allowed to bring the clothes we could wear and two toys to New York. Papa attached straps to Bruno so I could carry him like a backpack. I was trying to figure out how to transport the glass carousel horses without breaking them, when bricks slammed through the newspaper-covered windowpanes, followed by verbal assaults of rioters outside our bedroom windows.

*Tod von Juden.* Death to Jews.

*Schweine.* Pigs.

*Heil Hitler.*

Glad I wore socks; I swung my feet off the bed and onto the floor, Siegfried, four years older than me, jumped out of bed and hobbled over broken glass and rock shards toward the window. "What's going on? Ow. *Teufel noch mal.* Dammit. There's glass everywhere."

I followed him while Renate, two years my senior, hid under the covers. She shook like the mice that scurried into our apartment to escape the cold.

"Get back to bed," Siegfried scolded. "You're too young, and you're a girl."

"I'm as good as any boy," I protested.

Another rock flew through a window and narrowly missed Siegfried's eye.

"Fine." My brother's whisper fierce. "Stay low and don't tell Papa I let you out of bed."

With the newspapers destroyed, our room was lit by the rising sun and streetlights. We were in Vienna's Second District, the Jewish Quarter, called *Mazzes Insel* after our favorite bread.

I peered cautiously out a window. Protestors wore dark overcoats and waved fists as if they wanted to fight. With straight backs and pointed chins, Hitler's Brownshirts roved among them.

My siblings and I were dressed in white and yellow hand-stitched pajamas Mama had sewed from kitchen curtains. The icy wind cut through the fabric like razor blades.

I didn't understand what was happening, and I knew Siegfried and Renate had to feel the same.

A rock flew through the top frame of a window and another surge of cold pilfered my breath. Ducked below the window frame, Siegfried shook his fist at the crowd. Renate dug deeper under the blanket *Bubbe* had quilted. The sun climbed higher into the wintry sky and cast additional light onto the cobblestone street. The voices of the crowd blended into a rush of spewed venom. I recognized many of the demonstrators. The butcher and his son, my teacher from last year's class, Siegfried's co-captain on the swimming team and his mother.

They yelled, "*Juden raus! Auf nach Palästina!*" Jews out! Out to Palestine!

The rebbe's wife screamed. I looked up and saw Rabbi Ehrenfeld on his third floor balcony. Two Nazis held his arms and another pulled at his long black beard, sawed at it with the edge of a dull dagger, and yanked it off below his chin.

The Nazi held up the hairy prize. The crowd cheered.

"*Tod den Juden,*" they chanted. Death to Jews.

## CHAPTER EIGHT
## RUBY FRIEDMAN
## UNION HILL, NEW JERSEY
## KRISTALLNACHT DAY ONE

AT HALF-PAST midnight Ruby sat on a three-legged stool in front of a mirror in the dressing room he shared with seven other performers at the Hudson Burlesque Theater. The windowless room smelled of tobacco and Colgate Rapid-Shave cream. Ruby was the only mime among comedians and singers.

Built in 1907, the theater was located on the corner of Thirty-eighth and New York Avenue. In the dressing room, Ruby's theatrical cohorts gaped through loose wood boards at the showgirls in the next room. Ruby never partook in the voyeurism and refused to join in when the boys tittered about one dancer's ass or another stripper's tits. Such talk was disrespectful to the women, in particular to Dixie Lee, his partner in the skit he was preparing to perform.

Sweet Dixie, tall and buxom, her ribs arched like the span of a bridge when she danced in pasties and a G-string. Her hips curved like a racetrack. Her breasts were so large and firm the military boys came by busloads to gawk at "the twins." It was all Ruby could do not to linger in the wings of the theater after she took center stage and did her striptease. It was all he could do not to drop to one knee and pledge his love to her for all eternity.

Ruby was a head shorter than Dixie when she wasn't wearing

heels, even if at twenty years old he was two years older. He revealed to no one that he was in love with her. He didn't have a shot anyway. Why be embarrassed? After all, she dated that idiot ventriloquist, Harry Lester, who was the most famous clothed act at the Hudson.

Ruby studied his face in the mirror. It was plain and unmemorable, a little round, sort of oval. His nose pointed at the tip yet curved above the nostrils, and his eyes were dull, almost vacant, when he was not in character. Almost daily, people would stop him, snap their fingers and say "don't I know you?" With a photographic memory, Ruby recalled where he had met the cads but feigned ignorance. Why bother to explain when the person wouldn't remember him the next time either?

Ruby believed he danced as well as Fred Astaire, crooned like Bing Crosby, emoted better than James Cagney, and was funnier than, yes, his idol, Charlie Chaplin. Trouble was, no one gave him the chance to show his stuff. Not Sam Cohen, the general manager of the Hudson Theater. Not the talent scouts. Not anybody. He was stuck performing for a crowd of rowdy and drunk men eager for him to get off stage so a barely clad woman whose pasty might fall off could take his place.

"Hey, Ruby," Frank Byron, Jr. called.

Ruby forced his glance from the mirror. It wasn't that he liked looking at himself; it was that he barely recognized the face that crowned his body.

"Chaaar-leeee," Frank repeated in his snarky singsong way.

"What?" Ruby was not in the mood to converse with a dummy.

Harry Lester, or The Great Lester as he was called on stage, rarely spoke to anyone except through Frank Byron, Jr., his hand-carved ventriloquism doll that sat on Lester's lap.

"Do you know why girls don't fart?" Frank asked.

Ruby sighed. It was easier to play along and hope Harry would lose interest and turn his attention elsewhere. "No, Frank. Why don't girls fart?"

"Because they don't get an asshole until they're married."

Ruby glimpsed at a clock that hung crooked on the wall. He had less than thirty minutes until showtime.

"I thought it was funny." Frank looked at Harry. "Did you think it was funny?"

"A riot." Harry picked up a glass of water and drank.

"How about this one?" Frank asked. "A man goes to the doctor and says, 'Hey, Doc, I have ringing in my ears. What should I do?'"

"Don't answer," Ruby said, dryly.

Harry put the glass down. Frank sagged in his lap. "What's wrong, old chap? Don't feel like playing?"

"Tired, I guess."

"You're going to kill them tonight. Everyone's talking about your new act with Dixie. Is it as good as the hype?"

"I hope so."

"Well, brighten up. Dixie says it's great. You can't go on stage with that long face." He pulled Frank up on his lap.

"The American Medical Association did a study of why Jewish women like Chinese food so much," the dummy noised. "Do you know what they discovered?"

Ruby sighed. "No, Frank."

"It's because won ton spelled backwards is not now."

Ruby was silent.

"Not funny?" Frank asked.

"I'm not in the mood."

Ruby turned to the mirror; the bulbs that surrounded it cast him in jaundiced light. He opened a black case and reached in. First there was greasepaint, a flesh-colored paste he applied to his face to help his features stand out under stage lights. Next came face powder to give him rosiness, which he dabbed carefully on his sunken cheeks and sagging jowls.

True to his Austrian heritage, his hair was blond and his eyes blue. Using shoe polish, he dyed his hair black. He reached into the case, removed a tube of Brylcreem, and squeezed a bit into the palm of his hand. He rubbed his hands together and molded his tresses until the sides poked out and winged back. He then added a dab to the top of his head to give his straight hair a hint of curl.

Next came eye makeup. He applied liner along the bottom and top lids and then a touch of bronze eye shadow to accentuate his dark blue eyes. Since he didn't speak on stage, his eyes were a big part of his act. He tried not to regret all the efforts he made to rid himself of his Austrian accent, in order to appear more American. Despite hours of efforts, his Ws come out like Vs. Sometimes when it happened he forgot to be upset and smiled. He may no longer be in Austria, but Austria was in him.

He glued on bushy black eyebrows, knowing when it came time to take them off, the pain would be excruciating. From fastening the fake eyebrows on and then ripping them off, show after show after show, he did not have eyebrows of his own. *Maybe*, he considered, *I should leave them on permanently.*

He reached into the bag for one of the signature items that would complete his transformation. He held the caterpillar-like object, which was made from real hair. He had to wash it after each show so it wouldn't stink. As hard as he had tried, he couldn't grow the right kind of moustache, so he had to use a prop. He hated that it was a toothbrush moustache that looked like Hitler's. He hesitated every time he put it on, and thought of his younger sister, Amalie, his brother-in-law, Jacob, and his nephew and nieces in Vienna: Siegfried, Renate, and Liana. Oh, what they must be going through with the Nazis having marched into Austria to no resistance! He looked at the crooked clock on the wall and did a quick calculation. It was six thirty in the morning in Vienna. His family was fast asleep; the sun began a lazy rise.

Ruby had made arrangements with Madame Juliette, a friend of a friend of a friend of Dixie's, to have the family taken out of Vienna to Paris and then transported to New York by cargo ship. Today was the momentous day. Today they would start a journey that would take them to America. Ruby sighed and knew he had to trust that everything was going to work out.

It was so hard to get news from Europe. At least there wasn't a war going on, only Hitler and his men making a lot of noise about this and that. At least that's what the newsreels reported.

Once his family got to New York, he'd tell the truth. He wasn't a famous actor living in a brownstone on the Upper East Side of Manhattan as he had written in his letters. He labored as a lowly mime that worked burlesque shows; so minor they didn't allow him to speak on stage. He had yet to have a chance to prove himself as a song and dance man. He was certain his family would be happy to be free of Hitler that they would forgive his embellishment. Besides, Jacob was a good song and dance man in his own right. Maybe they could put an act together.

Ruby flipped the small, dark moustache over in his hand. Smaller in width on the top, it fanned out on the bottom almost to the length of his upper lip. He applied glue and carefully placed the hair under his nose. He exaggerated a smile, forced his mouth to a frown, flung his head back and mimicked a silent laugh. He opened his mouth wide and raised his eyebrows in surprise. The moustache and eyebrows stuck firmly in place and pinched his skin a little.

He stood, removed his short-sleeved button shirt, and glanced at his chest. An eight-inch red, bulbous scar glistened under the yellow theatrical lights. The wound was received from the slash of a switchblade in the hands of a man who believed he was hungrier and more desperate than Ruby. The combat occurred at the pinnacle of the Depression when Ruby refused to leave the warmth of a sewer grate. While Ruby had the gash on his chest as memory, the man who was faceless to Ruby had most likely received a trip to the morgue. Ruby didn't hang around to confirm if the gouge from the knife he had stuck in the man's throat had been lethal but he was certain it was a wound that couldn't be survived.

Not needing to linger on the memory, he pulled on a white long-sleeved button-down with a wing-tipped collar. Wrinkled and a size too big it gave him freedom of movement. He tucked the shirt into his black trousers, slipped his arms into a gray vest, buttoned it, and grabbed a black tie from his bag. He put the tie around his neck, under the collar, and fashioned a neat, tight knot. He tucked the tie into his vest. The matching suit coat was next, also slightly rumpled.

He took a dramatic pause, his mood lightened and as he morphed into character. He reached into a larger bag on the floor next to his chair and pulled out the final trappings that would make his transformation from Ruby Friedman to Charlie Chaplin complete.

The bowler hat and cane.

He placed the hat on his head. It popped up and came down. He rolled it from the top of his head, somersaulting down his right arm and up, landing squarely on his skull again. Ruby smiled, he was good at being Charlie Chaplin, much better than he was at being Ruby Friedman.

He thought of how in 1934, when he was sixteen years old, he had traveled by steamship from Vienna to New Jersey. He had come to America with his comedy troupe and then sneaked off and hid, refusing to leave when it was time to return home. He had been young and impulsive and believed if the world was going to appreciate the talents of Ruby Friedman, he'd have to make it in America. It was the middle of the Depression and hadn't anticipated the troubles he'd have obtaining proper work papers, the cold nights sleeping in door wells, and the demeaning, menial jobs to avoid starvation. He cleaned toilets, dug ditches at construction sites, shined shoes, and sewed clothes in a sweatshop. He even had an opportunity to run numbers for Dutch Schultz and other Jewish gangsters, but resisted despite the temptations of hot food, cool liquor, and a place to live. He was glad Dutch had died three years earlier because he had been aggressive in pursuing Ruby. Sometimes it had been hard for Ruby to say no, but he had never lost sight of his goal, for the world to learn his true talents as an actor and for him to be able to support his family once they arrived in New York.

He swallowed a lump in his throat. Regret for leaving his sister and her family behind was immense, like a boot stomped his heart. They were the only family he had. He shook his head and looked at himself in the mirror. Charlie Chaplin stared back. Amalie, Jacob, and the *kinder* were going to be fine. Dixie had assured him Madame Juliette was the real thing, and she had successfully transported several Jewish families out of Hitler's reach. They were going to be reunited. Soon.

When his sister and her family arrived in America, he would tell them the truth right away. He didn't live in a brownstone on the

Upper East Side of Manhattan. He wasn't a famous actor. He didn't lunch with Cary Grant. He wasn't short listed to star in a Howard Hawk movie. He didn't date Margaret Sullavan. He was Ruby Friedman, who worked as a mime at a burlesque theater in Union Hill, New Jersey for thirty cents an hour.

"Don't complain," Sam Cohen, the manager of the theater, liked to remind him. "That's five cents above minimum wage."

Ruby rented a room at a boarding house one block over from the theater. His landlady was Mrs. Bowen, a strict old woman who held fast to conservative views. Four dollars and fifty cents a week, paid every Friday no later than seven p.m., got him a one-room third-floor walk up furnished with a cot, a table, and two chairs. A shared toilet was two flights down. Breakfast and dinner were included, no noise after 8:00 p.m., and lights out by eleven. One person per bed was permitted in each room, unless a couple was married, legal proof required. Then there were Mrs. Bowen's boys, three sons with the size, strength, and savagery of rugby players, each known to use force first and never to ask questions. On the day Ruby moved in eight months earlier, the oldest and largest of Mrs. Bowen's boys threw a man down the stairs for being twelve hours late with rent. Ruby didn't know what happened to the man after he got up and ran away, leaving all of his possessions behind, his arm dangling sideways at the elbow.

What was Ruby going to do when his family arrived? Could he hide them from Mrs. Bowen until Jacob earned enough money for them to get their own place?

"Hey."

Ruby looked up and sighed.

Frank sat on Harry's lap, his wooden square jaw and big black eyes mocking. "The girls are awfully frisky tonight. I think they're going to have a pillow fight. Want to watch?" The dummy cocked its head toward the wall where two brothers who called themselves the Frat Boys and sang *a capella* peered into the ladies' dressing room.

"No, thanks."

A knock sounded, and the door to the men's dressing room flung open. The performers jumped to their feet, Ruby included.

"Dixie," Harry said.

She sauntered into the room; her low cut evening dress tight on her breasts and hips. She ran her long fingernails over Harry's cheek and walked past him.

She stopped in front of Ruby. "Ready?"

He nodded, unable to speak, captivated by the heat of her body and held hostage by her lavender perfume.

"Let's knock 'em dead, hot stuff." She walked out of the room, her gate long and elegant.

Charlie Chaplin shuffled behind her.

# CHAPTER NINE
## MICHAEL

I POUTED IN my small, one-bedroom rental apartment located across from the Empire State Building. My first significant foray into Gram's money, a twenty-five-thousand-dollar retainer to Erica, repulsed me. She's worth the fee, but it hurt. It hadn't been Gram's intention when she left me her two-million-dollar estate and her black cat Cardozo for me to expend the dough on something boneheaded like this. I know. Twenty-five grand off two million isn't much of a dent. I don't want to sound like some crybaby, but each penny of Gram's money I spend to defend myself against Sara's bogus allegations means I have disappointed Gram in the afterlife. Regrets suck.

I petted Cardozo who kneaded on my lap. "But if I win, Sara has to pay my attorney's fees."

Still, this battle wasn't one I longed for.

Cardozo arched his back, jumped off of me and sat on Sara's blue case file, the one I hadn't shared with Erica when I retained her earlier in the day.

"I need you to move, 'Dozo." I pulled on the edge of the folder and hoped he'd scoot. No luck. Gently I pushed him away.

Seated on the couch, the folder rested on my lap. I felt overwhelmed and sickened by the sight of the reports from Sara's parents' murders eighteen years earlier, by the sworn statements taken by the police during Uncle Charlie's murder investigation four years ago, and by the notes I made throughout my tenure as Sara's attorney. Documents I hadn't thought I'd have to look at again, pleadings and reports I never wanted to have to see again. My intestines lurched. My throat tightened. I ran to the bathroom and regurgitated a pretzel purchased earlier from a pushcart on the street. I flushed and watched the salted jumble circulate down the bowl, wiped my mouth with a towel, and sat on the toilet, seat closed. I wiped tears from my face, and I regrouped.

I went to the couch on shaky legs. Why was I being a wimp? I opened the case file again and removed Sara's spiral notebook with Batman on the cover. I considered returning it to her after the guilty verdict but was glad I hadn't.

Sara's diary covered her life from ages seven until twenty-four. I opened to the end of the notebook and read the final entry in 2007, written in a slanted scribble.

*A few minutes ago, I remembered finding my parents lying on the living room floor. I walked in before Soldier Boy did. The house was still. We always braced for yelling and screaming when we came in, and the stone silence scared me. It felt strange. I thought I should call out for them, but then I wondered if they were sleeping or passed out, so I said nothing. As soon as I saw them lying under the piano, I was compelled to go nearer. Was it curiosity? It seems funny now that I didn't think, "Oh no, Mommy and Daddy are dead." I was thinking about the mess on the floor and how Blanca was going to curse about having to clean it up. It was as if they weren't my parents or even human beings at all. They could have been two large flowerpots that tipped over, smeared soil staining the carpet.*

*As I hovered over my mother's body, I could see the blood gushing from her stomach onto the floor and spreading as it seeped deeper into the rug fibers. My sneakers were white, and I was afraid the blood would get on them. There was a gaping hole in my father's head. At the time I didn't think about a bullet wound, but instead of a cork shooting off a wine bottle into his skull. His eyes were open and he stared at the underside of the piano. I wondered what he would play if he could get up. It occurred to me that although he always talked about how well he could play, I'd never heard him strike a key.*

*My mother's torso was splayed across his legs, and her eyes were open too. They were moving. Her gaze was directed toward the back of the house, at the pool. I stared into her flexing and prancing eyes, wondering if this scene was real. I followed her line of sight and saw the sliding door was open. I stumbled toward the door, but no one was there. When I came back, my mother's eyes were no longer moving. The small pistol my parents had always cautioned us against touching rested near my father's right hand. I picked it up and put it in the piano. Apparently no one ever looked there.*

*After I closed the piano lid on the keys, I saw Soldier Boy standing in the doorway. He was looking down, and I hoped he hadn't seen anything. I ran him out to Aunt Claire and Uncle Eddie and told them to call the police. I don't remember much about that day after the cops arrived.*

*One week later, I wrapped the gun in a towel, put it in the basket of my bicycle, and rode out to the garbage dump.*

I closed the spiral notebook and knew Sara's recorded memories of finding her parents on the night of their murders contained lies; she was the ultimate unreliable reporter. I turned to notes I jotted during a telephone conversation with Sara after I first read that diary entry. The conversation started when I implored Sara to be honest. As she spoke I scribbled the following:

*Cops thought mother/father deaths were murder-suicide, cops wrong, murder-murder, someone ran out back door; Sara doesn't know who.*

And then notes from a later conversation with Sara:

*Uncle Charlie murdered Mom for Rest Well Inc. fortune. Sara saw him run out back door.*

Other notes I made also dotted the margins of the lined pages.

*Why would Charlie kill father too? Was he a witness to mother's murder? Why hadn't Sara talked to police? Why not tell me from the start? What did Soldier Boy know? Why the secrets? Why the lies?*

I rubbed the remnants of a dull ache in my abs and lay on the couch. Cardozo jumped on to my chest, kneaded and purred, his green eyes wide and intent. I rubbed his boney back. Like Gram while she lived, Cardozo wasn't much of an eater.

"What if I met Sara before Uncle Charlie's death?" I spoke out loud.

The cat quickened the alternate movements of his front paws. Left, right, left, right.

"Could I have prevented his murder? Would Sara and I still be together?" I imagined Sara as Mrs. Michael Tucker, shook my head, and chased the thoughts away. "I'm being stupid, 'Dozo. Aren't I?" I scratched behind his ear; he leaned toward me in response. "She never loved me. She used me."

Cardozo apparently agreed. He jumped on to the floor, curled up under a beam of sunlight and licked his privates.

Elaine, my first love and law school professor, had been correct. When she ended our relationship, she cupped my cheek and said, "You're a romantic. You don't deserve to be hurt, but this isn't going to be the last time."

"That's it," I pronounced to Cardozo, my only audience. "I'm done with women. It's going to be you and me."

Unimpressed, he continued grooming.

I looked at Sara's folder and scattered the notes and reports along the coffee table. I reviewed the summary I made after my second and last visit to Sara at Rikers Island after her conviction. This time my notes were not detailed, since I hadn't taken a pad and pen with me. I hadn't expected her jailhouse confession, or at least what I had interpreted as such. Instead, after leaving the jail I sat in my car and scribbled what I recalled while the shock throbbed in my chest.

I remembered her dull eyes and her monotone voice as she finally shared the truth about her parents' and Uncle Charlie's murders.

My notes went like this: *The day parents killed, Soldier Boy and Sara spent afternoon with aunt and uncle (paternal, Claire & Eddie Harpon). Uncle Charlie going to house to discuss Rest Well Inc. business with parents and wanted kids out. Sara forgot something (what? does it matter?). Asked Harpons to bring her home. Sara went inside and saw Mom drunk, pointing gun at Dad, Dad trying to get gun from her. Gun went off and Dad fell to the ground. Mom dropped the gun. Rage overcame Sara, who grabbed the gun and shot Mom twice in the stomach. Hid gun in the piano.*

I put the notes aside, giving Cardozo a landing pad to jump to and curl into my lap. I stroked him as I remembered being in the jail in a small private room reserved for attorneys and their clients, digesting Sara's confession and feeling sick.

"You wanted Uncle Charlie dead so you and Soldier Boy could have the entire Rest Well Inc. fortune," I ventured. "You let Soldier Boy believe Uncle Charlie killed your parents all those years ago so he would seek revenge. You knew with his experience in the Marines and his devotion to you he would do it. You used him."

She didn't respond.

I added one final piece to the puzzle. "Blanca knew everything. Soldier Boy killed Uncle Charlie in the Forbidden Room. Who else would clean up the blood but Blanca?"

Her cold stare the confirmation I needed.

In my apartment, I scanned the notes for an overlooked clue. Each page seemed to come alive, waved at me, cautioned, "Don't forget, Sara is an unreliable reporter."

What could I believe that she told me about the murders of her parents, about Uncle Charlie's death? What could I believe that she had said about us?

I stood and 'Dozo jumped from my lap, giving me the stink eye for interrupting his nap. I looked out the window of my apartment. Cars and taxis vied for spots on Thirty-fourth Street. Pedestrians scuttled up and down the pavement. A Korean couple pushed a hot dog and pretzel cart.

I turned to Cardozo. "Erica says Soldier Boy might help with my defense against Sara. Why would he ever testify against his sister?"

The cat ignored me.

"It's like some unbelievable movie plot." I reached for a pad and scribbled out the story line.

*1998, Mom, in drunken stupor, killed Dad. Daughter witnessed it, turned gun on Mom. Police close case as murder-suicide.*

*2012, seeking revenge for great uncle keeping family fortune, daughter lies and tells son (her brother, recently discharged from Marines) great uncle murdered Mom and Dad years ago. Sister encouraged brother to seek revenge, which he does.*

I wished I had Quentin Tarantino on speed dial.

I made myself a cup of green tea and offered Cardozo salmon treats, which he eyed with disinterest. I gave up trying to engage him and wondered where Soldier Boy could be, and I considered the question that nagged me: did I want to be the one to find him?

# CHAPTER TEN
## MICHAEL

TWO DAYS AFTER I retained Erica as my attorney, I drove out of the driveway of my parents' Bellmore, Long Island home and motored through the streets in the 1968 red convertible Ford Mustang Gram gave me before she died. Every time I visited the town where I was raised and lived until a couple of years ago, it seemed to be smaller and more rundown. What used to enchant me with its ranch-style homes, large parks, and access to the bay where Dad and I fished now felt outmoded.

Mom was happy to see me when I stopped in, and I was glad to see her too. She was a cool mother, not overbearing or needy, even-keeled and normal. We never talked about why Gram, her mother, hadn't left her anything in her will, but I knew. Mom agreed with Gram to leave it all to me. Mom and Dad had plenty of their own money.

Mom owned a knitting shop off Merrick Road where she sold imported yarns and patterns and held classes. The store was one large room with a sitting area in the middle where mostly women and a few older men sipped coffee, gossiped, and, naturally, knitted. She called the store Knit One, Talk Too. Mom didn't make much money from the undertaking, but it made her happy.

Dad owned a gas station on the corner of Bellmore Avenue and Sunrise Highway. He had owned several stations but sold them off to simplify life. He wasn't ready to retire and fantasized that I would take over the remaining station. He had a couple of mechanics but preferred to do most of the work himself.

While I grew up, Dad would smile through his Fu Manchu moustache and say, "If I'm not greasy when I get home, then it wasn't a good day."

I admired my parents because they had learned the secrets to life: keep busy, and if something doesn't make them happy, don't do it.

I turned onto Sunrise Highway and into Dad's gas station where I stopped alongside a set of tanks. I jumped out and was about to slide my credit card when he greeted me with a hug from behind.

"How's my boy?" His Russian accent was strong despite having lived in the United States for the majority of his life.

"Good, Dad."

"I see you're taking Gert's baby for a ride. The gas she is on me."

"I got it."

"Absolutely not. Want me to check her out?"

"Didn't you tinker with her last week?"

A hint of Dad's smile showed through an upturn of his moustache. "She's beautiful, Mikey." He traced his fingers along the hood. "You know a man can't keep his hands off a beautiful woman. What brings you to the old country?"

I smiled. He knew I preferred the City to the suburbs. "Work."

"You're taking cases on the Island now?"

"No, um…"

Dad's eyes hitched, he knew I was about to lie.

I switched gears. "I'm going to Sara's house."

"Sara? The woman who killed her uncle? Isn't she in prison?"

I nodded. "I need to find her brother."

"Military Man?"

"Soldier Boy."

"Why you look for him?"

I took half a second to decide if I would come clean. I never could lie to my parents, at least not with success. "Can we talk somewhere?"

He motioned to one of his employees to fill up Gram's car. I followed him into his office, a disarray of old furniture, paper receipts, automobile manuals, and old dog-eared magazines. Pictures of Mom and me hung askew on the walls along with dusty civic awards and local business honors. Dad took his seat behind a big, scuffed desk. I sat in a crusty chair. He pushed aside an adding machine, a worn ledger, a receipt book, and a manual credit card slide. When it came to accounting, Dad refused to enter the computer generation. The office smelled like him, a combination of grease, oil, and Polo aftershave. He leaned back in his chair and waited.

"Sara is suing me."

"For what?"

"I didn't tell you, but, well, we were in a relationship." I tried to read the twitch of his moustache.

He pushed aside invoices and rested his forearms on the desk. "Your grandmother she told us."

"How come you never said anything to me?"

"Do you know the fastest way to get your son to make a bad choice?"

I waited for the punch line.

"Tell him not to do something."

I shifted in the chair. "Yeah. I wouldn't have listened."

"We decided Gertrude would talk to you about it, and we hoped for the best."

"Well, she did and…" I searched for something to

excuse my behavior.

Dad rescued me. "It's hard to keep your hands off a beautiful woman."

I smiled slightly, sad I disappointed my family, and glad Dad wasn't going to give me a lecture.

"Tell me what she is suing you about."

"She's trying to say I screwed up her trial so she can get a new one."

"Did you?"

"No."

"Then you have nothing to worry about."

"It's not that simple. A couple of days ago I hired an attorney to represent me. Remember my old babysitter?"

"Sure. Ellen."

"Erica."

He chewed on the end of an already gnawed pencil. "She's a lesbian, no?"

"Yes, Dad."

"Good. You'll keep your *schmeckel* in your pants."

I laughed. "That's for sure."

# CHAPTER ELEVEN
## LIANA
### KRISTALLNACHT DAY ONE

THE CROWD OUTSIDE our apartment building grew rowdier, the throng resilient and relentless with its verbal lynching. Hitler and his Aryan army didn't like Jews. What I didn't understand: how an entire race could be bad. Whatever sparked the rage of the people outside my window and the fury of the Nazis on the Rabbi's balcony had to be about more than religion. It had to be *my* fault. They were outside *my* window, and I was the one always getting in trouble.

Had the other occupants of our four-story apartment building learned I fed and named the mice that crept in through the cracks in the floorboards? Had I been spotted sneaking to the Spanish Riding School in the Imperial Hofburg Palace to watch the Lipizzaner stallions train, when I was supposed to go directly home after school?

Several times a week since the Nazis stomped into Austria eight months ago, my parents sent me to bed without supper or wouldn't let me play outside, claiming it was "for my own good" and "one day I would understand." Rabbi Ehrenfeld was strict too. If I talked during a sermon, my punishment was to dust the outside of the ark where the Torah scrolls lived. I was a disappointment to Mama and Papa, to our Rabbi, to the members of our temple, and to God.

More rocks flew into the room, and I snatched the quilt off Renate. "Let's go." I pulled her out of the bed and toward our parents' room. Siegfried followed.

Renate and I flew into our father's embrace. He was half-dressed but held us, then let go and buttoned his black, long-sleeve shirt. Mama was already clothed.

In a voice too calm to match the urgency of our dilemma, Papa told us not to worry. "Remember the plan. Run to the attic and hide until this is over."

Why didn't he scold me for making God angry?

"I'm sorry," I said. "This is my fault."

"Shh, child." Mama placed a warm and wet hand on my cheek. The shaking of her sweaty palm belied the forced steadiness in her voice. "Do as your father says."

At Rabbi Ehrenfeld's command, escape plans had been prepared and practiced. With Papa and Siegfried in the lead and Mama in the rear, we ran in a line down the narrow hallway around a sharp corner, and into the small kitchen. Grabbing a knotted rope, Papa and Siegfried pulled down the stairs to the attic. Mama, five feet five inches tall and strong enough to carry four one-gallon glass bottles of milk at once, climbed up first. Siegfried handed her blankets, sheets, towels, and pillows. Renate went next, since she whimpered and shook so much she wasn't able to help. Papa, Siegfried and I formed a line from the refrigerator and the cupboard to the attic, where we passed up food and drinks.

Loud blows on the front door to our apartment halted our assembly line. I looked up at Papa, who was over six feet tall and broad shouldered, and then to Siegfried. My brother, a few inches shorter than Papa, was leaner and also well muscled. Siegfried's dark, floppy hair was mussed. His blue eyes glowed with intensity. His side curls swung as he looked from the door to Papa.

"Should we answer it?" I asked.

"No." Papa shoved me toward the attic stairs.

Tears built in my eyes, and I knew my instinct was correct. Papa *was* angry with me. This situation *was* all my fault.

# CHAPTER TWELVE
# RUBY
# KRISTALLNACHT DAY ONE

APPLAUSE GREETED DIXIE as she stepped onto the apron of the stage from off right. The heavy red velvet curtain closed behind her and shimmered like a flag in a balmy breeze. She wore gold spiked heels, a gold G-string, and white opera gloves pulled above her elbows. Her bleach- blond hair piled high on her head. Her stomach muscles flexed as she strutted across the front of the stage. Long calf muscles slinked in a sexy curve. Her buttocks hard, her body glowed with the benefit of being eighteen years old. With her left pasty in place, her right one had been positioned askew and offered a glimpse of a light pink areola. The service boys whooped, especially those in the front rows.

"Pantomimes have always been welcomed on our stage at the Hudson Burlesque Theater." She enunciated above the ruckus. "None have been more admired than that top banana, Charles Chaplin. Here, giving his impression of Charles Chaplin is Ruby Friedman."

With Ruby's back to the audience, the curtain opened. On stage left were a table and two chairs. On top of the table was a bottle of vodka, actually water, and two old- fashioned glasses. At the sight of Ruby, the audience erupted in laughter as if the real Charles Chaplin graced the stage complete with black suit, bowler hat, and a long and thin bamboo cane. Mac, at the upright piano stage right, played Scott Joplin's classic rag, "The Entertainer." Ruby pivoted, and the audience erupted at the sight of his small black moustache, thick eyebrows, and dark hair, which winged out from under the bowler. He tipped the hat and followed with a congenial bow.

Spinning the cane and taking short, stutter steps, he made his way to the table, tripping over nothing at all and then reacting as if something large had been in his way. Dixie pranced like a peacock toward Ruby to the cheers of the primarily male crowd. Hands on hips, she stood next to him. He moved his hands in a figure eight and gave a thrust of his pelvis. The audience roared.

Ruby reached out to her. Dixie extended her hand and Ruby's bowler hat somersaulted down and up his right arm. They repeated this routine several times. Ruby hung his cane on his forearm and balanced the hat on his nose as if a seal. Dixie clapped with exaggeration, her breasts bounced. The audience applauded with her.

Next Ruby bobbled his hat across his crotch, from pocket to pocket. Soldiers stood and clapped their hands above their heads. A hefty sailor with a crew cut who was seated in the front row roared louder than the rest.

*The skit is going well*, Ruby thought. *Focus. Stay focused. Don't let that idiot in the front row ruin this opportunity.*

He and Dixie played off each other like an accomplished symphony; he was no longer unknown Ruby Friedman but the marvelously talented Charles Chaplin. This moment could be his break out opportunity when everyone would recognize what a talent he was. Maybe there was a scout in the audience who would recognize his talent and help him make the move from Union Hill to Manhattan, from burlesque to vaudeville. Maybe he could be a famous actor by the time his family arrived in New York from Vienna. He wouldn't have to confess his lies, and they'd have a nice place to stay, rather than be crammed into his tiny one-room apartment where they'd have to hide from Mrs. Bowen and her goon sons.

Center stage he dropped the cane, picked it up, and it got caught in his fly and waved straight out toward the spectators. Ruby knew the young men, many who had teen attached to their ages, loved this part; certain some of the boys in the audience had actual hard-ons as they imagined a chance encounter with Dixie after the show.

Ruby reached into his pocket and pulled out a red rose. A rolled wad of cash dropped to the floor. He quickly picked it up and stuffed it in his pocket. He handed the rose to Dixie.

Hand on her cheek in surprise, Dixie pointed to his pocket and mouthed, "Oh my God." She dropped a lace hankie that had been stuffed in her G-string.

Ruby picked up the hankie. When he stood, his cane traveled up her leg. Ruby stepped back, a feigned look of surprise on his face, and hit the handle of his cane as if to punish it for being bad. The boys hollered.

Dixie demurely sat at the table, and Ruby waddled toward the other seat. Standing in front of it, he crossed one ankle over his knee and shimmied to a seated position. He mimed that they should drink, to which Dixie nodded enthusiastically. He sloppily poured them each a drink, the liquid spilled all over the tabletop and flung into the air. He put the bottle down and shook his hands, as if nervous. He poured the "liquor" again, and once more it flew all over. Dixie covered her face and arms and tried to avoid being splashed. Ruby sloshed the liquor off the table, into the palms of his hands, and then poured it into the glasses, wiping his hands over the glasses to get the last bit of pretend vodka into them, wringing each finger. The service men howled.

In the front row, the large sailor gyrated his pelvis as if hearing strip tease music. Ruby's face heated, and anger built. *How dare this clown ruin my show and mock the woman I love?*

The jerk pointed at Dixie. "Bring it here, baby. You need a man who speaks the language of love."

Servicemen laughed. Ruby pretended not to hear, and hoped it didn't show on his exterior that he seethed on the interior. He moved to the next stage of his act, approaching the climax, the moment when it would be revealed: does Charlie Chaplin get the girl?

At the table, Ruby and Dixie clinked glasses, the only sound of their performance other than Mac's piano, and Dixie pointed into the audience. Ruby looked to see what she pointed at, while Dixie produced a small vial from under the table and poured it into Ruby's drink. Unknown to Dixie, but known to the audience, Ruby saw her devious act.

This part was his favorite. Could he switch cups when she wasn't looking and fool her into drinking from the glass she had contaminated? It was a lovely cat-and-mouse scenario that would bring more laughs. Except for the imbecile in the front row, it was going so well maybe Sam Cohen would let him show his stuff as the song-and-dance man he was.

Ruby faced the audience, widened his eyes, and mimed what Dixie had done when she poured the potion into his drink. He put both hands on one side of his face and acted as if he was going to sleep; after all, that was why she had spiked his drink. He reached into his pocket and pulled out the wad of cash. The message was clear without words. If he drank from his glass, he would fall asleep and she would steal his money. He would not let that happen. He waggled his finger back and forth and returned the cash to his right front pocket.

"If you don't fuck her already," the crumb in the front yelled, "I'll do it for you."

Some spectators laughed; others yelled for the heckler to shut up. One of the men next to him tried to subdue him.

Ruby again ignored the agitator. As a mime, he had to be limber but the heckler made him tense.

Ruby took a long deep breath and hoped it appeared to be part of the show. He tapped his head to suggest he had an idea. He moved to clink glasses with Dixie, then jumped half out of his seat and pointed behind her. She looked away, and he exchanged the two glasses. The toxic one was now in front of her.

She was too smart to be taken by her own trick, though. She raised the contaminated glass as if to toast and then pointed over Ruby's shoulder. Ruby refused to look. He turned to the audience and tapped his skull again, because he wasn't falling for her ruse a second time. Meanwhile, Dixie picked up both glasses and banged them down on the table to their original spots. Confident that he knew which glass did not contain the sleeping agent, Ruby drank from his own. Soon his eyes grew wide and his head tilted to the side as if he was falling asleep. He pulled on his ear and spit a stream of liquid from his mouth, pushed on his nose and another stream shot out. He paused for the laughter.

The man in the front slapped his friend on his back, and yelled, "I can do that with my dick."

Ruby carried on, determined not to let him ruin the show. Pressing down on his hat and pulling on his finger, he spurted water from his lips. He then faked fatigue and his head fell to one side. He jumped up, trying to stay awake. He fought to keep his eyes open, fell into the chair, and then jumped up again. Soon he slumped forward and was asleep.

Dixie rose and inched her way toward him. She reached into his left pants pocket. With his eyes closed, Ruby shook his head and pointed to his right pocket. More laughter. She took the money and started to walk away, but Ruby wasn't finished with her yet. The money, on a rubber band, sprung back to him.

The audience cheered. Ruby jumped up from his seat, a wide grin on his face. Grabbing Dixie's hand, the act over, Ruby walked to the front of the stage. He bowed; she curtsied.

"Now are you going to fuck her?" The man in the front gripped his crotch.

The audience members yelled. "Yeah, fuck her."

"I'll do you, baby."

Others screamed for them to clam up. Papers and programs landed on stage along with apples, a banana, empty cigarette packages, and coins.

In the wings, Sam Cohen motioned for Dixie and Ruby to get off the stage. Behind Sam were Lester and Frank, Jr., and other performers and dancers.

As Ruby led Dixie off stage, the idiot in the front row threw copper Wheat Pennies onto the stage and plunged his hand down his pants. "Come and get this, whore."

Ruby stopped and shouted, "Show her respect."

"She don't deserve respect."

Sam and Lester ran onto the stage, grabbed Dixie and led her safely away.

The servicemen yelled and screamed, threw shoes and hats, and fought with each other. On the stage, Ruby dodged missiles from the audience. He knew what he wanted to do, knew what he shouldn't do, jump off the stage and pummel the Joe who started this.

"What the fuck's up with that moustache?" the sailor yelled. "You a Hitler want-to-be?"

Two burly men stepped from the wings and onto the stage. They were security, the fellows who were supposed to keep the women safe. It was assumed the male singers and comics could take care of themselves, or at least run fast enough to escape trouble.

Ruby held up his hand to stop the bouncers, and the most interesting thought popped into his mind. If I fight this man, I am no better than him, no better than Hitler who uses bully techniques to dominate and intimidate.

He stepped back, tipped his hat to the crowd, and walked like Charlie Chaplin, feet pointed out, penguin style, to the table, where he gulped from the vodka bottle. He returned to the front of the stage where the sailor in the front row yelled and grabbed himself. Ruby did a funny walk, side-to-side, heel-toe, heel-toe, rolled his hat up and down his arm, and twirled his cane. The crowd quieted and watched. He stopped in front of the man and leaned over as if he was going to tell him something. Instead, Ruby yanked on both of own his ears and squirted water from his mouth, a forceful stream curving like a rainbow into the man's face. The audience laughed and the security guards jumped off the stage and forced the man out of the theater.

# CHAPTER THIRTEEN
## MICHAEL
### 1994

MY TEN-YEAR-OLD SELF looked into the open casket, thick powder covered my paternal grandfather's stone face. Dedushka's arms folded stiffly across his chest. Red lipstick painted his downturned lips. His eyes were closed. If he could speak I knew he would say I was a disappointment.

"I'll find a way to make you proud, Dedushka. I promise."

In 1917, Dedushka was an infant when his mother and father emigrated from Russia to America during the Russian Revolution. They abandoned their belongings, fled the czar and the Cossacks on foot, were hidden by underground networks of Eastern European Jews, and made it across the Atlantic in the cargo hull of an ocean liner. They settled on the Lower East Side of Manhattan. As Dedushka grew, his father, who was my great grandfather, told stories of their escape, how they trekked across frozen rivers and lakes and traversed Poland and Germany to Holland. His mother, my great grandmother, tried to keep Dedushka from crying so they wouldn't be discovered. They had little food and water; they were cold, wet, dirty, and sick.

In America, Dedushka shared these stories with his son, my father, who then told them to me. Not in one long narrative, as I'm doing now, but in snippets spoken between flips of burgers on a grill, sips of lemonade on a hot day, and while Papa taught me how to change spark plugs. If I whined as a boy that I needed a new pair of sneakers, which was something I complained about often, Papa would say, "When Dedushka was a boy he had one pair of shoes for three years and cut off the fronts so his toes wiggled free."

Message received. Maybe that's why I'm a freak about my sneaker collection, more than seventy-five pairs. As long as I have a lot of shoes, as long as I don't have to cut out the toes to make them fit, I am okay.

When Dedushka left Russia as a baby, his last name was Turgenev. When he was carried off Ellis Island, his face hidden in his mother's chest, he was a Tucker.

"Easier to pronounce," said the immigration official who stamped several forms and called, "Next in line."

In Russia, and before the Revolution, Dedushka's father was a successful tailor with his own shop. He made clothes, ironically, for Emperor Nicholas II. In America he was another immigrant who couldn't speak English, had no connections, had little money, had a wife and a baby to support, and who had no job, so he did what every poor immigrant did. He located housing with another Russian family and took whatever work he could find. He scrubbed floors, labored in kitchens, cleaned stalls and washed sewers. He did everything but what he loved to do, which was sew. As Papa told it to me, Dedushka never complained.

Graced with stubbornness and dogged determination, on his thirtieth birthday, Dedushka opened his own tailor shop in Manhattan, near Bloomingdale's. My grandfather believed the greatest day of his life was when he opened the doors to his store in America, but modified that declaration to the day four years later when twenty-year-old Gertrude Pishkin walked in and asked him to make her a dress for her college graduation.

"Love at first sight," Dedushka would say, followed by a hearty laugh and look of bewilderment that a young, beautiful, free-spirited woman like Gram would agree to be his wife.

Gram also told me of her attraction to him when she stepped into the Third Avenue store. "His eyes sparkled when he discussed ideas for my dress. His hands were smooth and strong. His spirit was gentle. His speech, thoughtful. I was tired of dating men my age who were immature and couldn't handle a career woman. He encouraged me to go to law school. When I began earning more than he, when we attended the award galas and political functions where I was the center of attention, he never objected. He would say, 'What is there to complain about? I have Gertrude Tucker on my arm.'"

Dedushka and Gram married in 1957. Abram Tucker, my papa, was born in 1960. While he didn't fancy needle and thread, he took to carburetors, spark plugs, and brake pads. He owned his first gas station before his twenty-first birthday. He and my mother, Mariya, met in college at a Russian school club and married in 1982. I came along two years later.

Dedushka passed away in 1997. At his funeral, I listened intently to the eulogies from our family members, and his friends and business associates of all he had accomplished. Seated on the hard pew, I looked at Gram who was renowned in the field of law, saw my father who owned a chain of gas stations at the time, and viewed my mother who was head of the PTA, and who made and sold fine dresses that Dedushka taught her to sew. I realized I descended from a family of greatness, and I had to achieve great things too. It was in my DNA, right? After all my family had accomplished, I had no choice but to be amazing, and I wanted to make Dedushka, Gram, and my parents proud.

I attempted to excel in school but was nothing more than a B student, I played football and warmed the bench, I was decent at basketball but no star, I tried out for school plays and never got cast as more than a spear holder. I couldn't sing, I sucked at dancing, and I was an alternate on the debate team. When I started the Future Lawyer's Club in high school, no one showed up.

I graduated somewhere in the middle of my class at SUNY at Stony Brook with a degree in American literature and took the LSATs. I scored well enough to get in to some law school somewhere, not Ivy League, but I would be accepted into a lower-tier New York law school or into one of those law schools that popped up in Florida with names no one's heard.

With applications spread in front of me, deadlines imminent, I sickened. Even if I could get in to a third-rate school, I wasn't good enough to go. I didn't deserve to be a member of the profession that Gram was kicking ass in, and I would flunk anyway. How would that look? Not only couldn't Gertrude Tucker's grandson get into a *real* law school, but he also couldn't graduate. I'm not going to mention the terror I experienced of having to pass the bar exam.

After therapy and a lot of marijuana, I came to terms with who I wasn't and who I was. I wasn't gifted like the family members I had studied at my grandfather's funeral when I was ten years old. I was average, not made of the same stock as my relatives, a person who will not change the world.

When I told my parents and Gram I wouldn't apply to law school, and made it sound like I was delaying for a year when I had no intention of attending, Papa offered for me to work with him.

"You already know a lot about cars," he had said. "We've worked on them together since you were a boy. It's my dream for you to run the gas stations one day."

That wasn't the first time I politely rejected his proposal. Mama suggested I learn how to design clothes for twenty-somethings to complement my sneaker obsession. While that proposition interested me, it didn't make my heart race, so I did what every new college graduate wants to do: I backpacked around Europe.

Mama, Papa, and Gram chipped in, unaware I had accumulated a decent stash from selling pot throughout my college years. My family was patient with me, not dissuading me from taking the trip, not pressuring me to find a career. Perhaps they had come to terms that I was destined to be ordinary, a thought that brought relief. At least they knew the truth about their only offspring.

I bought a one-way ticket to Heathrow and began an adventure into I wasn't sure what. What I did know was that backpacking around Europe felt a lot less scary than failing law school or the Bar exam.

I stayed in hostels and, with the aid of a Eurail pass, explored Europe. Sometimes I toured alone, at other times I hooked up with newly made friends. Once, I met a cute coed from Southern Italy and we spent an exciting eight days traveling through France, having sex more than seeing the sights. Sartre wrote, "France was a woman." To that I would add, "Paris is an aphrodisiac."

Five and a half months of that whirlwind tour was invigorating and exhausting, but I wasn't ready to head to the States. I had to go to Russia to see where Dedushka escaped from, and to visit the homeland of the Turgenev family before we were randomly renamed Tucker by an hourly wage clerk at Ellis Island.

The Turgenevs hailed from Oryol, Russia, a city approximately 220 miles from Moscow. Our most famous member, not counting Gram who was a Turgenev/Tucker by marriage, was Ivan Turgenev, a novelist who died in 1883. His book, *Fathers and Children*, was an important work of the nineteenth century. I imagined my interest in literature came from that genetic connection.

When I got to Moscow and viewed the Kremlin with its daunting towers and imposing surrounding wall, I was overcome with awe, longing, and sadness. Awe for the magnificence of the structures, longing to know more about my ancestors, and sadness they and others had been forced to flee their native land. I walked east to Red Square and clenched my jaw as I imagined the terror of the people who lived before me and the horror and suffering of my family. My thoughts turned next to their courage and daring. In contrast, I saw my failures crank before me like a 1930s black and white newsreel. I knew, surrounded by that massive building and its amazing history, that I was nothing.

Two days later I boarded a plane home to New York. This man who had attended his grandfather's funeral as a ten-year-old boy would no longer accept being ordinary, not with the blood that coursed through my veins, and not with my parents and Gram asking nothing of me. Some average man with a government job might have caused my last name to become Tucker, but I was still a Turgenev.

Seven months after arriving home from my European trip, I started law school at NYU. Gram got me in. Except for taking criminal law with Elaine Weitzman as my professor and soon-to-be lover, and a constitutional law class that featured the Nuremburg trials, I hated law school. I didn't find the work challenging. Most of the professors were officious and cruel, and many of the students were stuck ups and show offs. I kept to myself and graduated with a solid C average. I passed the New York bar on my first shot and went about finding a job, *without* Gram's help. I wanted to do it on my own, not on her coattails.

I had interned at a large real estate firm and vowed not to enter the corporate law arena, since I had seen the questionable billing practices and lousy treatment of new associates at large firms. I applied to the district attorney's office but was not invited for a second interview.

I therefore hung out a shingle, as they say, in a rundown office building in midtown Manhattan on the same floor as my cousin's talent agency. I lived at home, worked for my cousin when the law business was slow, which in the beginning was most of the time, and had my dinners paid for by friends I didn't charge for getting their traffic tickets dismissed. I considered asking Gram for help in getting some real cases when I hopped on the Long Island Railroad and saw Sara.

# CHAPTER FOURTEEN
## SARA

THE KEY TO surviving incarceration is repetition and routine. Wake up at the same time, place the left foot down first onto the cold linoleum floor, and brush your teeth with thirty strokes, up and down, and then the tongue. Eat the same food, count the number of steps to the library, talk to no one, and lights out at nine p.m. Keep to yourself and read as much as possible. Start again the following morning.

A guard's voice boomed over the loudspeaker. "Inmate zero six two five three three to holding area four."

I put down the worn copy of *Grapes of Wrath* and sat up on the cot. Wire springs poked through the old mattress. A surge of giddiness flowed through me at the prospect that it was Michael visiting, but knew that was unlikely. My euphoria turned glum when I wondered if it could be Billy, again.

I stepped into holding area four and the door to the pod locked behind me. I watched the entrance to the visitor bay in front of me and waited for the "all clear," when the guard believed it safe to pass into the next bay. With a loud clank that no longer rattled me, the door opened. I stepped through.

Another guard pointed toward the third room on the left, visitor room 7b. I then knew I was meeting with my attorney, since those rooms were reserved for clients and their counsel. Trace probably wanted more money.

I didn't mind that Glen Trautman had passed my appeal to Trace. As the founder of one of the country's largest law firms, Glen Trautman spent most of his days lunching with powerbrokers and lobbying legislators. Trace, however, was a caustic go-for-the-throat litigator who yearned to win every case because he hated to lose.

Trace was seated behind a scuffed table. He greeted me with a nod, and didn't bother to stand. His belly tumbled over his belt but I'm sure that's not why he didn't rise when I entered the room. I was a convict, and while he respected the green in my bank accounts, he didn't regard me with value. I didn't need him to like me, just to get me out of my situation.

The woman seated next to him had dark skin, kinky hair, stunning green eyes, and a friendly and inviting face.

She stood and offered her hand. "I'm Elizabeth."

Her eyes were nonjudgmental and kind. She watched me with amusement.

I didn't recognize her at first. "You're Liz Trautman," I said.

"Nice to see you, Sara."

"It's been a long time."

"Fifteen years."

"Since I went to college."

"Sorry to see each other under these circumstances."

"Me too." I wanted to embrace her, but kept my face stiff. It wasn't easy to suppress the tears.

Elizabeth was five years younger than me, and the same age as Soldier Boy. When I was growing up, the Trautmans and the Goldsteins often celebrated holidays together, so the younger kids had been thrown together at family gatherings. Trace, who was eighteen years older than Elizabeth, wasn't around much in those days. Eventually I discovered they were half-siblings. Elizabeth was the product of Glen Trautman's second marriage to a much younger woman.

The dark-skinned girl who didn't look like the rest of us had fascinated me when I was young. I was twelve when curiosity overcame me. It was July Fourth when I asked the question that had nagged me.

"How come you don't look like the rest of your family?"

"I'm adopted," seven-year-old Elizabeth said.

We grew closer and talked about her heritage and how she didn't want to know her birth parents. Like many friendships, we lost touch. In the visitor's room at Rikers Island we were now found.

I looked across the table at her. "Forty percent Sierra Leone, thirty percent English and thirty percent Swedish."

"You remembered."

I didn't feel like a prisoner. I felt normal, as if the reunion could be happening in a coffee shop.

Trace broke my bliss. "What's that?"

"What's what?" I asked.

"That shit about Sierra Leone and England and whatever."

Elizabeth rolled her eyes. "My genetic history. I'm forty percent Sierra Leone, thirty percent English and—"

"Yeah, yeah. Well, I'm one hundred percent starving, so let's move on."

I frowned at Trace.

"What?" he asked.

I controlled the tremor in my voice. "Why are you here? Do you have information about my appeal?"

Trace pointed to Elizabeth. "You tell her."

"I've been assigned to your case," she said.

"To do what? You're not a lawyer, are you?" I racked my brain and tried to remember if I had heard Liz had gone to law school.

"I'm a private investigator. You didn't kill Uncle Charlie, correct?"

"Absolutely." I didn't flinch; no revealing blinks or twitches. I told the truth. I hadn't killed him.

"Okay," Liz said, "my job is to find out who did."

I leaned back in the hard plastic chair and then I laughed. It was a good rip, right from the gut.

Liz looked hurt. I tried to stop. It wasn't so much that I cackled because what she had said was funny as it was some kind of psychological reaction. My diaphragm convulsed and my eyes pleaded with Liz for forgiveness.

"What the fuck is wrong with you?" Trace's contempt beyond an empty stomach was obvious.

I hiccupped a few times, and finally calmed. I looked at Liz. "I'm sorry. I wasn't laughing at you."

"If you don't want me to help—"

"No, no," I interrupted. "Have at it. I'm not optimistic, that's why I agreed to let Trace attack Michael. I'm not hopeful of new evidence being discovered or getting the real murderer's confession."

Trace snapped his fingers. "That's it. Lizzie sees herself as some Nancy Drew, don't you? I thought finding the real murderer was a waste of time too, but Dad said I had to find something for her to do on this case." He looked at me and scoffed, making no secret of his belief in my guilt. "If you want to go undercover, Sis, go after Michael."

"What does that mean?" I tried not to screech.

"It means she's going to use her feminine wiles to get close to Michael and find what we can use against him. There has to be something."

"I don't know," I said.

"Well, I do." Trace clapped his hands. "Done. You up for it, Lizzie?"

"Sure."

"Okay, good."

I thought about mentioning Billy O'Brien. If I could make up a reason for them to go after him, maybe he wouldn't threaten me again and it would divert their attention from Michael. But I had agreed for them to file the appeal against Michael…

"Wait," I said.

"Wait for what?" Trace scowled.

"Nothing," I said.

"You want out of this fucking nightmare, don't you?"

"Of course."

"You agree trying to find the real murderer is a waste of time."

I hesitated, not sure if my agreement would insinuate my guilt. Truth was, I could save Trace and Liz the time and tell them who killed Uncle Charlie.

"Right." Trace further gleaned guilt from my non-response.

I'd never liked him and started to despise him.

"It's a done deal." He clapped his hands again and looked at Liz. "Do whatever you have to do, and I mean whatever. Find what you can, whether it will help us with the appellate court or in some other way. Everyone has secrets. Got it?"

"Understood."

"And I mean do anything." He raised his eyebrows up and down.

"Anything?" I asked.

Trace smiled. The bastard knew he was getting to me.

"All in the name of freedom, right, Sara? Isn't that what you hired us for? Now isn't the time to get soft about your boyfriend."

"He's not my boyfriend," I said weakly.

"Yeah, whatever. Okay, time to eat." He stood.

"Wait," I said.

"Nothing to wait for. We're unleashing my beautiful baby sister on Michael Tucker. When you throw enough shit against a wall, something's bound to stick."

Liz got up.

"Where are you going?" Trace asked.

She looked bewildered. "I thought we were leaving."

"I am, you're not. You have work to do."

"And what's that?" she asked.

"You, my dear, have to prepare to seduce Michael Tucker, and who better to teach the seductress than his paramour." He walked out.

Liz sat and we faced each other. I searched for something to say. From Liz's flustered look, I thought she also rummaged for words of reassurance. What did I want to hear from her? How about, "Don't worry, Sara, I won't sleep with your boyfriend."

"He's not my boyfriend," I mumbled.

"What?"

"Nothing."

"Okay." Her voice was a sigh. "Tell me everything you know personally about Michael."

"Like what?"

"Where he grew up, where he went to school, about his family."

"Is this necessary?"

She took out a pad and a pen. "I'm afraid it is."

# CHAPTER FIFTEEN
## LIANA
## KRISTALLNACHT DAY ONE

HARD KNOCKS ON our apartment door changed to powerful bangs.

"Into the attic. Now," Papa ordered.

"Wait." I ran out of the kitchen before he or Siegfried could catch me.

I sprinted down the hall as fast as my stocking feet would allow. I skidded into my bedroom and slid to a stop at the foot of my bed. Broken glass lay all around the floor, along with cragged rocks and bricks that pinched and sliced at my toes and heels. I wrapped my arms across my chest. Bits of the newspapers that had covered our windows blew like confetti.

"Open the door," a thickly German-accented voice bellowed from the building hallway.

More pounding. I grabbed my pillow and pulled off the case.

"What are you doing?" Wide-eyed and sweaty, Papa stood in the door to the bedroom.

I ran to him and wrapped my arms around his waist. "This is my fault."

"No, it is not."

"Everyone is mad at me." I cried and looked up at him.

Papa smiled despite the fear in his eyes. "This is Hitler's fault."

He unwrapped me from his waist and knelt. We were eye to eye. "You need to get into the attic. Now."

"The carousel horses. We have to take them." I ran to my bed and opened the pillowcase. "And I can't forget Bruno." I grabbed the stuffed animal and looped my arms through the belts Papa had attached. The bear hugged me like a backpack.

"There's no time for the horses."

"You told me I had to protect them. You said, 'When I am with them, I will be with you too.'"

"I know, but we can't take them." He reached for my arm.

I darted out of his grip and stretched for the white Arabian, one of four glass horses that sat on a rotating tray and moved like a real carousel when a person pulled the lever. Somehow my horses had not been broken like all of the windows to our bedroom; they were magical.

I was about to pick up the Arabian and put it in the pillowcase when Papa yelled, "You need to listen to me for once."

He grabbed me around the waist and threw me over his shoulder. I punched at his back and kicked at his front. My outstretched arms reached for the horses. As Papa turned to go down the narrow hallway to enter the kitchen, three storm troopers, their backs to us, blocked our path.

# CHAPTER SIXTEEN
## RUBY
## KRISTALLNACHT DAY ONE

RUBY STEPPED OFF the stage to chants of the crowd, "Ruby, Ruby, Ruby." He didn't know if they cheered for him and how he had embarrassed that rude sailor in the front row, or for Charlie Chaplin, but he didn't care. He had saved the day. He had prevented a riot from breaking out in the theater. He had used humor to quell the crowd, like Chaplin would have done.

Sam, the general manager, short, round, and smelling of salami, waited in the wings. "Good job, Ruby. You're fired."

He laughed. "Good one. Did Frank Byron Jr. put you up to that? That's something the dummy would do."

"I'm serious. I was supposed to tell you before you went on, but I couldn't do it. We're in a recession, kid. People don't have disposable income to spend on burlesque like they used to. The owner of the theater waited as long as he could, but now he has to let someone go."

The Frat Boys took the stage. The crowd quieted as Mac began playing the opening notes to "Whistle While You Work".

Ruby watched Sam and searched for the crack of a smile, a brightening of his eyes, something to let him in on the joke. "You're serious," Ruby said.

"Afraid so."

"Why me?"

"It was between you and the Frat Boys, but they agreed to take a pay cut, and—"

"I'll take a pay cut." Ruby thought of his family on their way to New York. He had to be able to support them, at least until Jacob found work. "My act is so much better than the Frat boys. They can't even carry a tune."

"You're not going to hear any argument from me on that one, kid, but it's too late. The Frat Boys are also the owner's second cousins once removed or something like that. You never stood a chance. I haven't told any of the fellows or the gals. I'll leave that up to you." Sam walked away, and called over his shoulder, "You killed 'em out there, kid. You done Mr. Chaplin proud."

On stage, the Frat Boys sang off-key.

# CHAPTER SEVENTEEN
## MICHAEL

I DROVE FROM my father's gas station to Sara's home, nauseated like a schoolboy about to ask a girl out on a date. I knew Sara wasn't there, but anxiety and fear shook my nerves. Fear as if she might open the front door, anxiety as if her brother might knock me senseless. I wasn't taking the journey to reminisce or to beat myself up over stupid choices. The trip was to find Soldier Boy and was probably a waste of time.

I pulled the Mustang into the long drive that abutted Sara's mansion and tried to convince myself I was engaged in character building. It was good to confront what scared me, or some self-help mumbo-jumbo like that. I put the stick shift into first gear, shut off the car, and lifted the brake. No cars were in the driveway.

My throat tightened, pressure behind my eyes built. Were those tears? Damn it. Elaine Weitzman was right. I'm a never-ending romantic, and I asked myself, When Sara told me many times prior to her conviction that she loved me, had she done so as an unreliable reporter?

Two large columns with four-foot-high stone lions at the bases guarded the front door. I remembered when I leaned against one of the lions with Sara in my arms. As much as I tried to convince myself otherwise, I missed her mouth, the shape of her lips, the taste of her kiss, and her sweet words. I would miss the lies, I'm sure, if I knew which ones they were.

Perhaps this visit would penetrate my stubborn heart. She was no good. Her actions against me weren't solely a product of her lawyers' strategies but of her own volition.

*Get over her, Tucker.*

I pushed open the car door. I had to make things right. I had to help Erica defend me, I had to guard Gram's money, and I had to protect my reputation and my family's honor.

I stepped between the columns and in front of the massive door. The stone lions seemed to eye me with suspicion. Overgrown bushes shadowed the steps. The grass was several inches too high and weeds peeked through crevices in the marble landing. The shades on the windows were drawn.

I leaned into the doorbell and a cacophony of bells greeted me. As the last chime faded into the late morning air, I waited. Who would open the door, if anyone? Soldier Boy? Blanca? As far as I knew, they were the only options.

I rang the bell again. It was a large house, and someone upstairs, in one of the bedrooms, or even in the Forbidden Room, might not initially hear the chimes.

No response.

It was a waste of time, indeed. I headed to the Mustang, mildly disappointed I hadn't come face-to-face with Soldier Boy and mildly pleased, because I had no idea what I would say to him and how he would react to me.

I'd have to think of a new plan. I could Google Soldier Boy and see if his name comes up, search a list of Army personnel to see if he's re-enlisted, and check the jails, prisons, hospitals and mental institutions.

I slid into the Mustang and was about to reverse out of the driveway when a pickup parked behind me, probably maintenance workers. I waved my arm out the window and indicated they needed to move so I could back up. No response. I got out of my car. The driver of the pickup stepped out of his. I stopped, considered rushing into the Mustang and driving away, but I was trapped.

"Michael Tucker," Billy O'Brien said.

I don't know why I was afraid of him. He had never done anything to me, but over the years I had heard what prison had done to him, how it had made him hard, and how he was a suspect in murder investigations.

"Hey, Billy," I sounded casual. "You doing work for the Goldsteins?"

"You could say that."

"Lawn maintenance?"

His laugh was odd, stilted. "Call it what you like."

"Great. Um, think you can move your truck? I have an appointment."

He was taller and broader than when I saw him last. He wore black jeans and a black T-shirt.

He stepped closer to me. "You do know Sara is not home. As best I can recall, she's in prison and it's your fault."

"I don't want any trouble." I held my hands up.

"Trouble you got, Michael Tucker, and it's spelled B-I-L-L-Y."

"I thought we were friends."

"Friends, I don't think so. Your charity project, maybe. I don't need no favors from you, never did."

"Okay. Fine. I want to make it to my appointment on time, that's all."

He moved into my space. "You know that appeal that Sara filed? Tell the court you fucked up and she's not guilty."

I sucked in a laugh. "I can't do that."

He reached behind him and produced a gun from his pocket, maybe. He tucked it into the front waistband of his jeans. His hand rested on the grip of the gun. Sweat shined on his forehead.

"Sure you can."

I stepped back. "It doesn't work like that. She had a trial. If the appellate court finds legal reason to overturn her conviction then—"

"If you say one more thing that I don't understand, I swear I'm going to shoot you."

"Okay, okay." I stepped farther away. "Whatever you want, I'll do it."

"Good." He slithered into the pickup and backed out of the drive and away, the wheels screeched on the Basalt paver tiles.

I bent over and put my hands on my knees and caught my breath.

"He's a real bastard," came a voice.

I spun toward the front of the house and blinked at the sight before me. He was a wisp of a man so frail and pale I questioned if he were a ghost. Surprisingly he stood straight and tall. He fidgeted with a black lanyard around his neck that had several keys attached. I walked toward him, and hoped the shaking in my legs would stop. As I got close I saw his fingers swelled with arthritis. He had no eyebrows.

"I'm friends with Soldier Boy," I said, "I mean, David. Is he here?"

The man let out a small laugh. "Can't keep that boy in one place for long. If you're his friend, I don't have to tell you that."

I detected an accent. German?

"He's always traipsing off somewhere." I tried to sound like I knew Soldier Boy.

"Who should I say is calling?"

My heart rate quickened. "You mean he's here?"

"Not at the moment. He should return soon."

"Do you know when?"

His eyes narrowed. "You one of his army buddies?"

"No, I know him through Sara."

"My niece sure got herself into a pickle. I'm not saying plenty of people didn't want Charles Carrara dead, but Sara didn't do it. She should have hired an attorney with more experience. It's not like she doesn't have the money."

I shifted on the stoop, glad he didn't recognize me as Sara's inexperienced attorney. "You knew Uncle Charlie?"

"Knew him? Of course. He was Alfonso's half-brother, about

thirty years younger since Big Al's old man took a fancy to a dancer. Young, pretty women have associated with old rich men since the beginning of time."

"Wait." I tried to sort through this information. "You knew Alfonso *and* Charlie?"

"Alfonso and I were business associates and friends. In those days, you had real friends, and you were friends for life. None of this fake Internet friend crap." He swiped his hand across his forehead, and looked pallid.

I was processing the family connections when the old man slapped me gently on the arm. "Don't work off too many brain cells and try to figure that out. Trust me, you're going to need all of them if you're going to live as long as me." He teetered.

I grabbed him until he steadied.

"Isn't easy being an old man. Guess how old I am."

I hated that game, can't win unless you're within a couple of years older or you underestimate. Was he Gram's age when she died? I figured he looked about how she did with loose skin, watery eyes, and shaking hands. Yet, like Gram, he had a fresh mind.

I took a guess. "Eighty-six."

"Ninety-seven."

"No shit."

"Can't believe it myself. If you knew the things I'd been through and the people I've associated with, you'd be shocked."

I reached out. "Michael Tucker."

He looked at me quizzically.

I dropped my empty hand to my side. "Sara's former

attorney. The inexperienced one she shouldn't have hired."

Darkness covered him. "Sometimes I don't see so well in sunlight. What do you want with David?"

"To ask him a few questions."

"He might want to pop you in the mouth. Come to think of it, I might want to also."

The old man's eyes rolled back and his knees buckled. I grabbed him before he hit the ground. Carrying him, I stepped over the threshold into Sara's home and laid him on a couch in a grand sitting room. I checked his pulse. Before I could call 911, he opened his eyes. I helped him sit up.

"Fucking blood sugar. I have to eat every couple of hours or else I faint."

I ran to the kitchen and returned with a glass of orange juice. After a few moments, healthy color restored to his face.

"Thank you." He held out his hand, which I took. "Ruby Friedman." He palmed his forehead. "If you will be so kind and help me to my room."

He stood, wobbled, grabbed my arm and leaned on me for support. Ruby shuffled toward the stairs like an aged Charlie Chaplin.

At the summit, I asked, "Which room is yours?"

He pointed to the second room on the left.

My breath sucked in. "Are you sure?"

"I may be old, young man, but I know which room is mine."

"I didn't mean any offense, it's just—"

"That's the room where Charles was murdered. I don't believe in ghosts. If I did, there'd be a whole host of goblins swarming me. You kids have no idea what it was like during the Depression, the things we did to survive, what we saw, the people we ran with."

He held my arm and we made our way along the hallway until we stood in front of the closed door to the Forbidden Room.

I pointed to a small, rectangular object nailed to the upper corner of the doorjamb. I hadn't seen it before.

"What's that?"

"A mezuzah."

"A what?" I asked.

"Where is your family from?"

"Russia. My great grandparents escaped the czar."

"Your family religion is Orthodox Christianity."

"Yes, but I don't practice it."

"A mezuzah is parchment inscribed with the Jewish verse, 'Hear, O Israel, the LORD is our God, the LORD is One'. It's nailed to the front of Jewish doorways to remind us of our faith and to fulfill a mitzvah."

"What's a mitzvah?"

"It's a commandment of Jewish law."

I wanted to ask how the paper with the verse written on it fit inside that little case, but my heart jittered with thoughts of what was on the other side of the door. My nerves shook but it was no longer from my run in with Billy, or from fear of seeing Soldier Boy. Would the carousel horses prance in the middle of the room, displayed on a stand like a museum object? Would Stephen Goldstein's beloved Lionel trains circle tracks? Would my memories of where Sara and I first made love be heightened? Could I mount the horses for another ride?

"I would like to go to sleep." Ruby looked up at me.

"Oh, yeah. Sorry."

I pushed open the door. Inside was like any bedroom, with a queen-sized bed, a dresser, and two end tables. Even the glass shelves in the corner might exist in any other room, except for what was displayed.

Ruby held on to me as I led him to the bed.

"I tell you, Big Al and I saw our share of characters. Meyer Lansky. Bugsy Siegel." He sat on the bed, bent, and slowly removed polished leather shoes.

I kept my eyes on the shelves. "You knew Meyer Lansky and Bugsy Siegel?"

"There weren't many young Jewish men on the Lower East Side of Manhattan in the 1930s who didn't run into those guys. Me, Alfonso and Meyer, we knew each other real well. Meyer was instrumental in Alfonso starting his hotel business, the reason for all of this." He waved a skinny, blue-streaked arm. "In fact, if it weren't for Meyer, Alfonso would have been just another *schmuck*. Loyalty meant something in those days." He pointed a crooked finger at me. "Survival was about who you knew, who you didn't cross, and using your noggin." He tapped his head and then laid his upper body back in the bed.

I lifted his feet at the ankles. He shifted until his head rested on two fluffy pillows, the satin pillowcases stitched with the Rest Well Inn emblem: two gold leaves that framed a carousel horse in flight. Ruby closed his eyes and soon snored. I walked to the five-shelved octagonal display case.

# CHAPTER EIGHTEEN
## LIANA
## KRISTALLNACHT DAY ONE

"THIS WAY." PAPA jerked me into the bathroom, away from the storm troopers who blocked our path into the kitchen. I hoped Mama, Siegfried, and Renate were safely hidden in the attic, the ladder and the knotted rope up, and the hatch closed.

Even though Papa pulled so hard I thought my arm would pop out of its socket, I got a good look at the brown shirts of Hitler's men and the swastikas sewn on to bands wrapped around their left biceps. I recognized one of the Nazis, a teenage boy who lived on the next block.

Papa quietly closed the door to the bathroom in the rear of our two-bedroom apartment. Outside the window was anything but scenic, especially during the winter months when the trees were bare with no snow to offer the illusion of a magical time. Our bathroom window overlooked the rear walls of other brown, drab apartment buildings, iron fire escapes, and a great deal of concrete. There was one plot of land that Mama, Renate, and I weeded each spring and then seeded with basil, parsley, thyme, tomatoes, beans, and cucumbers. Narrow streets on either side of our building allowed cars and horse-drawn wagons to traverse single file.

A storm trooper growled. *"Die unerwünschten Personen."* Find the undesirables.

"What about Mama, Siegfried, and Renate?" I asked Papa who

locked the door and clamped his big, clammy hand over my mouth. His palm was rough and smelled like sweat.

"Shh," he whispered. "They're safe in the attic." He dropped his hand to his side.

My lips parted to speak. When he raised his hand to cover my mouth again, I choked the words down my throat.

Just large enough for Papa and me to stand in, the bathroom had a toilet, a pedestal sink, and a bathtub with a shower spigot. An iron gate guarded a window above the tub. The gate rolled over the window like the elevator door at Papa's office where he worked as an accountant until Jews weren't allowed to work anymore. On the other side of the window was a fire escape. I think he installed the gate, which locked with a key, so I couldn't climb out the window and play on the fire escape. I had tried to climb the fire escape from the outside, but I was too short to reach the bottom rung of the ladder.

Papa eyed the window. Bruno hugged my back and the straps looped over my shoulders.

"We can't leave without Mama, Siegfried, and Renate." I spoke so soft he had to be proud of me. "And the carousel horses, we have to take them with us."

"Forget the carousel horses." Papa's eyes were wide like the rims of our teacups.

"What are we going to do?"

He dropped to his knees, put his hands on my shoulders, and looked into my eyes. "You're going to climb out that window, go down the fire escape, and run."

Tears came to my eyes. A bulge wedged in my throat. I swallowed hard so I could talk. "You all will follow, right?"

He spoke as if he hadn't heard me. "Stay close to the buildings and in the shadows." He unbuttoned his long-sleeved black shirt and slipped Bruno off of me. He draped his shirt around me, pulled my hands through each sleeve, and then looped my arms through Bruno again. "This will keep you warm and cover those bright pajamas."

"I understand, Papa." I tried to sound grown up. "Renate is a big scaredy cat. I'll help her jump off the fire escape." Tears skimmed the bottom of my eyelids.

Papa's bare chest heaved and tears dropped off his chin. He tried to wipe them away but there were too many. "Run and don't look back."

"I'm not going without you, or without them."

He stroked the dark hair from my eyes, leaving a wet trail of salty tears on my cheek. "Don't talk to anyone who is not a Jew, even if they used to be a neighbor, your friend, or your teacher." He held me with one arm and tugged on the window grate, which rattled but did not open. "*D'amyt.*"

"Papa!" I scolded.

Mama hated when Papa cursed in any of the three languages my family spoke: German, Hebrew, and Yiddish. I hated it when he cursed too. He swore when something bad happened or was about to happen.

"The key." He scanned the interior of the bathroom. "Where's the key?"

I didn't know. They never told me, on purpose I'm sure.

Outside the bathroom door, feet shuffled. Male voices with strong German accents mumbled. Papa yanked on the back of the toilet and reached inside. He tugged on the toilet seat. He jerked the medicine cabinet open. No key.

"*A broch!*"

Another curse. I cried.

He knelt in front of me and wiped my tears with thick thumbs. "Don't cry, *bubeleh*. Now is the time to be brave. Can you do that for me?"

I sniffled and nodded.

"I'm going to find where your mother hid the key, and then you are going out that window."

"I'm not going alone. We can wait for the Nazis to leave and then we can go to the attic. Here, take your shirt back. I don't need it." I started to remove his black shirt.

"No." He stopped me. "The day has come. The Nazis are not going away."

The doorknob jiggled. Papa stood to his full height and pushed me behind him. We watched the bronze knob rattle. It shook and then stopped.

"The bathroom door is locked," a Nazi said.

Papa opened the medicine cabinet and grabbed four straight-razor blades. He put them in the front right pocket of his black shirt, which I wore.

One of the SA men sniffed loudly and then laughed. "The smell of shit from the inside of this bathroom is not from a toilet. I know you're in there, *Juden.*"

From the medicine cabinet, Papa grabbed a horsehide leather strop, folded it, and tucked it under one of Bruno's straps.

Somewhere inside the apartment, glass shattered. I jumped and my heart raced faster. More sounds of shattered glass were followed by footsteps as the Nazi who had been at the bathroom door ran toward the kitchen. I heard bangs and thumps, a loud crack, and a crash. I figured our dining room buffet and hutch were toppled and the contents spilled on to the floor. The crush and crunch of china dishes echoed into the bathroom and I feared my beautiful teacups were destroyed.

"The key?" Papa ran his hands over the sides of the doorjamb and along the top. His large fingers emerged with a small gold key.

The crashing and banging stopped. Footsteps approached. The doorknob jiggled again.

Papa pushed me aside and lunged for the iron gate. "You're going out this window."

The bathroom knob rattled. "Come out, come out," a strong male voice boomed in singsong.

Papa's hand shook as he tried to fit the key in the lock. "Go to the train station and wait for Madame Juliette. She'll take you to Paris."

"I don't know what she looks like." I watched Papa's bare back as he tried to unlock the metal gate. "I'm not going without you and Mama." My tears drowned out my brother and sister's names. My legs buckled. I grabbed onto the toilet with both hands and my dinner hit the sides with a violent whoosh. I sat back and wiped my mouth with the sleeve of Papa's black shirt. "I'm not going," I whimpered.

A shoulder, or something else, was rammed into the bathroom door. "It's best you come out. We promise a swift death if you don't force us to break the door down."

Despite how his hands trembled, Papa slid the key into the hole, twisted it, and pushed the gate to the side. He grabbed me with one hand, and with the other he pushed the window open.

I held on to the porcelain sink with all my strength. "No!" I screamed.

"Last chance, dirty Jews."

More banging, kicking, ramming, the sides of the door and the wood frame splintered.

"Let me knock the door down."

I recognized the voice of the teenage Nazi.

"Karl," I whispered so low I don't think Papa heard.

"Stand back," one of the SA men said, "I'm going to shoot."

"Wait," yelled a male voice, one I knew perfectly well. Siegfried.

Two shots fired. Papa and I didn't move. Couldn't. Finally I looked down at Papa's shirt and expected to see blood oozing from my body. I hadn't been shot, and neither had Papa.

Papa came to, as if getting a whiff of smelling salts. Roughly, in a way he never handled me before, he pried my fingers from the porcelain sink and lifted me. I kicked my feet and swung my arms. He pushed me through the window. My stocking feet landed on the metal grate of the fire escape. Papa's dark shirt wrapped me in the smell of his sweat.

"I hate you," I yelled with all the strength I had left.

He slammed the window shut. Behind him, the door to the bathroom flung open and the two older storm troopers rushed in and grabbed him from behind.

The men dragged Papa into the hallway. Papa fought, kicked,

screamed, and flailed his arms. Siegfried? Where was Siegfried? I didn't see him. Two shots fired. Siegfried?

The two Nazis lugged Papa out of my view. Seconds later, the Nazi boy ran into the bathroom and opened the window. Inches apart he thrust his head and arms into the early morning air and grabbed for me.

I stepped out of his reach. "Karl, it's me, Liana Krochmal."

He hesitated. "I, I, I know who you are, and you're a dirty Jew."

"You and Siegfried are friends. I've played with your sister. We've always been Jews. Why does it matter now?" I rambled, desperate.

He blinked, considered my question, I supposed. His posture slumped and then straightened again. "Hitler says Jews are evil." He looked over his shoulder toward where I could hear Papa grunt in battle, and then Karl rotated toward me. "Go, Liana. I'll say you got away."

"But my family?"

He pushed me. I fell on the fire escape. The window and the gate slammed shut.

# CHAPTER NINETEEN
## RUBY
## KRISTALLNACHT DAY ONE

RUBY SAT IN front of the mirror in the dressing room. The Little Tramp looked back. *What made me think I could be as good as Chaplin*? He ripped off the eyebrows. His skin stung as he peeled the glue from his face. Red marks remained above his eyes like theatrical battle scars. He took a damp cloth and wiped away the greasepaint and face powder. Around him, performers stretched and practiced vocal exercises in preparation for shots at fame. There was Sycamore the Clown, who rode a unicycle across a tight rope, Dapper Joe who looked like Clark Gable and sang like a sick cat, and, of course, The Great Lester and his dummy, Frank Byron, Jr.

*And I am the one who got canned?* Ruby thought.

"Hey, Ruby," Frank called from his perch on Harry's lap. "Did you hear about the man who was told by his doctor he has six months to live?"

Ruby swathed a wet cloth across cheek. He wasn't going to respond, but then thought, *Why not one last time*? "No, Frank."

"He couldn't pay his bill, so the doctor gave him another six months."

"That's not bad," Ruby said.

"What? Are you sick?" The dummy looked at Harry. "If Ruby likes that one, we should strike it from the act. How about this one? Why are Jewish men circumcised?"

"Because Jewish women like things that are twenty percent off."

Frank laughed. "Ruby has a sense of humor tonight."

"Can you be quiet for one second, Frank?" Harry said, and the dummy sagged in his lap. Harry looked at Ruby. "You were spectacular out there." He stood, put Frank down, and then sat on a stool next to Ruby. "Can I tell you a secret?"

"Frank's not real?" Ruby unbuttoned his vest.

"Funny, chap, but no."

"I need to tell you something too."

"Me first." He reached into his pocket and took out a small black box. Ceremoniously he opened it.

Ruby looked at the gold band with a small, clear diamond set high.

"I've been saving for almost a year to buy this beauty. It hasn't been easy, with the recession going on. Good thing Frank doesn't eat much." He slapped Ruby on the back and sprayed him with stale cigar breath. "I'm going to ask Dixie to marry me."

"Well, uh, that's swell. Congratulations." Ruby's limbs weakened, shakier than when he learned he had been fired.

"Are you just saying that? I mean, me and the guys know you have a thing for her."

"We perform together, that's all." He tried to keep his voice steady.

"That's never all there is when a man and a woman have an act together."

"We make a good pair," Ruby said. "Behind the curtain, that is. Nowhere else, I swear."

Harry hit him on the back again. "Don't worry, old chap, I know Dixie is a fine-looking woman. Every man in this room is in love with her, and many of the women she works with too." He let out a belly laugh. "Do you think she'll say yes?"

"She'd be a fool not to."

"I cannot tell you how excited we are."

"We?"

"Me and Frank."

"Harry, Frank's a doll."

"I know, but he's like my child. So what did you want to tell me? I hope your news is as good as mine."

"Um, yeah, I have a great idea for my next act."

"That's fantabulous, my friend." Harry rose. "I'll let you know the wedding date. I want you to be my best man, and Frank too, of course."

Two hours later, the dressing room was empty and the theater dark. Ruby sat in front of his makeup mirror and lingered, unsure if he would find another job on the stage. He was eager to savor everything about the theater, the stale smell of cigar smoke that hung in the air like a rain cloud, the pungent reek of mold on the ceiling and walls, the tang of greasepaint that burrowed into his nostrils.

He tumbled the bowler hat up and down his right arm and thought of the countless hours he had spent practicing the trick. He wiggled his toes in the dark loafers, carefully scuffed as Chaplin had done to his shoes so he would be considered *every man*.

Ruby spoke again to the mirror. "This might be the last time I am Charlie Chaplin." He slipped his makeup into the duffle. *"Was werden Sie jetzt tun?"* What are you going to do now?

Pleased to have spoken in his native Austrian tongue, pronouncing the W's as V's, and for a few seconds being who he truly was, the satisfaction dissipated. He had no job, no prospects for work, and two days to come up with rent money. He had no way to support his family when they arrived.

"You've been down before. You survived. You can do it again." He reached into his bag and grabbed a scratch pad, on which he wrote. He folded the note in half. Being unemployed wasn't as disappointing as knowing Dixie was going to marry Harry. He was sure she would accept his proposal. Why not? She would have security and a man who adored her. Correction, a man and a dummy that thought she was swell.

He got up and threw the duffle over his shoulder. He started for the exit, stopped, and went to his dressing station. He hooked his hand around the handle of the bamboo cane that leaned against his chair and gently pressed on it until it bowed out à la Charlie Chaplin.

Twirling the cane, he walked out in Chaplin's famous waddle, and left the note at Harry Lester's makeup table. *Congratulations, old chap, you got the girl.*

# CHAPTER TWENTY
## MICHAEL

WITH RUBY ASLEEP, I walked to the five-shelved octagonal display case. A black bowler hat, worn and torn in places but appearing to have its original shape, sat on the bottom shelf. Next level up and displayed on a triangular stand was a worn book, its leather cover frayed and bent at the corners. I leaned in to get a better look.

*Mein Kampf. Why would Ruby have Hitler's autobiography outlining his plans for Germany's domination of the world?*

Next to the book were long white candlesticks, upright in gold-plated holders.

On the third and middle shelf, a black-and-white photograph of a beautiful woman, statuesque, barely dressed, and standing in front of a sign, *Hudson Burlesque Theater.* Scrawled in a corner was a date, 1938. The fourth shelf contained another framed black and white photograph, this one of a family: a mother and father, an oldest son, and two younger daughters. In the background a river flowed.

I opened the glass door on the cabinet, reached in, and took out the photo of the family, turned it around, and read the penciled scribble on the coffee-colored rear. Amalie, Jacob, Siegfried, Renate, and Liana, Danube River, Vienna, 1935. I rotated it again to take a closer look. Liana, the smallest and youngest, appeared to be about ten years old. She cradled a stuffed bear and held her head high and her chin outstretched, the appearance of a young girl who yet knew fear.

Vienna, Austria, 1935. I looked at the family again and asked softly, "Where were you three years later?"

Had they been in Vienna when Hitler's army marched into Austria? Were they asleep in their beds when *Kristallnacht* began? Were they sent to concentration camps?

It became apparent Sara told me little about her family. My inner spoiled child emerged. We hadn't been only lawyer and client; we had been lovers. Wouldn't she have shared her family's involvement in the Holocaust with me? Is this an example of her unreliability, or had she saved me from learning a difficult history?

I replaced the frame in the cabinet and looked to the top and fifth shelf. There they were. Four glass carousel horses mounted on a rotating platform: the white Arabian, palomino, chocolate bay and spotted appaloosa.

The feelings that overcame me were no strangers, foreboding, coupled with longing. My thoughts flooded with memories of the last time Sara and I made love, visions of Charles's blood on the carpet, which Blanca tried to remove with bleach, police reports of the investigation into his death, images of the boys who found his body, my visit to Gram in the hospital room, and holding her hand as she released her least breath.

The glass menagerie once again evoked mixed emotions of fear, love, dread, and hope.

"What is it about you?" I asked the horses.

I checked on Ruby again. He snored with his mouth wide open. I turned to the cabinet, reached in, and removed the Arabian. With the delicate mount in my palm, I transformed, as if in a time machine. I gently placed the Arabian on its side next to the photograph of Sara and Soldier Boy's family and then gripped each horse in turn.

With each horse placed on its side and surrounding the framed photograph, I picked up the platform and examined it. Also made of glass, its design seemed simple. It had a turnstile with a music box and a lever that, I presumed, when switched on rotated the platform and played music. I had never looked closely at the horses before, had never gotten this near. I flipped the base over and read the markings on the bottom.

Oskar Glasman Gloggnitz Austria 1791.

# CHAPTER TWENTY-ONE
## MICHAEL

I PLACED THE carousel platform on the top shelf and then restored the horses to their perch. Questions abounded. Was 1791 the year the carousel horses were crafted? Was Oskar Glasman its creator? Were the horses really 225 years old? I clenched my fists. Rage over the end of my relationship with Sara clamped my intestines. Fury over the lawsuit she's filed against me cauterized my nerve endings. Why couldn't she love me like I loved her? Why hadn't she listened when I told her I was not experienced enough to defend against a murder charge? Why did everything have to be so complicated? I looked at the horses again. Why did they bring out in me this array of extreme emotions?

I wanted to pull on the lever to hear what music might play but didn't risk waking Ruby. I sighed. This was stupid. What was I doing, imagining the horses held inner meaning and mystic power created from days gone by? Why would Soldier Boy help me against Sara? The carousel horses weren't anything but glass and jewels and nothing more, fantasy. And Soldier Boy was a man who abandoned his sister when she needed him most.

Enough romanticizing Sara and her family, better to let Ruby sleep, better to go home and have Erica handle my defense since that's what I paid her for.

Lights on the carousel flickered blue, red, yellow, and green. The platform rotated and a sad melody emitted from the music box, one I recognized from concerts I attended with Gram, Papa, and Mom. It was Mozart's final requiem. The lever was slightly pushed back. I must have hit it when I put the carousel away.

Worried the music might wake Ruby I looked at him. He slept soundly. I took the Arabian from the slow revolving carousel and held the glass horse to my heart, closed my eyes and swayed, the piano notes so stunning they sounded as if played by Mozart himself.

"What are you doing here?" Soldier Boy stood in the doorway.

"Shh. He's asleep," I whispered.

"Then shut that music off and put the horse down." His voice was a low growl.

I clutched the Arabian to my chest. "Have you ever held one of them?"

He stepped into the room, his movements short and controlled, military-like. "Put it down, or else I'm calling the police."

I replaced the Arabian onto the rotating platform. Mozart's final orchestration played in the background. I was glad Soldier Boy stood about ten feet from me.

While I was wiry and fit, Soldier Boy was thick and muscular and possessed the training and instinct of a Marine. He was about five inches taller than me. He blocked the door to the room. I looked over at Ruby, asleep.

I hesitated and determined my next move. Gram used to say it's not the mistake you make that's important but the choice you make after.

"You know your sister is suing me."

"Yeah. So?"

"I didn't mess up her defense."

"You should leave."

"She wouldn't let me call you as a witness."

"My sister is a complicated woman. What are you doing here?"

"I came to see you."

"She didn't kill Uncle Charlie."

"Did you?"

He stepped toward me, favored his right leg. I backed away.

"Is that why Sara wouldn't let me call you as a witness?" I asked. "She was afraid you'd confess on the stand?"

"My sister is as much of a mystery to me as I am sure she is to you, but to answer your question, I didn't kill Uncle Charlie either."

"She told me you did it to get revenge for him murdering your parents."

He moved farther into the room. I was surprised when he didn't advance toward me and sat on the bed. His shoulders slumped. Ruby stirred. The Requiem played.

"Is that what she told you? That I killed him?" Soldier Boy asked.

"Yes."

"Well, she's mistaken." He spoke calmly. "It wasn't me."

"Blanca?"

He shook his head.

"Ronald McGuiniss?"

Soldier Boy stood. "I'm done with twenty questions."

"We need to find out who did it."

"No, we don't."

"Yes, we do." I moved toward him, my confidence raised. "Don't you see, even if her claim I sucked as her attorney gets her a new trial, the evidence was there to convict her the first go round and it'll be there the second time too, and even on the slim chance she's found not guilty she's going to sit in jail for years before she has a new trial. The legal system moves slowly."

Solder Boy showed no reaction, his face etched in stone.

"You don't want to help your sister?" I prodded.

"She's in prison for life without a chance for parole because she protected you."

"Her choice, and that's not why she's in prison. I didn't kill Uncle Charlie, and I never would have asked her to take the fall for me if I had."

Mozart's final requiem ceased playing mid-note. Soldier Boy and I looked at the horses. The carousel stopped rotating.

"Have you ever held one of them?" I repeated the question that started this conversation.

"Maybe. I don't know."

"They're like..." I searched for the right words.

"Magical and demonic all at once."

"Sara and I used to ride them out the window into the night air. All over Long Island." His mouth contorted and he looked sad.

"Will you help her? Will you help me find who murdered Uncle Charlie?"

His eyes turned steely. "To get you off the hook for being a crappy attorney? No way. Shouldn't you have tried to find the real killer the first time around?"

I looked down. "I never thought she'd be convicted."

"Do it," Ruby said.

We looked toward the bed. The old man was partially propped on an elbow.

"Come, David. Help me sit," he said.

Soldier Boy guided Ruby until he was seated on the side of the bed.

Ruby addressed Soldier Boy. "Michael's motives to find out who killed Charles are irrelevant. Is it to help Sara? Is it to help himself? It doesn't matter. Your sister needs you. Family comes first."

Ruby slid his feet to the floor and stood, wobbly. Soldier Boy and I stretched toward him. He waved us away. With pained steps, he walked toward the cabinet. I thought he was going to reach for one of the horses, maybe tell a tale or two, but instead he bent for the bottom shelf, opened the glass door and grabbed the bowler hat. He reached next to the side of the cabinet and retrieved a battered cane. He opened the top drawer of his dresser and took out a small satchel. With delicacy, he extracted what looked like a black worm. He placed the worm between his upper lip and nose. He twirled the cane, rolled the hat up and down his arm, and shuffled along the foot of the bed. Charlie Chaplin brought to life.

His act fascinated me, but I grew impatient. "What does that have to do with who killed Uncle Charlie?"

"Everything. The past reveals the present and the future."

"Fine." I sighed. "Where do we begin?"

"There is no we." Soldier Boy huffed and hurried out of the room.

I started to chase after him.

"Let him go," Ruby said.

I faced Ruby, wondering again what I was doing. Why couldn't I hand my defense fully over to Erica? I paid her a fat retainer so I wouldn't have to agonize. Why did I have to re-open everything, not just the facts surrounding Uncle Charlie's murder, but also my feelings for Sara? And what about that threat from Billy O'Brien? Was he someone I had to fear?

I sighed and asked again, "Where do we begin?"

"With the carousel horses and with Liana," Ruby said.

"Liana from the photograph?" I looked toward the cabinet and the fourth shelf from the bottom where the black and white photo of the family from Vienna, taken in 1935, leaned.

"Liana was my niece, and Sara and Soldier Boy's grandmother."

"Hasn't she been dead for decades?"

"Doesn't matter," he said. "She'll tell you everything you need to know."

I studied the old man. Not only did he speak like a crazy person, he did so dressed as Charlie Chaplin.

He cupped his hand to his ear. "Listen."

I strained to hear.

# CHAPTER TWENTY-TWO
## LIANA
## KRISTALLNACHT DAY TWO

I AWOKE ON the fire escape with the sun a blurry ball high in the sky, forgetting my predicament for one sweet instant. It wasn't long before I unfurled and remembered everything, including my last words to Papa.

*I hate you.*

Embers and smoke floated and crackled around me. The evil words spewed at Jews like poisonous darts had stopped, replaced by chatter on the streets to the sides of our building. I had to get into my apartment. In all the excitement, maybe Papa forgot where I was. He, Mama, Siegfried, and Renate probably sat around our wood kitchen table, where I had carved my initials and was punished by not being allowed to visit the Lipizzaner horses for one week, and worried about me. I had to get inside.

I put Bruno on the grate floor of the fire escape and removed the razor blades from the pocket of Papa's shirt. I laid the strop next to Bruno. I took off Papa's shirt and wrapped it around my right hand, my stronger hand. While I wrote and ate with my left, I used my right to throw balls, punch Siegfried when we were play fighting, and flip cards. I took a deep breath and punched as hard as I could on the glass of the bathroom window.

"Ow." I recoiled and fell to my knees. Pain shot through my knuckles as if burned by a hot iron.

I waited for the tears to clear and looked at the window. It was intact, not broken, not cracked, not even a slight web to suggest the glass had compromised in any way. I punched the glass again and again and again. Pain worsened with each attempt. The glass was unforgiving in its steadfastness. I remembered how Siegfried would kick like a martial arts expert when we played. I flung my foot out and landed the sole on the window. Stinging, burning pain shot through my heel and into my ankle and calf. It didn't stop me. Nothing could stop me. I needed to find my family so they wouldn't worry about me. I kicked at the glass repeatedly and then alternated, three kicks, two punches, five rapid-fire kicks, seven punches. My knuckles bled through Papa's shirt. My feet ached and swelled. My stockings bloodied.

Barely able to see through the tears that stung my eyes, I fell to the grate, tired, helpless, and sad for my family. They had to be petrified that the Nazis had gotten me. With Papa's shirt, I wiped tears away and faced my nemesis. "Damn you, window."

I leaned in and looked closer. It was tiny, but a spider web of a crack in the middle of the glass sparkled in the sunlight.

With renewed vigor, I went to work again. Kick, kick, kick, punch, punch, punch, over and over. I couldn't tell if the web spread. I needed a marker. I unwrapped Papa's shirt from my hand and, using a bloody knuckle, drew a circle of red around the tiny crack. Kick, punch, kick, punch, the thin line was still corralled by my trail of blood. My feet swelled. My hands bruised black, blue, and yellow.

"Aaargh!" I roared like sweaty boys when they tried to hit a ball with a stick and missed. I thought that was sound only boys made, but as I stared at the window I knew it was something animalistic. The snarl came from deep within, from inside my belly, from a place I've never known.

My breath drew in and out so violently the inhales stung at the bottom of my lungs. Sweat poured off my face. The crack had spread a little outside the circle of blood. Hope faded since I had smacked the window a gazillion times with my fists and feet. How come Mama and Papa didn't hear me hit the window? How come they didn't run to get me?

It then occurred to me. They weren't looking for me. The last words I said to Papa were "I hate you." Had he thought I meant it? Did he hate me too?

"I don't hate you, Papa," I yelled. "I love you. I love all of you. I love you, Papa, Mama, Siegfried, and Renate. I'm out here, on the fire escape." From a strange place within me, I screamed. "I hate you, Liana Krochmal. You are the worst person in the whole wide world." I punched the right side of my head. "I hate you. I hate you. I hate you." With each word of hate, I hit my head. Warm liquid drizzled down the side of my face, over my ear. "You deserve to die, Liana Krochmal." I raised my fist to hit myself again.

"Hey!"

I looked down and to the side street where two Brownshirts pointed gloved hands up at me.

"Are you a Jew?" one of the SA men barked.

I breathed heavily; blood trickled into my mouth. I wanted to ask: "Why does it matter? Aren't we all just people?" Instead I puffed out my chest and declared, "This is my fault."

The men laughed. "What is?"

I waved my arms as if explanation enough.

"What is your name?" the other asked.

I was about to answer, knowing I would reveal my Jewish heritage by telling them my surname, but I didn't care. I was a Jew and I was proud. They couldn't hurt me. They couldn't harm all of us.

The Nazis looked to the main street and then at me. Without another word, they ran away. To where and why they suddenly left, I didn't know and didn't care. I stepped to the edge of the fire escape, and with all my might, I took three quick steps toward the window, ramming it headfirst. I fell, and landed next to Bruno. The window was intact. I took Bruno in my arms and cried softly into his fur. A pop sounded. The web expanded until the entire window shattered. Glass tumbled over the fire escape, over my stuffed bear and me.

I laughed wildly, shook glass off of me, out of my hair, and off Bruno. I pushed on the iron gate. It was locked.

# CHAPTER TWENTY-THREE
# RUBY
# KRISTALLNACHT DAY ONE

RUBY STEPPED INTO the four a.m. chill, the kind that plunged through every nook and cranny of his worn clothes and jabbed like razor blades at his skin. The streets were quiet; light snow dazzled. He had his duffle thrown over his shoulder, the bowler hat in one hand, and the bamboo cane in the other. He did not walk with the clown-like confidence of Chaplin but with the hunched shoulders and hesitant steps of the unemployed and frightened. The one room he rented from Mrs. Bowen lurked a few blocks away. He did not want to go there and to be alone.

One block over, he smelled burning embers and heard murmuring. He figured what he would see down the alleyway, six or seven men huddled over a steel barrel, fire blazing, trying to stay warm. They wouldn't be men who were killing time because they didn't want to go home. They would be men who had no place to go, among the legions of the homeless.

Ruby stood at the mouth of the alley as the snow began to shower in large, chunky flakes. Lit by an overhead streetlight as if he were on stage and in the spotlight, he wondered. *Could that be me one day? Again?* Years ago, when the Depression was in full swing, he had slept on his share of sewer grates to keep warm and had huddled in subways, a time in his life he did not want to revisit.

"Hey," one of the guys called.

Ruby thought to walk away and go to his pathetic one-room hole-in-the-wall, but he didn't move. Maybe there was time for another Charlie Chaplin routine; maybe he could bring a little happiness to the men with a few waddles and hat-and-cane tricks.

"What are you looking at?" A beefy man took gorilla steps toward him.

"Nothing." Ruby fixed his duffle tighter on to his shoulder.

The man and his buddies surrounded Ruby. From their dress, the musk of their colognes, and their burly physiques Ruby realized that food and funds were plentiful in their lives. He had misjudged who the men might be.

"What do you have in that bag?"

"Nothing," he repeated.

"Nothing? Nothing? Is that all you can say?"

Ruby moved to walk away. A brick building of a man blocked his way.

The beefy one grabbed him by the arm and spun him around. "Who are you supposed to be, Hitler?"

Ruby brought his fingers to below his nose. He had forgotten to remove the moustache; he ripped it off and stuffed it in his pocket. "Charlie Chaplin."

"Charlie Chaplin? Make us laugh."

"No."

"Did you think that was a question?" The man tightened his grip on his arm.

Ruby smelled the rancid combination of onions and liquor on his breath. He stretched out his arm, the one the man didn't squeeze, and with little enthusiasm rolled the bowler hat up and down.

"I don't know," a man wearing a well-tailored suit said. "You look more like Hitler than Chaplin."

"I certainly do not. I'm a Jew from Austria."

"A Jew from Austria?" he mocked. "I'm a German from the Bronx."

The men laughed.

"Can you please let go of my arm?" Ruby asked.

The man tightened his grip. "Say 'Heil Hitler.'"

"I will do no such thing. Let. Go. Of. My. Arm."

The man drew him closer until they were nose to nose. "Have you heard of the German American Bund?"

Ruby knew it was an offshoot of the disbanded Friends of the New Germany, which had been a group of German citizens that lived in America and a branch of Hitler's Nazi party. In 1935, all German citizens were ordered by the Nazi party to leave the FOTNG and its leaders were required to return to Germany. Three months later, the German American Bund was formed, an American Nazi organization.

"You know what, Jew boy? You interrupted our meeting. That wasn't very polite of you."

The snow fell harder, crashed into Ruby's cheeks and landed on his eyelashes.

"I don't want trouble."

"You killed Jesus."

"What?"

"That's right. Because of you, Jesus was hung on the cross and crucified."

"I did not—"

"You're a Jew, aren't you?"

Ruby puffed out his chest. "Yes, I am."

The fist hit him in his solar plexus and his knees buckled. When he was on all fours on the sidewalk, a foot met his chin and reeled him backwards. The cane and hat flew. Fists, feet, and knees pummeled him, swift, forceful, and vicious. The snowy sidewalk grew dotted with blood from Ruby's nose and then puddled with blood from his mouth. He curled into a ball, took the blows, and lost his breath, his head dizzy and then foggy.

*What the hell is happening? This is America. If this is going on here, what is happening to my family in Vienna?*

Tires screeched, car doors opened, male voices grunted, and the blows ceased. Ruby heard groans and snorts, the smacks of fists against bone, and heads hit against the sidewalk. Two rapid shots came from a gun. Ruby was lifted and then thrown, surprised when he landed on a soft cushion. His duffle, the cane, and the hat fell into his lap.

He opened his left eye, the one less swollen, and gradually took in his location, the back seat of a black 1938 Buick Century. There was a man in the driver's seat, another in the front passenger seat. Ruby looked out the window at the sidewalk. The beefy man lay face down in the snow. Blood circled his head like a hellish halo. The others must have run away. In the distance, police sirens. The driver plowed down on the gas pedal, and the car jumped forward. Ruby's neck snapped back and a wave or nausea overcame him. It passed quickly, and he looked at the man next to him in the back seat.

The man held out his hand. "Meyer Lansky."

Ruby managed to extend his own hand.

"I hate those fucking Nazis. You okay, kid?"

"Yeah." He pulled a white handkerchief from his pocket and spit blood into it.

Meyer laughed. "You're going to live. Ain't he going to live, boys?"

"For sure," the driver said.

"He's definitely going to live, Boss."

"We saw your show at the burlesque theater tonight. You were funny as hell, wasn't he?"

"Hysterical," the driver said.

"A riot," the front passenger added.

"The way you handled that idiot in the front row with humor was beautiful."

"Thank you." Ruby spit blood into the handkerchief and saw one of his teeth in the mound of red.

"We heard those Nazis were having a meeting on New York

Avenue and we were on our way to break it up. Imagine our surprise when we saw them beating up Charlie Chaplin." Meyer laughed again. "You have to admit, it was kind of a funny sight."

"Funny, Boss."

"Actually," Meyer said, "it wasn't funny at all."

"Not funny."

"Sad."

"I mean," Meyer continued, "why beat up America's greatest comedian?"

"He's British," the driver said.

Meyer shot him a scornful look.

The driver's eyes widened in the rearview mirror as the windshield wipers thumped snow off the front window. "I mean, he was born in Britain, but he's an American treasure."

"We can't have Nazis beating up Charlie Chaplin, now, can we?" Meyer asked.

"Certainly not."

"Where do you live, kid?"

"Off of thirty-eighth," Ruby said.

"Take the man home," Meyer ordered.

The sedan lurched forward and they drove for a few blocks.

"That's the apartment building." Ruby feebly pointed.

The Buick stopped out front.

"You need help? My boys can help you."

"Yeah, we can help."

"Whatever the boss wants."

Ruby shook his head. If Mrs. Bowen saw the gangster Meyer Lansky and his thugs helping him to his apartment, she wouldn't wait for sunlight to kick him out. He pushed the car door open, and managed to get his feet out, the drop endless before his scuffed shoes hit the pavement. He held on to the doorframe with both hands and bolstered himself to an upright position, the cold air and falling snow refreshing. He reached in and grabbed his duffle, the hat, and the cane.

"You performing again at the Hudson tomorrow night?" Meyer asked.

"No, I, uh, they let me go. You know, the recession and all."

"No way. Me and my boys thought you and that dame were terrific."

"Great," the driver said.

"Amazing," the front passenger added.

"You got too much talent to waste, kid. We'll pick you up at ten."

"Yeah, at ten," the driver said.

"That's like in six hours," the passenger added.

*A job? Is Meyer Lansky offering me a job?* Ruby quickly weighed his options, knowing whatever Meyer was going to have him do would be illegal. Ruby also knew his family was on its way and he had no way to support them, but he had avoided aligning with gangsters so far. Shouldn't he stay on that track and make an honest living?

The driver of the car leaned out the window. "I suggest you don't say no to Mr. Lansky." He opened his coat, the handle of a gun evident.

Decision made, Ruby looked to the well-appointed man in the back seat. "Should I dress like Charlie Chaplin, sir?"

"What's your real name?" Meyer asked.

"Ruby Friedman."

"Dress like him."

# CHAPTER TWENTY-FOUR
## MICHAEL

I GRIPPED THE black-and-white photograph from the middle shelf of the glass cabinet and looked at Ruby. Soldier Boy was still out of the room.

"Who's the woman? She's beautiful. Was she your…?" I couldn't think of a word suitable for the time period.

"Paramour?" Ruby lay in bed propped up by several pillows. "Regrettably we were never lovers, but Dixie Lee and I did kiss once." His face lit up. "She was my best friend."

"The Hudson Burlesque Theater." I read the sign behind her in the photograph. "Did you perform there?"

Another wide grin filled his wrinkles. "Sometimes you don't know the best days of your life until they're over. Dixie Lee and I did this incredible act where I was Charlie Chaplin and she was a call girl." He affectionately fingered the bowler on his lap before his expression went limp. "That was during the tail end of the Depression. Germany occupied Austria, but it hadn't invaded Poland yet. I had arranged for my family to get out of Austria." His thoughts trailed off.

"What happened to your family?" I hesitated to ask.

Ruby sighed. The skin on his face sagged. He gestured and waved the past and me away.

I changed the subject.

"Oskar Glasman Gloggnitz Austria 1791." I recalled the inscription on the underside of the carousel. "Who is that?"

Before Ruby answered, Soldier Boy returned. My muscles tensed. I looked to Soldier Boy, prepared for him to order me out of his house. I tried not to show fear.

"Sara and I have always wondered who Oskar was," Soldier Boy said as if we had not had words. "Our father told us stories of our family history but never mentioned Oskar Glasman."

Ruby looked toward the window. "The sun is setting."

"What did your dad say about the carousel horses?" I asked.

"Our grandmother, Liana Krochmal, brought them to the States from Austria when she escaped the Nazis. She gave them to our father when he was six years old."

"Hand me those candles." Ruby pointed toward the cabinet.

I grabbed the candles next to *Mein Kampf.* Ruby set them on the side table. He reached into a drawer and took out a matchbook. I looked to Soldier Boy for an explanation.

"It's Friday at sundown," he said. "The beginning of the Sabbath."

Ruby reached into the drawer again and placed a yarmulke on his head. He handed one to Soldier Boy, who took it. Ruby then stretched his arm toward me. I hoped he didn't notice my hesitation before I accepted the beanie.

Ruby lit the candles and then waved his hands over them.

"What's he doing?" I whispered to Soldier Boy.

"He's welcoming the Sabbath."

Ruby covered his eyes. "*Barukh atah Adonai, Eloheinu, melekh ha'olam.*"

"Blessed are you, Lord, our God, sovereign of the universe," Soldier Boy said.

"*Asher kidishanu b'mitz'votav v'tzivanu.*"

"Who has sanctified us with his commandments and commanded us."

"*L'had'lik neir shel Shabbat. Amein.*"

"To light the lights of Shabbat. Amen."

"Amen," I said.

Ruby removed his hands from his eyes.

"You know Hebrew?" I asked Soldier Boy.

"Some."

Ruby laughed. "Don't be modest, David. He knows rabbinical and modern Hebrew. Ask him how many languages he speaks."

I looked at Soldier Boy, who turned away.

"He reads them too," Ruby said. "German and Yiddish, of course, they're in our blood. He knows the romance languages, and others, right? The Marines wanted him to learn Mandarin and Hindu but he refused."

"I joined to fight," he said.

"Problem is, the kid doesn't know when to stop fighting."

"Uncle Ruby, please." Soldier Boy looked markedly uncomfortable by the attention tossed his way.

"You should be proud of your talents."

"Can we talk about the horses?" I tried to change the subject once more. "What do you both know about Oskar Glasman? He must have made the carousel horses, right? Have you ever Googled him? Do you remember Liana telling you anything about him?"

I looked from Ruby to Soldier Boy, who both appeared unimpressed by my curiosity. Still, I didn't stop.

"Will you talk about Sara? About Uncle Charlie?" I took off the yarmulke and fidgeted with it between my fingers.

"Enough," Ruby spoke. "Not during the Sabbath. 'God blessed the seventh day and sanctified it, because in it he rested from all his work, which God had created and made.' During the Sabbath, we rest." Ruby lay back.

Frustrated, I tossed the yarmulke onto the table.

Ruby enlarged his eyes. Behind the watery whites and the dark pupils, his glare gave me a glimpse of the man he used to be. "You can leave now."

"I'm sorry." I picked up the yarmulke and put it softly down again.

"During the Sabbath we rest for twenty-four hours. From sundown on Friday until sundown on Saturday we celebrate who we are. No work, no cooking, no driving; we don't even brush our teeth."

"Well, I do." Soldier Boy smiled slyly.

"Some follow it more closely than others, but one thing is constant," Ruby said, "and that's faith. So, Michael, if you will excuse us, we'd like to continue saying our prayers."

"Oh, right."

"You know the way out," Ruby added.

"Yes, of course."

I left the room, unsure if Ruby had hoodwinked me into not asking any further questions or if he really was a man who believed in the Judaic ritual. I strode down the hall and passed the linen closet where Sara and Soldier Boy hid when their mother and father fought, and then I walked down the winding stairs with the snake-shaped railings on either side. At the bottom, I entered the room where their parents' bodies were discovered under the baby grand. I hesitated, imagined the gruesome scene, and then double-timed it out of the house.

# CHAPTER TWENTY-FIVE
## LIANA
### KRISTALLNACHT DAY TWO

THE SUN THAT dangled in a light blue sky warmed the winter morning. I stood on the fire escape and gripped the iron gate; broken glass bit at my toes and the bottom of my feet. My blood painted the iron grated floor, a breeze blew cinders around me. Bruno was crumpled in a corner. Under other circumstances, an unseasonably warm November day like that one brought families outside, to picnic and frolic in the park. Mama and Renate and I might stitch on the front stoop while Papa and Siegfried tossed a ball.

I closed Papa's shirt more tightly around me, warmed by the sun but still chilled. I had put the razor blades in the front pocket, and the strop rested on my lap. In the distance, the sounds of a parade and the smell of a bon fire. A band played *Koniggratzer Marsch*, the Nazi Military March. Boots slapped on concrete in precision, percussive, getting louder, closer.

Through the iron gate and the window, inside the bathroom, cracked glass littered the linoleum floor. The mirror above the medicine cabinet was shattered and the sink was pulled from the wall. Remnants of my vomit floated in the toilet. The wood door to the bathroom was splintered and hung on one hinge. In the hallway outside the battered door, on the floor, a bare foot turned sideways, toes pointed at me.

"Siegfried!" I screamed and shut my eyes as tight as possible. I prayed for a miracle and then looked into the bathroom and toward the door again. The foot was still there.

No sounds or movement came from inside the apartment, nor had anyone passed by the back or sides of the building in some time.

I cried again, this time silent, tears dropped to my chin and onto Papa's shirt. How many tears does a little girl have? What happens when there are no more?

"I hate you, Nazis."

I rattled the iron gate, and recalled that idiot Karl who had slammed the gate shut and who must have the key. I stuck my hand through the gate. If I had the key, I could unlock it and join my family members who probably, most likely, definitely, hid in the attic and waited to join me.

If only I hadn't gone back for the carousel horses and Bruno.

I shook the gate, pushed and pulled. "I hate you, Nazis. I hate you, Liana Anna Krochmal, this is your fault."

"Hey."

I looked down, toward the voice.

"Liana, c'mon down from there."

"No, Karl."

"I have something for you." He held up the key.

"Throw it up here."

"You'll drop it."

"No, I won't." I let go of the gate. "I can catch it, like when you and Siegfried would throw a ball around." I held my hands out, hoping to prove I could play catch.

He walked closer to the fire escape, his neck craned as he looked up. "I can't risk you missing. This is an important key."

"I know. My family needs me."

"Yes, they do. So come here and get the key."

I shook my head. "If I get off the fire escape, I won't be able to get back up here."

He stood under me, his hand on the bottom rung of the ladder.

"Oh, I see. You can't reach the ladder."

"I'll be able to soon, when I grow a taller."

"I'm sure you will."

"Is my family's okay?"

"They're fine."

"Are they in the attic?"

"Yes."

"Good."

"If you come down, I can let you in the front door."

I tried to judge if he was a liar. He had always been a funny-looking kid with yellow hair like straw and ears that stuck out too far. He wasn't good at sports, and he didn't seem smart in school. At least that's what Siegfried had said. I tried to recall his exact words about Karl.

*He's the kind of guy who makes up for his shortcomings by being a bully.*

*Then why do you play with him, I had asked.*

*Papa and Rabbi Ehrenfeld say it's important to have a lot of friends now, especially non-Jews.*

*I don't understand, I said.*

*That's okay, Sieg responded, you don't need too. You're too young.*

"Don't you want to go in the front door and be with your family?" Karl prodded.

Noises of the parade grew louder. Music played, and cheers of the crowd mixed with the slap of metal-bottomed boots on pavement. I pictured Nazis moving in synchronized straight lines, their legs kicking into the air, their arms rigid and swinging by their sides. I didn't want to see another Nazi again.

"I think I'll take the key and go in through the window," I offered.

"If you won't come and get it, I'll have to bring it to you."

"I can catch it. I promise."

Karl put the key in his front pants pocket, jumped a few feet, grabbed onto the ladder, and climbed. His thick boots distressed the fire escape, which groaned. He paused on the first landing and then ran up the stairs two at a time until he stood in front of me. The fire escape landing was just large enough for the two of us.

I held out my hand, hoping he'd drop the key into my palm.

"You know," he said, I always thought you were cute."

"Can I have the key, please?"

"Sure." He didn't move.

"Please?"

"Go ahead, take it."

I looked at his pants pocket. "Can't you hand it to me?"

"I'm kind of tired. Reach for it."

Slowly I slid my hand into the front left pocket of his brown trousers. "It's not there."

"Oh." He laughed. "Must be in the other pocket." He pivoted his right hip toward me.

I reached in and wrapped my fingers around the cold metal, also feeling a bulge. I pulled my hand out of his pocket.

He snatched the key from me.

"You said I could have it."

"For a price."

"I don't have any money."

"It's not money I want."

"What do you want?" I kept my eyes on the key, my prize.

"Put your hand back in my pocket."

"No."

He dangled the key in front of my face. "I guess you don't want this."

I grasped for it.

He snatched it from my reach. "Everything has a price, *kleines mädchen*." Little girl.

"Fine. Give me the key, and when I go inside I'll give you money. I know where Mama and Papa hid the grocery money."

"I told you, I don't want money." He grabbed my hand and put it over his crotch.

I pulled away.

He grabbed my throat. "If you want to survive, you're going to need friends. I can be your friend or your enemy; your choice."

I gagged, barely able to breathe. He squeezed my throat harder. "Okay, okay," I croaked. "What do you want? I'll do anything."

"That's better." He looked around and then unzipped his pants, reached in and grabbed his penis. "Suck it."

I had never seen a penis before. It was thick, short, and white with brown spots like coffee stains. Skin grew over the tip. His private part was hard and jutted from a sloppy mound of yellow hair. *Ekelhaft*. Disgusting. Why would anyone want to suck that thing?

He thrust himself at me. "Suck it, I said." He put his hand behind my head and pushed my face down, toward him.

"No." I pushed away.

I reached down and grabbed the leather strop and snapped it at Karl's eyes.

He jumped back. His hands covered his eyes. "Awwww."

I snatched a razor blade from the pocket of Papa's shirt. With the straight edge, I slashed his penis. Blood surged. He doubled over and wailed. I struck him again and again, not sure if I hit him but too panicked to stop. Blinded, he flung his arms to hit me, to grab me. His body blocked my way off the landing, up or down. The key. The key. Where was it? There, on the floor of the metal grate. It gleamed in the mid-morning sun, balanced like it could fall at any second.

He opened one eye and snarled. "I'm going to kill you."

With the razor edge between the pad of my thumb and the knuckle of my forefinger, I struck out and slashed him in a deep line across his neck. Blood spurted and he pivoted and fell over the rail onto the ground two stories below. The key teetered on the lattice-shaped landing of the fire escape, inches from my feet. I grabbed it and clamped it into my palm.

I looked at Karl's body below, face up, one arm by his side, the other arm unnaturally twisted over his head. His legs were strewn as if mounted a horse.

He was dead. I should feel sad, but no remorse consumed me. The hardening of Liana Anna Krochmal began.

# CHAPTER TWENTY-SIX
## LIANA
### KRISTALLNACHT DAY TWO

I FLIPPED BRUNO over my back, tucked my arms through the belt straps and opened my left fist. The key was dull and tarnished yellow with a long and thin shank. A heart-shaped bow topped the metal, and a small rectangular piece cut with triangular grooves jutted at a right angle from the stem. I wished it were the key to a dollhouse where Mama, Papa, Siegfried, Renate, Bruno and I could live. Uncle Ruby from America could visit and bring his movie star friends. The carousel horses would have their own special room. In the backyard, which would be covered with dark green grass that had no end, we'd sit on lawn chairs and drink lemonade. When it was dark and I couldn't sleep, I would ride the carousel horses until we took flight.

I reached through two of the metal bars, curled my wrist, and slipped the bit into the lock. The metal gate swung open.

"Look," a male voice yelled.

Two Nazis on the side street ran to Karl's body. They were the ones who had been in my apartment, broke the glass, knocked down the bathroom door, and fought with Papa.

The taller one looked up and pointed. "You."

I dove into the apartment, sliced my palms on the jagged edges of the windowsill, and landed hands down on the floor. My legs and feet hung out the window. Like a snake, I wiggled until my stomach and legs belly flopped onto the bathroom floor. I rolled over and sat up, stunned that I had actually made it inside, eager to find my family. I jumped up, wiped the glass from my pajama bottoms and from Papa's shirt, and took a step forward, then stopped.

The foot, the calf, the shin, they were right outside the busted door in the hallway. Now that I was closer, the coloring of the body parts wasn't right. They were greenish-blue and didn't look human. The smell of rotted meat hit my nose, how Mr. and Mrs. Goldhaber and their Pekingese, Jumbo, had smelled when we found their bodies after they ate rat poison.

Did I want to know who was attached to the foot? It hadn't moved for hours. My breath sucked in and I held it there, forgetting how to exhale for a long, painful moment.

I blew air from my lungs, coughed, and heaved from the stench.

I dreaded the next deduction. If Karl had fallen off the fire escape, and the two other Nazis that had been in my apartment were outside, that dead foot had to belong to—

"*Anhalten.*" Halt.

Through the window, a large hand gripped my wrist and twisted. The pain excruciating, I fell to my knees.

# CHAPTER TWENTY-SEVEN
## LIANA
## KRISTALLNACHT DAY TWO

"I AM LIANA Krochmal. This is my home—"

"Shut up." The tall Nazi yanked me by the arm, hauled me out the bathroom window and onto the fire escape.

My body scraped along the window ledge. Broken glass cut my hands, my face, and stuck in the folds of Papa's shirt. The Nazi dragged me down the fire escape, Bruno cinched to my back. My thighs, knees, and calves smacked against the metal stairs as I tried to gain footing. He moved too fast, too rough. I couldn't regain balance. Pain shot through my arms and legs as they slapped against the rails. On the bottom rung of the ladder, he jumped and I landed on top of him. He scrambled to his feet and pushed me aside.

Pointing at Karl, he bellowed, *"Schauen Sie sich einmal an, was sie getan hat!"* Look what you did!

I blanched at the sight of the neighborhood boy. His neck was sliced open with stuff coming out that looked like soft-boiled eggs squished and colored red and purple. Blood, like thick ink, pooled around his head and groin. I turned away from his hacked penis. His face was stiff, his eyes wide, and his mouth frozen and egg-shaped.

The shorter soldier bent over Karl.

The tall Nazi shook me. "You killed him, you murderer."

"No, no. I didn't. He was my friend."

Through gritted teeth, he seethed. "Nazis and Jews are not friends." He spit on the ground.

"Karl and I were friends, before this."

"Before what?"

"Before Hitler."

The Nazi bolted upright, raised his right arm in the air, no bend in the elbow, his hand straight. *"Heil, Hitler."*

The other Nazi, the short one, also saluted.

But for the height difference, they looked the same, brown uniforms, short greased-back blond hair, and a sidearm holstered on their belts.

"You like Hitler, little girl?" the tall one asked, his voice creepy and high-pitched.

"I've never met him."

"She is a smart aleck, Udo," the tall one said.

Udo walked toward us. "Yes, Werner, I would say she is many things and not just a Jew." He spit.

"Hitler does not want to meet you, dirty Juden. He knows you are filthy excrement."

I looked at the grounds at the rear of the apartment building. No one else was near. It was the two horrible Nazis, dead Karl, and me. I looked up toward the bathroom window. *Papa, rescue me.*

"I think I would like Hitler if I met him," I said.

The Nazis laughed.

"If you were to meet the Fuhrer, would you sing the Nazi anthem to him?" Udo asked.

"Oh, yes, '*Horst Wessel-Lied*' is my favorite song." I didn't know what else to say, what to do. Run? Scream? Who would hear me? Music from the marching band played from the street in front of the apartment building, the parade ongoing. *What was celebrated?*

"Let's hear it."

"What?" I asked.

"'*Horst Wessel.*' Sing it," Werner said.

Tears came to my eyes, thick like syrup, blinding. They dropped down my face and stung like pelts of freezing rain. I didn't want to sing *that* song. Rabbi Ehrenfeld had made us all learn it. He had predicted knowing the song might save our lives.

A few weeks after the Germans occupied Austria I had protested to mother while we were in temple. "Why do we have to learn that horrible song?"

"Because our Rabbi says so," came Mama's stern response.

A disapproving glance from Papa told me to do as I was told. With all the mishaps I had gotten into, stealing books from the library because Jews were no longer allowed to have library cards, watching the Lipizzaner horses train in violation of the Jewish curfew, Papa had never looked at me in that way, a stern, tight stare that dared me to betray him. That is, except one other time, when he had ordered me I had to climb out the bathroom window, alone.

"*Ja*, let's hear '*Horst Wessel*,'" Udo echoed.

I looked again toward the bathroom window.

"Jew," Werner spit, "your family is gone. No one is going to help you."

"They are not gone. They would never leave me."

"You are stupid. Your family is dead."

"No, they're not." I jumped onto Werner and hit him with closed fists.

Udo laughed as Werner grabbed me by the wrists and twisted my hands until I fell to my knees. He let go, and I stumbled a half step back.

"Stand up," Werner ordered.

I was on all fours, crying, sobbing violently I no longer heard the parade music, no longer saw Karl, was no longer at the mercy of those two horrible men. Nothing mattered if what he had said was true.

*Is my family really dead?*

"Get up now." Werner's voice was deep, cold, void of emotion, which frightened me more than the uniform, his sidearm, and how he twisted my wrists until I crashed to my knees. He was no longer human.

I rose and clasped my hands in front of me to stop them from shaking. My legs felt like they would betray me and I would fall again. My throat tightened and I could barely squeeze breaths out.

Werner pointed a black handgun at me. "*Singen*."

"*Die Fahne hoch*." I spoke softly.

"Sing it louder."

"*Die Fahne hoch! Die Reihen fest geschlossen! SA marschiert mit mutig-festem Schritt. SA marschiert mit ruhig festem!*" The flag on high! The ranks tightly closed! The storm battalion march with bold, firm step. The storm troopers march with calm, firm step.

I stopped.

"Keep going," Udo ordered.

"I've forgotten."

"You must never forget. Sing, and march in place. Go."

I lifted my knees. "*Kam'raden, die Rotfront und Reaktion Erschossen—*"

"*Nein*," Werner demanded. "From the beginning. Swing your arms while you march."

"*Die Fahne hoch!*"

At gunpoint, the Nazis forced me to sing their stupid anthem. Four stanzas from start to finish, over three minutes long. My arms swung at my sides and I marched while Karl's body stiffened, while the parade roared, while Germans and gentile Austrians cheered, while Jewish household goods burned in a giant bonfire.

"*Aufs neue.*" Again.

I lost count after I sang for the twenty-seventh time.

# CHAPTER TWENTY-EIGHT
## RUBY
## KRISTALLNACHT DAY ONE

CANE IN HAND, bowler hat pushed down on his head, Ruby dragged his feet up the stairs to his third-floor room of Mrs. Bowen's boarding house. Every step hurt. From stinging pain when he stepped on his heels and curled his toes to soreness in his shins, stiffness in his knees, and throbbing in his thighs. He took no pleasure in how Meyer Lansky and his boys had rescued him from the German American Bund and how they had likely killed one of the members of the American Nazi party. It's not that he minded a dead Nazi; he was in too much agony to take pleasure from anything. In about five hours Lansky and his goons were going to pick him up, expecting him to do what? Tell jokes? Commit crimes? He groaned as he stepped onto the second-floor landing. *What have I gotten myself into?*

"I'm not going." He spoke to the chipped lead paint on the stairway walls and the worn wood steps beneath his loafers.

Despite the threat from one of Lansky's hatchetmen, when ten o'clock in the morning rolled around, he wouldn't be waiting outside, not as Charlie Chaplin, and certainly not as Ruby Friedman.

Finally to the third floor, he slid the key in the lock to his room and smiled at the daily charade he made of locking and unlocking the door whenever he left or arrived, knowing the bolt hadn't worked since he moved in eight months earlier. He made some mild complaints to Mrs. Bowen early in his stay, but not wanting to incur her wrath, he let it go. Instead he created a unique pantomime each time he entered and exited the room. Sometimes he was a lover who slipped away from his mistress before her husband arrived. Other times he opened the door to a surprise party. His favorite charade was to find his family seated inside, safe and happy. The sound of their native German cradled him like warm bath salts.

This time he was too sore to pretend. He pushed the door open as himself, Ruby Friedman, unemployed, beaten by Nazis, saved by gangsters, who missed his family, and who lost any shot he had with Dixie, the love of his life. He stepped in and was surprised by who sat on his cot. He had been wrong. Despite his anguish, there was something, no, someone who could give him pleasure at this moment.

"Dixie?"

Her face revealed in a tilted, one-quarter view, immersed in the gloom of the small, dank room. He knew it was she, not only from her floral perfume but also from her stiletto heels, nude stockings, satin G-string, and pasties.

She cocked her head toward him, her face lit by the fluorescent glow that seeped in from the hallway. He was quick to register that her visit was not for the romantic encounter he had dreamed of.

Yellowing framed her right eye, which was to be black and blue before long. A gentle trail of dried blood trekked from her left nostril to her lips. Her cheeks were red and scratched. He grabbed the blanket from the cot and placed it over her shoulders, and then closed the door and rushed toward her, bending on one knee.

"What happened? Are you okay? Did anyone see you come in?"

Her lips moved, but if words came out, he couldn't hear them.

He reached for one of the two glasses he had sponged from the Hudson Burlesque Theater and filled it with water poured from a glass bottle, also *borrowed* from the theater.

She flinched when she put her mouth to the lip of the glass, and sipped until it was drained. She handed the empty glass to Ruby.

"Thank you." Her voice was soft, hoarse. Her body seemed small, deflated. She was markedly different from the woman who had taken the stage with him a few hours ago.

"What happened? Did Lester do this?"

She shook her head.

"Then we have to tell him what happened."

"I called off the engagement."

Ruby's eyes widened. "So he *did* do this."

"No. I called it off at the theater." Her speech was hesitant. "I told Lester I would marry him and not Frank Byron, Jr., too. He said they were a package. I take both or none at all." Tears pooled in her eyes. "I can't do that, Ruby. That doll sits at the table when we eat. He's on the bed when we…" She wiped her eyes. Black mascara trailed down her cheeks like tiger stripes.

"I'm sorry."

"Lester and Frank Byron, Jr. took it well when I told them. They offered to walk me home, but I said I was okay. I've walked home by myself many times, and at all hours."

Ruby waited, he didn't want to rush her. He tried to assess her condition without appearing obvious. Knuckles on her left hand were bruised and scraped. A road rash formed on her right arm and traveled from the side of her hand, along her forearm and bicep, and to her shoulder. Dried blood caked on her thighs.

"Who did this, Dixie?"

She adjusted the blanket to cover her legs as well as her back and shoulders. "There were two men, soldiers, I think. They said they had seen our show earlier in the evening and loved it. They said they wanted my autograph."

"What did they look like?"

"I didn't get a good look."

"Think about it. You can't identify them?"

She shook her head, her sadness profound.

"Mr. Friedman." The hearty figure of Mrs. Bowen filled the

doorframe. "You know the rules, Ruby Friedman. No women are permitted in your room if you're not married, and certainly the door is never to be closed."

"But, Mrs. Bowen—"

"You're to be out by daylight, and seeing what time it is, you'd better start packing."

"It's not his fault," Dixie said.

"I've heard every excuse possible, Missy, so don't bullshit this bullshitter. Rules are rules, and there are no exceptions."

"Mrs. Bowen, my family is on its way here from Vienna, and Dixie, I mean Ms. Lee, and I work together at the theater and she ran into trouble."

"He was helping me. I swear."

"Out by morning." Mrs. Bowen pushed the door farther open until the knob smacked the wall and made an indent. "If this door is closed one more time, you'll be out immediately." She sized up Ruby and Dixie.

Dixie drew the blanket more tightly around her.

"Better yet," Mrs. Bowen growled, "why don't you and your hussy leave now?"

"Now? Can't you see she's been hurt?"

She wagged a finger at him. "This is a respectable boarding house, Ruby Friedman, and the likes of vaudeville men and their loose women are not going to bring cops and gangsters into my establishment. I'll be back with my boys in ten minutes to make sure you're gone."

# CHAPTER TWENTY-NINE
## LIANA
### KRISTALLNACHT DAY TWO

BRUNO ON MY back, I trudged along the streets where I used to play. Many of us were there from my temple, marching, Rabbi Ehrenfeld, his wife and their daughter, Bettina; Mrs. Adler and her two children; Mr. and Mrs. Kandel and their daughter, Birgitt; and Lulu Wittgenstein and her younger brother, Maximilian. Many were missing. Where was Mr. Adler? Olof Hammerstein? Lulu and Max's parents? My family?

We marched past the main square and two Nazis lit a bonfire. Piled high in the soon-to-be conflagration were furnishings, lampposts, a bicycle, and clothes. On the top of the pile was a placard with the Ten Commandments written in Hebrew. Next to that, scribbled in large letters, was a sign: *Rach fur Mord au vorm Rath!* Revenge for the murder of vom Rath! *Tod den International.* Death to the International! *Juden und Freimauren!* Jews and Freemasons!

"What's that about?" I looked up at my rabbi.

"Ernst Vom Rath was assassinated earlier this morning in Paris. "

"Who's that?"

"He was a German diplomat."

"A Jew?"

"No. He was killed by a Jew."

I slowed. "Is that why the Nazis are doing this?"

"That is what they will claim, but the truth is, Liana, Hitler has planned this action for some time."

The butt of a rifle jabbed me in the back. I didn't look behind me. I knew who would be at the other end, a despicable and disgusting Nazi.

"Have you seen my mama and papa?" I asked Rabbi Ehrenfeld for the millionth time, but he was no longer next to me.

I swung my head and looked for my family. I broke the line and ran to people I knew and asked anxiously, "Have you see my family? Do you know where Siegfried is? Is Renate okay?"

The people of my community wouldn't answer. Some pretended I wasn't there; others pushed me away, only few made eye contact.

"Get in line," a Brownshirt yelled.

I resumed marching, left foot, right arm, right foot, left arm, and never stopped looking for my family. They had to be in the crowd. It was hard to know how far in front and how far in back the sea of people traveled. The Jewish men and boys wore hats; the women and girls wore head coverings. Those on the sidewalks cheered and yelled nasty things at us.

*What is going on? Could all this be about that Vom Rath guy?*

After Werner and Udo had tired of the game of having me sing the Nazi anthem, I told them about a mysterious man who had jumped Karl and slit his throat. I wasn't sure if the Nazis believed my tale. When cheers erupted on the street Werner grabbed my arm and pulled me to the front of the apartment building where lines of Jews marched. Nazis in their brown uniforms held machine guns, pistols, and rifles. Rabbi Ehrenfeld had made us learn about guns, even how to fire them.

Non-Jews screamed horrifically. *"Die Juden."* Die Jews.

*"Sie riechen wie Schweine."* You smell like pigs.

"You cannot speak to us like this," Mr. Kandel yelled.

A Nazi pushed him to his knees and shot him in the head, blood and chunky matter flew and hit the side of a building. Mrs. Kandel and Birgitt screamed and tried to run to him; others held them back.

I found Rabbi Ehrenfeld again and clung to his coat, his daughter Bettina on his other side. I did not look up to see where we headed. Mr. Kandel's murder chilled me. Eventually, I peeked up as we marched around a corner, and I saw our synagogue. Germans stood on the steps and yelled anti-Semitic statements.

Werner stood at the door to the temple. *"Hut ab!"* Hats off!

Germans grabbed our hats and head coverings and flung them away. They corralled and forced us into the synagogue where we were ordered to sit. The women headed for the stairs, as it was an orthodox temple where the men and women sat in separate sections, but the Nazis stopped them. Men, women, and children sat together, maybe three hundred Jews for half as many seats, stacked on each other, under benches, between legs. The aisles required to remain clear for the Nazis to patrol up and down. I sat next to Rabbi Ehrenfeld and buried my face in his side; Bettina next to me clung to her mother. People murmured and wondered what they were supposed to do, what would happen next, but no one spoke out as Mr. Kandel had done for fear he too would get a bullet in the head.

"Quiet." Werner yelled.

A Nazi took the stage and leaned on the lectern where Rabbi Ehrenfeld delivered sermons. Behind him was the Holy Ark, a large cabinet where the Torah scrolls consisting of the Old Testament, written Jewish law, were stored. At the *bimah*, the Nazi opened a book and began to read. I stopped listening when it was clear the lecture was filled with hateful language. If anybody complained, if anyone allowed an expression of distaste or dissent to shadow her face, the butt of a gun met her head or a loved one was threatened or harmed.

After reading for more than an hour, the Nazi on the podium closed the book and asked, "Where is the rabbi of this temple?"

Rabbi Ehrenfeld peeled me off of him on his left side and moved his young daughter away when she grabbed for him.

Head held high, he announced, "I am Rabbi Solomon Ehrenfeld."

"Come." The Nazi beckoned toward the stage.

Johanna Ehrenfeld grabbed his arm, but the rabbi also gently pushed his wife away. He made his way down the row, along the aisle, congregants reached for him as he walked toward the stage.

"Read." The Nazi thrust a book at him.

Rabbi Ehrenfeld looked at the spine. "*Nein.*"

As if shot out of the sky, three storm troopers barreled down the row where I sat with the rabbi's family. One snatched his wife, the other his daughter, and the third grabbed me.

"Okay, okay," the rabbi said from the stage, "I will read."

The storm troopers threw us onto the hard wooden bench where we huddled, shook, and whimpered. I took Bruno off my back and hugged him to my chest.

Rabbi Ehrenfeld opened the book and began reciting from *Mein Kampf*, Hitler's autobiographical manifesto.

Three hours later, Rabbi Ehrenfeld continued to read. If anyone in the audience fell asleep, a Nazi smacked him in the face. If a child cried, the parent was hit. If a parent complained, her child was taken away. When Rabbi Ehrenfeld's voice began to lilt due to exhaustion, four Nazis gathered around him, screamed, hit him, and forced him to continue.

"Enough," a Nazi finally yelled. "This way."

The doors to the synagogue opened and we were ushered out of the temple. Those that were old and sick were pushed to the side. Others loaded onto trucks.

Someone dared to ask, "Where are we going?"

"Dachau," said a Nazi.

I had never heard of Dachau, but knew it couldn't be a good place after the way the Nazis treated us. No matter what, I didn't want to go, not without my family. I couldn't get on one of those trucks, surely then I would never see my family again. They had to be at the apartment, with the carousel horses, waiting for me. I had to get to them.

As people stepped onto the trucks, squeezed in, sat, and stepped on each other, and Nazis threatened to shoot if anyone disobeyed, I saw my dad's head, or what I thought was his hair. I shoved my way through the crowd and screamed, "Papa, Mama." Ignored and pushed aside in the chaos, I yelled, "wait for me." I tried to get to the truck; I had to get on. I had to be with them.

Before I could mount the truck, the man I thought was Papa rotated his chin, he didn't have side curls.

Next to me, Max Wittgenstein threw himself on the ground. "I'm not going."

His sister, Lulu, tried to pick him up, but the squirming child was too much for her. Udo picked Max up by the hair and shot a bullet into his skull.

I jumped away, unsure where to go. Which direction was the truck? Where was the temple? Nazis pushed people forward, some Jews moved stoically, others fought, and many were murdered. Lulu howled. Rabbi Ehrenfeld grabbed her around the waist and carried her like a sack of grain away from Udo, who waved his gun and screamed, "What Jew pig wants to die next?"

I ran until I saw the front stairs to the synagogue. I slipped into the emptying temple, stayed low to the ground, and ran up the aisle and toward the stage. I looked around, unsure where to hide, and saw the perfect place. I climbed and slipped into the Holy Ark and nestled between the scrolls of the Torah.

# CHAPTER THIRTY
## LIANA
## KRISTALLNACHT DAY TWO

HUDDLED IN THE ark between the two sides of the opened scroll, in a cabinet, I prayed and asked for forgiveness. I was, after all, hiding between the Torah scrolls, the "how-to" manual, as Rabbi Ehrenfeld instructed, which taught Jews how God expected them to lead their lives. The Torah included the five books of Moses, beginning with Genesis, the creation of the world, and ending with Deuteronomy and Moses's death. If God was going to be anywhere, I thought, he was going to be right there with me.

"Dear God," I whispered so the Nazis wouldn't hear, "please forgive me for all the wrongs I have done, for all the times I didn't listen to my parents, for when I cut the hair off Renate's favorite doll, and for the time I put shaving cream in Siegfried's new shoes. And God, please don't be mad at me for killing Karl. I didn't mean to do that. Oh, and one more thing, keep my family safe and tell the Nazis to go home. Amen. Your friend, Liana Krochmal."

A thin beam of light shone into the cabinet where I hid, and I had a sliver of a view into the temple. As best as I could tell, the trucks had been loaded and my Jewish friends, neighbors, the shop owners, and teachers were off to a place called Dachau. I hoped they'd be back soon, that all of this chaos would be over before long and the kids could return to school, the mothers could shop in the big markets again, and the fathers could have their old jobs again. Rabbi

Ehrenfeld's beard would grow longer than ever, and he would once more lead our community. Mama and Papa would be thankful to him for the way he watched over me while the Nazis made us sit in the temple, while they gave that evil talk, and while they forced Rabbi Ehrenfeld to read from Hitler's idiotic book.

Through the slit I couldn't discern anything for certain, except the shapes of long and dark figures moving in and out and across the light. I heard German, never Hebrew or Yiddish. I could identify by the accent if an Austrian or a German spoke. All the voices I heard were male, and they were all of Hitler's army.

I didn't know how long I had been stuffed between two sides of the scroll. I gripped Bruno to my chest. My eyes were heavy, but that fact didn't tell me anything about time. I hadn't slept in forever, I longed for my bed, to hear Renate talking in her sleep, and Siegfried snoring. I missed the carousel horses.

"Are you out there, God?" I whispered.

I waited for his response, a sign, a voice, something, anything. I couldn't leave my hiding place yet since the Germans wouldn't let me go home if they caught me. I had to wait until they were gone, and then I had to reunite with my family. I had to make sure Papa knew I didn't hate him.

"I'll leave when it gets dark, God. Is that a good plan?" I waited, heard nothing so I continued, undeterred. "I'll sneak through the streets until I get to my apartment building. I hope I can go in through the front door since I don't want to go around back. Do you think Karl is still under the fire escape?"

Two figures converged on the stage before me.

One greeted the other. "*Heil Hitler.*"

"*Heil Hitler.*"

"Are the trucks gone?"

"*Ja*, the last one left."

"*Gute. Ist alles bereit?*" Good. Is everything ready?

"*Ja.* Should I make sure the temple is empty?"

"No need. Get started."

"*Ja, Herr.*"

The unmistakable sound of the Nazis' calf-high jackboots with leather soles and heel irons struck the floor with sharp authority. I jumped at each step, like fearing the snap of a belt or the cock of a gun. I hugged Bruno tighter. The shadow of one Nazi remained on the stage. I wanted to open the door to get a look at him. It might be Werner. I imagined jumping out from the ark to stab him to death with the rods from the scroll. I'd stick one into each side of his neck, and wouldn't care if the blood shot in my eyes.

The lone Nazi walked around the stage. His boots clomped along the wood platform. He stopped in front of Rabbi Ehrenfeld's podium, and I heard "*Ffffft.*" It was a sound I had heard before but could not place. I smelled rotten eggs, like when Mama ignited the gas stove or when Papa lit his pipe. Heavy steps ran off the stage, lights flickered around the rabbi's podium, and wood burned.

I pushed open the doors to the Ark. Flames expanded rapidly, swallowed the stage, and devoured the pews. There was no time to wait for dark to make my escape. I slung Bruno over my back, ran out of the cabinet, and then back to it. I ripped a portion of the Torah, folded it, and stuck it in the front pocket of Papa's shirt. The ground grew hot underneath my socks.

I knew the rear of the temple well since my classes were held there after shul. I ran toward the rabbi's office. Flames lapped at my feet and legs and at the flap of Papa's long-sleeved shirt. Smoke burned my lungs and stung my eyes. I headed for a side door, the one where deliveries were made, pushed it open, and jumped into the early evening chill.

In the soft light of dusk, the streets were quiet, while behind me, fire raged. I had expected something different on the street, mayhem and Jews fighting Nazis and refusing to succumb to their bullying. There was nothing more than the smoldering of a bonfire in a park half a block away and the scattering of furnishings and kitchen supplies that hadn't made it into the cinders. Where was everyone? Even the Nazis were gone. Had they moved on to the next quarter?

I scampered away from the burning temple. Remnants of smoke

pricked my eyes; my legs cramped. I was weary. A few blocks from home, as the streets fell away, I picked up my pace. Renewed energy spirited through me at the prospect of being reunited with my family.

# CHAPTER THIRTY-ONE
## LIANA
### KRISTALLNACHT DAY TWO

ON MY BLOCK, the five-story apartment building, that was next door to my apartment and that housed the butcher and tailor shops on the bottom floor, leaned. The first and second floors crushed, the remaining three stories askew like a fallen cake. Rubble taller than me littered the street. The red brick and mortar of the building flared.

The building on the other side of mine had met a similar fate. Smoke hung in the air like a heavy blanket, but not the comfortable kind, the kind that itched and suffocated so you couldn't breathe. It was like time had jumped forward in an instant. One block earlier, the sun had gently lighted the street as it started its descent into the horizon. Now the murky air made it seem as if night had collapsed on all Jewish dreams.

I climbed over bricks and rocks, using my hands as much as my feet to scale the ruins. Adrenaline fueled me, whatever pain I experienced from earlier injuries was nonexistent. I looked up, amazed that but for broken windows, my apartment building was upright, intact. I eyed the second-story window where my siblings and I had our bedroom. I scrambled across the debris with more determination, eager to find my family, cutting my hands and feet on glass and rock, opening the wounds that had started to close from earlier in the day, but still no pain.

The front door was open. Closer, I realized the door was missing.

I then heard a sound that made me stop. It wasn't loud; it was different, not the noise of Nazis or the confusion of panic or the creak of rubble, but the soft cry of need.

"Help us," came an exhausted moan.

I looked to a mountain of debris, unsure if I had heard a real voice, or was that my imagination, or the wind perhaps. I moved on and worked to scale the wreckage to get to my apartment building, when I heard it again.

"Please help us."

I stopped, knowing it was for real, not a dream.

"Where are you?" I called.

"Here," came another voice.

"I can't see you."

"Down here."

I looked at my feet, rocks and ruins below. A piece of a cement block next to my left foot moved and a hand shot up. I jumped and fell. I regained my balance and looked where the hand had been. As the realization hit me, I inhaled sharply as if struck with a fist in my stomach. People were buried alive. I moved rocks aside, threw them off the pile, and made another heap instead. I reached down and a small child was handed to me, a little girl I knew from the neighborhood, her face wet with tears. I handed the weeping child to an older girl who had climbed out from the mound. Behind her, a teenage boy poked his head out. His face and hair covered with soot and dust.

"How many are you?" I asked the boy, who handed another small girl to me.

He wiped dirt from his eyes with the short sleeve of his formerly white T-shirt. "Not sure, maybe fifteen or twenty. The building collapsed, and this kind of cave was made. Parents threw their kids in. Then there was gunfire and screaming, and then all the adults were gone."

As he spoke, children scrambled out of the hole, climbed over rocks, and screamed for their parents.

"There are no adults down there?" I yelled above the cries.

"Not as far as I can tell. I think I'm the oldest." He handed smaller children to me and to some of the bigger kids who had climbed out of the rubble cave.

Bettina, the Rabbi's daughter, ascended out of the hole, and we nodded hello.

"I think that's it." The boy lifted himself onto the top of the stone mountain, his height and bulk similar to Siegfried's.

 I pointed at his brown pants and the bottoms tucked into his calf-high boots. "You're a Nazi." I fell and smacked my tailbone on a sharp stone. Stinging rose up my spine.

"No. Yes. I mean no." He balanced on top of the rocks.

A four-year-old boy that I knew clung to his leg. He picked up the boy, who wrapped his arms around his shoulders and buried his face in his neck.

"Put Johann down!" I yelled at the Nazi to release my neighbor.

"You know him?"

"He lives on the fourth floor. His family goes to my temple. I know most of these kids." I bent, picked up a rock, and raised it above my head. "Put him down."

"Okay, okay." He put Johann down. The child grabbed his leg again. "It's not what you think."

"Are you a member of the Nazi party?" I asked.

"Yes."

"Are you German?"

"Austrian."

"Do you hate Jews?"

"No."

I lowered the rock. "Liar. All Nazis hate Jews."

"I never wanted to join the Nazi party, but my father made me. He said if they knew I was Jew-loving, the Nazis would kill me."

"How can you be a Nazi and love Jews?"

"I'm not a Nazi. I mean I'm wearing the uniform, but that's an act. In school, some of my best friends were Jews. I don't understand what's bad about them. Look what I did here." He waved his arms at the children around them. "I saved them. I found the hiding place. The parents didn't ask me if I was a Nazi when they handed their children to me."

"How old are you?"

"Fifteen."

"Two years younger than Siegfried."

"Who?"

"My brother. He and my mama, papa, and sister are waiting for me in our apartment." I pointed toward the building that stood among the wreckage.

"They are?"

"Yes."

"Go get them, but first tell me your name."

"Liana Krochmal. And you?"

"Wilhelm Goldenstein. Now go."

I ran, not sure if I should believe Wilhelm or not, but I was more concerned to reunite with my family. I treaded among the rocks and debris until I found a clear path to enter my building. Inside, I ran along the front foyer. Glass and broken wood jabbed at my feet, which were bare on the bottom since the socks I had worn were tattered. I sprinted down a hallway and up stairs to the second floor. My heart pounded with excitement at the sight of the familiar *Willkommen* mat in front of our door.

I stepped over the splintered wood of the broken doorjamb and ran toward the kitchen. I skidded to a stop when I saw him in the hallway in front of the bathroom. I had forgotten about the feet and calves I had been able to see from the fire escape. I had refused to believe that the motionless limbs had belonged to Siegfried or anyone in my family, but there was no mistaking his long legs, the white-and-yellow pajamas that Mama had sewn were bunched around his thighs and upper body, the shock of dark hair on his head, the long side curls, and his lean and muscular frame. I fell to my knees and threw myself at his body. I recoiled at the sight of two holes in Siegfried's chest, at the red stains on his pajama top.

"Mama, Papa, Renate, where are you?"

Tears trailed behind me as I raced toward the kitchen. I stopped at the entrance. The table and chairs were upended, the icebox toppled, the contents of the pantry strewn all over the floor. I looked into the dining room and saw the curio cabinet flattened, all of Mama's china smashed, our teacups obliterated.

The ladder to the attic was down, the attic door open. I climbed over smashed cans of food, kitchen supplies, and bent and shattered baking dishes until I reached the ladder. I scaled it and slipped on some of the rungs. My entire body shook.

At the top, I stuck my head in. "Papa? Mama? Are you there?"

Nobody. Nothing.

I climbed into the attic. "Mama? Papa?" I waited for a response, listened extra hard for a sound, nothing.

"Renate, this isn't funny. You can come out now."

Nothing again. No Mama. No Papa. No Renate. Siegfried dead.

I sat heavy on the attic floor and trembled. I screamed and punched myself in the head. Bruno clung to me. The pain was delicious, the delirium sweet like sugar straight from the jar. I kept my eyes shut tight, afraid to open them, terrified of all I wouldn't see, who I wouldn't see. Blood dripped down the sides of my face, into my eyes, and seeped into the corners of my mouth, chunky on my tongue. Blood from the partially healed wounds on my hands mixed with tears, saliva and snot. I brought my knees to my chest and rocked.

"*Anhalten.*" Halt.

A hand wrapped roughly around my thin bicep and yanked me to my feet.

"Let's go."

I hung like a rag doll in his grip and prayed the Nazi would choose mercy and end my life rather than make me live another moment without my family.

"Get up."

"I hate you," I shrieked. "Shoot me." My fists and feet flailed and I tried to make contact with the Brownshirt, hoping to anger and annoy him so much he'd rather kill me than bother with putting me on a truck to that place, that place whose name I couldn't remember.

"Stop it, Liana."

I opened my eyes. "Wilhelm?"

"What have you done to yourself?" He took off his T-shirt and wiped blood and gunk from the sides of my face and from my hands. He looked at the blood on the front of Papa's shirt. "Are you hurt?"

I shook my head. "It's Siegfried's blood."

"We have to go."

"Where?"

"Somewhere safe. It's going to be dark soon. Me, you, the others, we can't stay here. In the hallway, was that Siegfried?"

Tears raced down my cheeks and he had my response.

"I'm sorry," he said.

"Do you think my *mutter, vater,* and Renate are…" I choked on the word, coughed and hacked.

Wilhelm held my arm, kept me upright as my knees buckled.

"Maybe they're on one of the trucks," he said.

"To where?" Using his shirt, I dabbed more blood from my face and hands.

"Work camps."

"What's a work camp?"

"Where the Jews are going to live so they can help the Germans build things."

A brightness splashed through my body. "So they'll be okay? I mean, not Siegfried, I know, but the others?"

"I'm sure." He let go of my arm. "Are you coming or not?"

"Yes, but first I need to get something." I looked at his bare chest and at his Nazi-issued pants and boots. "Why are you dressed like that, if you're not a Nazi?"

"My papa said it was how I would survive."

"Have you hurt any Jews?"

"No, no. Of course not. I've saved many."

I climbed down the ladder, and he followed. I picked my way across the kitchen and down the hallway, past the bathroom. I stopped at Siegfried's body, bent, and kissed the top of his head.

Wilhelm gently grabbed my shoulders to lift me. "We have to go."

I lingered over Siegfried for a final look at my brother and then forced myself to hurry down the hallway and into my bedroom.

"Where are you going?" Wilhelm chased after me. "What is so important that we can't leave right now?"

In my bedroom I released a long sigh. There they were, miraculously intact amid shards of glass, twisted window frames, and chunks of brick and stone. The carousel horses.

# CHAPTER THIRTY-TWO
## RUBY
## KRISTALLNACHT DAY ONE

AT SEVEN IN the morning nearly one foot of snow covered the sidewalks on New York Avenue while a steady stream of sleet pelted Ruby and Dixie. Ruby didn't have many possessions so it hadn't been difficult to add layers of clothes over his Chaplin costume and throw everything else, bathroom supplies and a few letters from Amalie, in a sack and over his shoulder. He had two dollars and twenty-seven cents in his front right pocket. He carried the bowler hat and cane.

Dixie wore two pairs of his pants, both cinched at the waist with rope, a couple of his shirts, a pair of his boots with the toes stuffed with socks, and a blanket wrapped around her shoulders. Their heads were bent and their eyes half closed against the whiz of ice that hit them like pellets shot from a BB gun.

They had a plan. Ruby was to follow Dixie to her apartment a few blocks over to make sure she got home safely. He couldn't stay with her very long. People would talk, and her landlady was as bad as Mrs. Bowen, which was one of the reasons Dixie hadn't gone home after she was attacked. As she had explained to Ruby while they piled his clothes on, she had witnessed other women be blamed for their assaults.

*If you hadn't dressed so provocatively, this wouldn't have happened.*

She hadn't been able to say the "r" word. Ruby knew from the blood and bruises around her thighs that the "r" word was involved.

"Don't blame yourself," he had said as he layered one last sweater over another.

Loud footsteps on the boarding house stairs sounded. They stopped dressing and looked toward the door, expecting to see Mrs. Bowen and her sons.

"It wasn't your fault," Ruby persisted.

"Shh." Dixie put her index finger over Ruby's mouth and then brushed her lips against his.

The oldest and burliest Bowen son's broad shoulders occupied the doorframe. "Out."

Behind him Mrs. Bowen and the other boys jeered.

Ruby threw the sack over his shoulder and took Dixie's hand. He pushed past Mrs. Bowen and her sons and led Dixie down the stairs and into the morning snow.

Dixie showered down the hall while Ruby stood outside the bathroom door and waited. Back in her apartment, she crawled into her bed.

"Can I take you to the hospital this afternoon?" Ruby asked.

Because she has already refused this request several times, he predicted her response; however, he hoped after a hot shower she might feel differently.

"You know how I make my living, don't you?" she asked, her eyes kind.

"You're a dancer."

"A burlesque dancer. No one is going to believe I didn't invite this upon myself."

Ruby was saddened but knew she was right.

"I've been violated once, I can't be violated again." Exhausted, her words trailed off.

"I won't let anyone hurt you." Ruby kissed her on each eye, on the tip of her nose, and then on her lips, thrilled when she kissed him back.

Her lids heavy, she succumbed to their demands.

Ruby managed a few hours shuteye twisted like a pretzel in a chair. He awoke with a start and peeked at the clock next to Dixie's bed, nine a.m. He regarded her sleeping form huddled in a blanket in deep slumber.

He hated leaving but she was warm and safe.

"I'll be back soon."

She slept and didn't hear but he didn't care. Having the ability to say to Dixie Lee "See you soon" invigorated him. He ran out her door, down the stairs, and into the chilled air.

At the corner, he stood under a streetlight, looked up and marveled at the sleet that had turned to snow. Each falling flake seemed to be crowned with a halo and kissed by the wings of an angel. He had no friends or family in New York except for Dixie. He wasn't sure where his sister and her family were; he hoped they would arrive from Vienna soon, yet euphoria overcame him.

He was in love, and maybe she loved him too.

He put the bowler hat on and tapped the cane on the snow-covered sidewalk. He shuffled back and forth like Charlie Chaplin, rolled his hat along his arm and on to his head. "A day without laughter is a day wasted," Ruby quoted Chaplin. "I'm not wasting another single day. I love you, Dixie Lee."

He spun, his arms open wide, then pretended to walk down stairs. He waddled along the street and laughed from his belly, hard and long.

The Buick Century rolled up next to him. Meyer Lansky leaned out the back window. "What's so funny, Ruby?"

The driver put down his window. The same fellow as from a few hours earlier leered in the front passenger seat.

"Nothing's funny, Mr. Lansky." The elation drained from Ruby's body like blood from a wound.

"What are you wearing?" Meyer asked.

"Uh, my clothes."

"Looks like you're wearing all of them at once. That's an odd way to keep warm. Get in." From inside the sedan, Meyer pushed open the door to the car.

"No, thanks." Ruby continued to walk.

The car rolled next to him.

"Excuse me?" Meyer said.

"I'm late for an appointment."

"Do you believe him, boys?"

"No way."

"Not me, boss."

"I have something important to do," Ruby said.

"What's her name?" The driver chuckled.

"Shut up," Meyer said. "What is her name?"

"Um, I don't know, I, uh, pay by the hour."

"You don't need a two-bit whore, Ruby. You're a nice Jewish man. Cheap whores are rubbish; they don't deserve respect. You work with us, and I promise you won't have to pay for another woman again. They'll be begging to suck your dick for free."

Ruby sped up his pace on the sidewalk with the car staying next to him on the street.

"I know what you're thinking, Ruby. I can read your mind," Meyer said.

The driver leaned out the window. "He can read your mind."

"He can read minds," the goon in the front passenger seat confirmed.

"Don't think about turning me down," Meyer said. "We got a job for you. One job, and you'll be done."

The driver exposed a nickel-plated gun. Ruby took off the bowler hat and got into the car.

# CHAPTER THIRTY-THREE
## RUBY
## KRISTALLNACHT DAY ONE

RUBY LIKED THE city best in the early morning when the streets were quiet. One of the pleasures he found from working in burlesque theater was when his job was done and he walked home, it was like Union Hill was his alone. Whatever the time of year, whatever the weather, except for a smattering of people sleeping off the night before or having nowhere to go and curling up in a shadow, at that hour, Union Hill should have been renamed Ruby's Town. When Amalie, Jacob and the kids arrived, at least one time he'd wake them up at three in the morning to show them his city, the one that seemed indestructible, the one where in the early morning fog dreams came true.

As the Buick bumped over potholes and along the George Washington Bridge, Ruby wondered if Union Hill would ever be his again.

"Where are we going, Mr. Lansky?" he asked.

"Ruby Friedman is a good Jewish name. I had a cousin named Ruby. He was a jeweler in Belarus. That's where I'm from. Grodno. Heard of it? What about you? Where were you born?"

"Vienna."

"Ah, a Viennese. Mozart was born in Vienna."

"He was born in Salzburg. He died in Vienna." Ruby regretted correcting the gangster.

Meyer looked at him sideways. "Tough thing about that broken glass."

"About what?" Ruby asked.

"You haven't heard? Well, I guess you wouldn't. Papers aren't reporting it yet. I get my news over the A.P. wire so it comes in almost real time. I have to stay up on the goings-on."

"What broken glass?"

"They're calling it *В ночь битого стекла.*"

"I don't speak Russian," Ruby said.

"What languages do you speak?"

"German, Yiddish, Hebrew, and English, of course."

"*Kristallnacht.*"

"The night of broken glass?" Ruby mused.

"You have family in Vienna?"

Ruby nodded. "My sister, her husband, my nephew and nieces, and cousins too."

"Not anymore."

Ruby grabbed him. "What does that mean?"

The driver hit the brakes and the sedan skidded to a stop in the middle of the icy bridge. Driver and front passenger pointed guns at Ruby.

Ruby removed his grip from Meyer's lapel and held his hands up for the bad guys to see. "I'm sorry. I don't know what you're talking about. Broken Glass. I don't have relatives in Vienna anymore. What does that mean?"

Meyer nodded and the henchmen put their weapons away. Meyer smoothed his suit jacket. The sedan rolled again.

"A Polish Jewish student killed the German secretary, von Rath," Meyer said. "Hitler took it personally and began a pogrom in Austria and Germany. You know what a pogrom is, right, kid?"

"Yeah." Ruby's thoughts were fuzzy.

"I grew up in Russia where anti-Jewish mobs ransacked our home and shook my parents down for loose change. I hated those sons of bitches."

"Are you saying Hitler is hurting Jews in Vienna?" Ruby tried to make sense of what Meyer was saying.

"All I hear is he wants them out of Austria and Germany."

"What about my family?"

"Tough break, kid."

"I have to go to them."

"How do you plan on doing that? You're across the ocean, and the Nazis occupy Austria and Germany. Who knows what will fall next?"

Ruby sagged, and his body flushed with heat. He wrenched off the three layers of sweaters he wore. "Maybe Madame Juliette already got them out."

"I don't know who this Madame lady is," Meyer said, "but I hope so, kid, for your sake and for theirs. What you have to do is not think about it. You can't control what you can't control, right? Think about taking a vacation to Hallandale Beach."

"Hallandale Beach?"

"Florida. You've heard of Florida, right, kid? It's always sunny there. Sometimes New York feels too crowded, and a fellow needs to get away."

"A vacation isn't in my budget."

"Stick with me, and that will change. I'm the butter and egg man."

"Why me, sir? I mean, why give me this opportunity?"

"Anyone who can pull off Charlie Chaplin like you do fits into my business plan."

Ruby sat back in the leather seat, immersed in thoughts of his family. He had to speak to Dixie, find out how to contact Madame Juliette, figure out where his family members were. Perhaps he could call or send a cable. Post would take too long.

*Please, God,* he prayed silently in Hebrew, *let the children be safe in Paris or on a ship to America. Let Amalie and Jacob be with them.*

The limo drove across the George Washington Bridge and the sun sparkled orange and red. The upper level of the suspension bridge opened in 1931 and traversed the Hudson River connecting Fort Lee, New Jersey with the Washington Heights neighborhood in northern Manhattan. A mammoth creature, 3,500 feet long and constructed of steel and cables, it had been the longest suspension bridge in the world until the Golden Gate won the accolades by 700 feet in 1937.

Ruby had taken off all layers of his clothes except for one, the black trousers he wore on stage as Charlie Chaplin, the button-down shirt and black jacket. The rest of his clothes, along with the bowler hat and bamboo cane, were folded on the floorboard of the sedan.

The car exited the bridge and drove downtown along the Manhattan streets, through Harlem and along the Hudson River.

Ruby continued to pray for his family.

"Turn here," Meyer said. A few moments later, he added, "Park over there. C'mon." He slapped Ruby on the chest. "Let's get some grub. We're going to need the energy."

The group was in Yorkville on the Upper East Side of Manhattan where George Washington stationed much of his troops in 1776 and where Gracie Mansion, the home of the New York City mayor, was built in 1799 as a private residence. In 1938, on this first day of *Kristallnacht*, Yorkville was the home base for the German American Nazi Bund, the notorious American Nazi group.

Ruby followed Meyer and his two thugs into a twenty-four-hour diner where they feasted on eggs, lox, whitefish, bagels, and cream cheese. Every few minutes breakfast was interrupted when someone came to shake Meyer's hand.

Breakfast over, the table mostly cleared, they sat, drank coffee and said little, until Meyer stood and his boys followed.

"What are we doing now?" Ruby looked up at them.

"We're leaving. You're staying here."

"What am I to do here?"

"Wait and watch," Meyer said.

"What am I watching for?" Ruby asked.

Meyer left without an answer. Ruby observed them through the big front window as they got into the sedan and drove off. Ruby sat in the booth, not knowing what he waited and watched for. A waitress kept his coffee mug filled. The owner checked on him. Neighborhood people vigorously shook his hand, their two hands cupped over his one. Many were Jews who addressed him in German and Yiddish.

"Everyone is so friendly here," he marveled when the waitress placed a hamburger platter he hadn't ordered in front of him.

"This is Meyer Lansky's table," she said. "They know you are his friend."

Ruby hoped all Meyer wanted of him was to sit at the table, a respectable-looking Jewish man with a slight resemblance to Charlie Chaplin who made his constituency feel protected.

"Easy as pie," Ruby said.

"Be back in a moment." The waitress returned with a plate of hot apple pie, a scoop of vanilla ice cream melted on top.

Around four p.m., Ruby realized why Meyer had stationed him at the diner. Outside the window and across the street in front of an empty storefront, men dressed as Hitler's Brownshirts jumped out of cars and vans and emptied boxes from trunks and beds. They carried large photos of Hitler and flags with swastikas. They erected a stage on the sidewalk using feed boxes and planks. They set up a loud speaker and a sound system. A crowd gathered, not getting too close. Ruby recognized some people from the crowd as those who had shaken his hand during the day. One hour later, Meyer rejoined Ruby along with his boys and eleven additional men.

Outside the diner, Meyer slapped Ruby on the shoulder. "You did good, kid."

"I didn't do anything."

"You kept an eye on things so nothing got out of hand before we returned. You let the people of Yorkville know Meyer Lansky watched over them."

A couple of decent-looking fellows with greased-back hair sidled up next to them.

Meyer pointed to the more handsome man. "Ben Siegel, this is Ruby Friedman."

"Call me Bugsy." He extended his hand.

Meyer slapped the other man on his back. "This is Alfonso Carrara, we call him Big Al. Don't mess with him. He's from Sicily."

Across the street, a slight man with a booming voice took the stage. Others, twenty in all, stood before him. The leader's voice easily carried. He praised Hitler and called for the annihilation of all Jews. Meyer seethed, his eyes intent on the Brownshirts.

"Now?" Bugsy asked.

"Not yet."

"They outnumber us," Ruby said.

Meyer's eyes did not leave the speaker. "I know." After a few moments, he said, "Okay. Now."

Ruby hung back as the other men stormed forward. They grabbed Brownshirts, kicked and punched them. A few of the Nazis tried to run away but Meyer's men stopped them, punished them with vicious blows. Ruby was mesmerized by the brawl in front of him. He had fought for survival before, like on the subway grate, but had never been in an organized scuffle.

The slight man, the one who spoke on the podium, looked at Ruby. Their eyes met, and the German American Bund leader charged.

Ruby took a wrestler's stance and waited for the man to ram into him. When he did, Ruby flipped him over and took him down. On the ground, Ruby kicked him a few times and then let the man get up and hobble away.

The Brownshirt rally had been broken up in minutes.

Meyer, Bugsy, and Alfonso stood next to Ruby, panted heavily, smiled, and congratulated each other. The high of the conquest surged through their veins.

Meyer crashed his fist into the palm of his hand. "Now they know Jews are not going to sit around and accept insults."

"Yeah." Ruby's adrenaline surged.

"Sicilians have the backs of all Jews," Alfonso proclaimed.

"Good job, kid." Meyer slapped Ruby on the back.

"I think you're ready?"

"Ready for what, Mr. Lansky?"

"The adventure of your lifetime, what else?"

Ruby surveyed the men next to him. Meyer Lansky, Bugsy Siegel, and Alfonso Carrara, all dangerous and connected men. He wanted nothing to do with them, and everything to do with them too. He yearned to relive this feeling of elation and accomplishment, breaking heads of more Nazis.

"C'mon, kid." Meyer started toward the sedan. "Let me take you home."

Ruby hesitated, but then followed.

# CHAPTER THIRTY-FOUR
## SARA

IT WAS FRIDAY evening, Shabbat. A few hours after I had shared Michael's personal details with Elizabeth, I tossed on my cot. My throat tightened and my lungs spasmed. Emotionally and physically exhausted I coughed several times, and then tried to breathe through my mouth to stave off a panic attack.

"Pipe down, Goldstein," a guard yelled.

Complaints from my pod mates flew.

"Put a lid on it."

"Shut the fuck up."

"Sounds like you're choking on your boyfriend's cum."

"She's choking on the truth."

Laughter.

My esophagus burned like a metal pipe edged into a furnace, molten glass, and red hot and glowing.

This evening, Elizabeth was going to edge up next to Michael, how she'd find him and where she would do it, I didn't know. I hadn't approved of tricking Michael but when Trace suggested it I hadn't objected either. I assented by silence. I hated the idea since I didn't know how Elizabeth sidling up to Michael would get me out from under this life sentence, and I feared Michael would show interest in her. What would the chances be of beautiful Elizabeth randomly meeting Michael and he not wanting to hook up? He had no reason to stay loyal to me. I was suing him, and then there's that thing about my being sentenced to life in prison. How could I expect Michael to dwell on me, on us? How could I expect him to wait for me when I had shown him no signs of interest?

I forced myself to be tranquil; I needed to sleep. I imagined Uncle Ruby at home lighting the candles and then settling in for twenty-four hours of rest. I pictured Soldier Boy with him. Images of Ruby and Soldier Boy saying the Friday night prayers comforted and relaxed me. I closed my eyes, and hoped when I awoke this nightmare would be over, my prayer every time I went to sleep in this prison cell.

That same guard who told me to shut up called, "Goldstein, you have a visitor."

I unfolded my legs from the cot and threw off the blanket. "It's not visiting hours."

I wore a sweatshirt and prison bottoms. Barefoot, I followed the guard. The tiled floor was cold, the individual cells of the pod locked down. Who could come see me at this hour? I had successfully bribed everyone who could hurt or harm me in the prison system, but I never believed it would be enough for this sort of violation of the rules, a visitor when it wasn't visiting hours.

"Over there." The guard pointed toward a door, one I've never seen. It was metal and gray and had four bar locks across it. "Go on, Goldstein." She shoved me.

I stood in front of the exit. "It's locked."

"Whatever." She laughed.

I reached out and the doorknob was frozen to the touch, the kind of cold where if my fingers had been wet they would have stuck. I flinched and drew my hand away. I looked at the guard.

"Don't be such a chicken shit." She walked away.

The bar locks on the door slid open, one clank after another. I put my hand on the knob again, prepared for the cold sensation. It was hot. Startled, I pulled my hand away, told myself to toughen up, and then pushed the door open. It closed with a loud bang behind me. I was wrong. I had been through that door before.

The carousel horses neighed and beckoned. My father's train set chugged, puffs of smoke trailed the caboose. The room smelled like home, dad's cologne, mom's perfume, newly mowed grass, and the metallic scent of fresh, flowing blood. My chance to escape, mount the Arabian for another ride out of there. But to where? To Long Island and my home? To lower Manhattan in the 1930s to watch Ruby from above? To Vienna during Kristallnacht when my grandmother's life was shattered? To Michael? Oh yes, to Michael.

"Remember what I told you?" My mother stood near the glass cabinet in Uncle Ruby's room.

I ran to the door, rattled the knob, and pushed on it. It wouldn't open.

"Let me in," I screamed.

I wanted my cell, the safety of routine and the security of consistency.

"Do you remember what I told you?" she asked again.

I knew what she referred to. I had been eight years old. How could I forget?

"You're no different from me." She smiled wide with satisfaction, the ultimate *I told you so*. "Look where you are. Incarcerated, like I was."

"No," I yelled. "I am nothing like you. You are a mean drunk. You killed Daddy. That's not me. That'll never be me."

"We all have our prisons, Sara."

"I hate you," I said.

She laughed and disappeared. I walked to where she had been, smelled her perfume, and her beloved bourbon. I contemplated the five-tiered shelf with the black bowler hat on the bottom, the copy of *Mein Kampf* next to the Shabbat candles, the photographs of my family and of Dixie Lee who had been Uncle Ruby's love. On the top shelf, the carousel horses. I mounted the Arabian for another ride.

# CHAPTER THIRTY-FIVE
## MICHAEL

THE LONG ISLAND streets were quiet for a Friday night as I motored Gram's Mustang along the winding roads that framed Sara's home. I wasn't ready to go to my parents' house and call it a night, and I didn't feel like hopping the train into Manhattan. I could drive but parking was so expensive in the City that I preferred to keep the Mustang in my parents' garage.

I was eager for answers, Sabbath or no Sabbath. I thought to return to the movie theater, which had been the location of Sara's alibi at the time of Uncle Charlie's murder, to see if there was something new I could uncover, but almost four years had passed since Charlie's death making the likelihood of finding new evidence nil.

"What are you doing, Tucker?" I asked myself.

Why was I focused on exonerating Sara as opposed to defending myself from her baseless accusations? Wasn't that why I went to her home to begin with, why I wanted to speak with Soldier Boy?

I switched on the radio to drown out my thoughts. David Bowie sang of a starman waiting in the sky.

I could hear Sara telling me not to be so hard on myself, which is what she had said several times when I voiced doubts of my ability to defend her. Once when I was particularly forlorn about my legal skills, we walked through the woods behind her house.

"You're as good as any attorney out there," she had said. "Even better, since you're one-eighth Gertrude Tucker."

I laughed at her math. "I hope that's enough."

"It's more than enough." She stopped and drew me into her.

Her kiss was passionate, soft at first and then harder. My hands rested in the curve of her hips. My lust swelled, until I realized where we stood. I pulled away.

"What?" she asked, confused.

"This is where…" I couldn't say it.

"Oh, Michael, get over it," she barked.

I can't think of when I had felt lonelier than when I stood in the woods behind Sara's house and watched her storm away. A light rain began to fall and her kiss camped on my lips. My feet were planted where Charles' body had been discovered.

"Get over her, Tucker." I commanded as I drove the Mustang around my old stomping grounds, past the ninety-nine-cent movie theater I used to frequent while growing up and was now a Starbucks, past the ice-skating rink where I had my first date with Tracy Robinson, toward McCloskey's Steak House, which had the best fried onion strings on the planet.

Honking startled me and I looked to my right, Billy in his pickup truck drove next to me on Sunrise Highway. Recalling our run-in at Sara's house, I stayed in my lane, steady. He rolled down the driver's window. I hesitated but then did the same with my passenger's window, maybe he wanted to apologize or say he had been joking. Instead, a large gob of spit landed in my passenger seat and sprayed on me.

"Fuck," I screamed and tried not to swerve.

"Next time it'll be a bullet." He sped away.

Shaken and disgusted, I drove into McCluskey's parking lot, threw the Mustang into neutral and snatched up the brake. On the radio, the Rolling Stones sang, "You Can't Always Get What You Want".

"No shit."

I switched off the music and looked at the gob of phlegm on the seat, the splatters on my arm. I reached into the glove compartment and grabbed napkins I had saved from a late night trip to Taco Bell's drive-through, and wiped the seat and my arm. I gagged.

I grabbed my phone and placed a call.

Major Kurt Higgins of the Nassau County Police Department answered quickly. "Michael, everything okay?"

"I think so. I'm sorry to bother you on a Friday evening."

"That's okay. I'm working. Are you on Long Island? Do you want me to come to you?"

"No, that's okay. I've been harassed lately by this guy named Billy O'Brien. You know him?"

"Sure. Drove the car for an armed robbery that left a store clerk dead. I think he got fifteen years."

"He's out."

"Already?"

"He's got a beef with me. Has to do with the murder of Charles Carrera, as best I can tell."

"What's he done?"

"Mostly threats."

"Take them seriously. The guy did hard time for murder. Let me do a little checking around and I'll see what I can find out."

I ended the call, glad for the friendship Major Higgins and I had developed during Uncle Charlie's murder investigation and Sara's trial. While advocates, we had also gained respect for the other. He called me with lawyer questions, and I called him with cop questions. After thirty years as a police officer, he would retire soon.

I looked up, the McCluskey Steakhouse sign beckoned. I hopped out of the Mustang, and walked through the parking lot, vigilant for Billy's black pickup. No sign of it, I pushed through the double, wood doors and into the restaurant.

Nothing seemed to have changed from my childhood days. The same wood décor, plastic menus, aged wait staff decked in black slacks and white shirts, and those glorious smells. I opted for a seat at the bar and discovered something else hadn't changed. The service was amazing.

"Beamish Stout," I called to the bartender at the end of the mahogany bar.

He responded with an affable nod, and within moments my fingers linked around the handle of a cold mug. I lifted it to my lips. The flavors of caramel and coffee hit the taste buds on the tip of my tongue, then slid to the back of my throat for a neat, bitter finish.

"Will you be having supper with us this evening?" The bartender wiped the area in front of me.

I looked past his gray beard and wire-rimmed glasses. It wasn't his face that I recognized but his voice. "Mr. D'antone?"

He cocked his head and took a good look at me. A broad smile lightened his eyes. "Michael Tucker."

"Sixth grade."

"You won the spelling bee."

"And you canceled our performance of 'Pippin' because..." I searched to recall. "I can't remember why."

He laughed. "You kids were impossible. Couldn't sing. Wouldn't learn the dance steps. I was frustrated."

"You teaching?"

"Retired ten years ago. Got hit hard by the downturn in the market, so I've had to pick up extra work. You know how it is. I don't need to ask you what you've been up to."

I had no response. Anyone who read the newspapers or surfed the web knew what I've been doing.

"You okay?" he asked.

"Yeah. It's nice to see you."

"You too." He patted me on the shoulder. "You're a good kid, Michael. Your parents are proud of you. I know Gertrude is smiling down from heaven and watching over you. Let me know when you're ready to eat. If you're like your dad, I have a prime rib with your name on it. End cut."

He moved to another customer before I could ask how he knew what my parents and Gram thought of me and what dad liked to eat, and then it made sense. While more than 16,000 people lived in Bellmore, it was a small town. People shared the good and the bad while they rolled shopping carts down grocery aisles, stood at checkout counters, and sat at the bar at McCloskey's.

I drank the stout. I had to regroup, come up with a new plan. I had to find out why Billy threatened me, even promised a bullet. I had to keep trying to get Soldier Boy's help.

"What do I do next?" I asked out loud.

"You need something, Michael?" Mr. D'Antone asked.

"No, thanks."

It had been crazy at Sara's house, with Ruby getting lightheaded and then sleeping, me examining the carousel horses, and Soldier Boy coming home. What about Ruby and that whole Charlie Chaplin thing? What was with the copy of *Mein Kampf*? If he were a Jew who celebrated the Sabbath why would he have a copy of Hitler's manifesto? There had been too many distractions. I needed to speak with Soldier Boy alone. I needed to give it another shot.

My phone vibrated, and I pulled it out of my pocket. I had a text from a source I did not recognize. The message was simple, Ok, it read. I looked at the phone number I had received it from, ten numbers beginning with 516, a Long Island area code. I stared at the phone for several seconds as if Siri would tell me who had sent the text. I could search online and link the number to its subscriber but my gut screamed that it wasn't necessary. It had to be from Soldier Boy. I quickly typed a reply with my thumbs.

*I'm at McCloskey's. Steaks and beer are on me. Meet me at the bar.*

"It's worth a shot, Tucker," I said.

I drained the mug and held it up. Mr. D'Antone brought another. I looked to my right. The barstool next to me was empty; I hoped it would soon be filled.

# CHAPTER THIRTY-SIX
## MICHAEL

THIRTY MINUTES AFTER I sent a text that I thought was going to be received by Soldier Boy, I got no response. I sipped on my third beer at the bar at McCluskeys, and considered ordering the end cut prime rib that Mr. D'Antone said was my dad's favorite. I'd eat and bunk at my parent's home, start again tomorrow.

"Is this seat taken?"

Not to be dramatic, but my heart skidded at the sight of the woman who stood next to me.

"Only if you're alone." I wished to take the words back, I sounded like a fast-talking jerk.

"Alone," she said, "but not lonely."

"Touché." I dragged the stool out for her.

She sat, examined the beers on tap, and took out her phone, reading e-mails or something, signaling our conversation had ended. I studied my lager, not too upset the seat I had hoped would be filled by Soldier Boy was occupied by a beautiful caramel complected woman.

*Wait. Had that number I texted been hers? Stop it, Tucker.* Paranoia is not my best color, but I had to be sure. I took out my phone and sent a smiley face to that same number. I waited for her phone to buzz or beep, after a few seconds, nothing. I relaxed, sipped my beer, and decided to give it another shot. "I'm Michael."

She hesitated, looked me over a bit, and probably evaluated the motivation behind my introduction. Was I an innocent flirter, a dude with an endgame, a serial killer? When she grinned a little, I figured she had eliminated murderer from her list of possibilities of who I could be. At least that was a start.

"Elizabeth."

"Nice to meet you."

"What are you doing alone on a Friday night?" she asked.

"Alone but not lonely." I stole her line. "What's your excuse?"

"Hungry and thirsty. McCloskey's has the best—"

"Onion strings." I finished.

"Yes." She smiled.

I raised my hand. "Mr. D'Antone, would you put in a large order of onion strings, please?"

"You got it."

"What are you drinking?" I asked.

She peered behind the bar. "There are so many choices. I miss those dives where you only had to choose between Bud and Miller. What do you have?"

"Ireland's finest." I signaled Mr. D'Antone again. "A Beamish stout for my new friend."

"Anything for you, Michael."

"You a regular?" she asked.

I shook my head. "He was my sixth grade teacher."

"No kidding. Where?"

"Reinhard Elementary, class of nineteen ninety six."

"Two thousand," she said.

"You don't look familiar. Maybe I know your family. What's your last name?"

Our eyes locked. "Innis."

"Like the beer? That's ironic. We should be drinking that."

Mr. D'Antone put her pint on the bar.

She sipped the Beamish. "I like this one. Kind of chocolaty."

"I guess you didn't have Mr. D'Antone."

"I had Mrs. Pollard in sixth grade. Think she works here too?" She playfully looked around the bar for her.

"Don't be surprised if you find her greeting you at Walmart. The market killed people's retirement dreams in two thousand and eight." I hoped not to sound like a geek.

"September twenty-eight, two thousand and eight, the biggest market crash in a single day." Her dark eyes averted. "I'm a news junkie."

She looked anywhere but at me. My realization wasn't as swift as I would like, but at least it came to me. I should have figured from the start. I'm not that charming.

I no longer cared if I appeared like a jerk. "Did you know who I was before or after you asked if the stool was available?"

She brought her gaze to mine. "You're not hard to spot. Most everyone in this restaurant has probably noticed you. Can't avoid that when your picture was on the front page of most local newspapers for one year straight, and that's not counting the Internet and national news coverage, and now you're front page again."

What I thought would be a pleasant diversion was another round of shells aimed at my already bullet-holed ego.

"I'm sorry." She gently touched my hand. "I thought it'd be interesting to talk to you. If you want, I can sit somewhere else."

"No, no, that's okay. I'll go." I slid off the stool.

"Here you are." Mr. D'Antone placed the onion strings between us.

"Can't go now." She half-smiled.

I looked toward the door. It had been almost forty minutes since I'd texted the number I believed belonged to Soldier Boy. Sara's house was no more than seven minutes from there. If he was coming, he surely would have arrived by then.

"C'mon," she encouraged. "What could be better than a plate full of onion strings and a good beer while seated next to a fellow Reinhard Elementary School graduate?"

I plopped onto the stool. She was right. I had nothing better to do, and she was awesome to look at.

# CHAPTER THIRTY-SEVEN
## LIANA
### KRISTALLNACHT DAY TWO

"LIANA, YOU CAN'T take those with you."

I held a pillowcase and was about to put one of the glass carousel horses inside. I looked at Wilhelm and considered a myriad of responses from "mind your own business" to crumbling into tears. I couldn't leave the horses behind. It was enough I had to leave Siegfried in the hallway and go on without knowing where the rest of my family was. Instead of finding my voice, instead of telling Wil how devastated I was and how I needed to bring some part of my family with me, I pushed rocks, bricks and broken glass off my bed, sat and wept.

He stood over me. "I know this is hard. It's hard for all of us, but you're going to have to help the younger kids, and the horses are going to break anyway. You have that stupid bear on your back. Isn't that enough?"

*Stupid?* I jumped up and pummeled his bare chest with my hands. How dare he tell me what I couldn't take? How dare he suggest that Bruno alone was a sufficient reminder of my family? As I hit him with my fists and his chest blushed red, he didn't restrain me, didn't step away. He was several inches taller and two years older. His chest had broadened into that of a man, his shoulders wide and muscular. His blond hair razor short, he had a day's growth of stubble.

He grabbed my wrists and brought his face close to mine. "You're not the only one who lost her family today."

"Fuck you."

My neck craned so I could look up at him, dared him to show his true colors. He was a Nazi, not my friend, not someone who tried to help us Jews.

"What's your plan?" I snapped. "Pretend you're helping us, when you're taking us to a work camp?"

He let go of my wrists and pushed me onto the bed. A jagged edge of glass dug into my hip, but I didn't let out a sound of distress. I wouldn't give him the satisfaction.

"Think what you want. It's getting dark." He rotated on his heels and with the cadence of a soldier walked out of the room.

I jumped up and caught him in the hallway before he reached the front door. "Wait." I needed to look in his eyes, and when I did I glimpsed what I first saw when he handed children to me from under the rubble cave. Sincerity. At least that's what I thought I saw in his light brown eyes, the color of Bruno's fur. I recalled Papa telling me not to trust anyone who wasn't a Jew, but Papa wasn't there. I had no family, friend, or neighbor to turn to. I could stay in the apartment and wait until it was light and then find Madame Juliette, but Siegfried was there, in the hallway. I couldn't bear to see him one more time. I could take the others to meet Madame Juliette at the train station. Maybe she could help all of us. I knew most of the kids that had hidden in the rubble cave. How could I abandon them, and why would Wil have helped them if he were a Nazi? Why would he have given me his shirt to wipe blood from my face when it was cold outside?

I looked at Wil, who wore the German brown pants and boots, and then ran into the room I had shared with Renate and Siegfried. I opened a drawer, grabbed some things, then went into the closet and chose a pair of shoes. I ran to the hallway.

"Here." I tossed Siegfried's pants and a shirt to Wil. "I'm not going anywhere with you dressed like that."

He stripped to his underwear. I watched, fascinated by his transformation from looking like a Jew hater to a regular teenage boy, like Siegfried. I imagined him tossing a ball and wearing a cap lopsided, the brim high on his head the way boys liked to wear them. A lump jammed in my throat as I thought of my brother who would never get to be a boy again.

Dressed, Wil held out his hand. "Let's go."

"Not without the carousel horses," I said.

# CHAPTER THIRTY-EIGHT
## LIANA
## KRISTALLNACHT DAY TWO

THERE WERE SEVENTEEN of us, and we ranged in age from four-year-old Johann to fifteen-year-old Wil, sixteen Austrian Jews and one Austrian gentile who was a member of Hitler's army. I hadn't spoken those words to Wil, but there was no need. If he were caught helping us, he would be killed instantly.

The air was thick and black, and made it difficult to breathe. It smelled of embers and smoke. We climbed over rocks and cement blocks, ash and soot landed on our clothes and darkened our skin. Wil carried Johann while I helped the younger children scale mountains of stones and debris. Wil had been right; to take the carousel horses would have been a grave mistake. I wouldn't have been able to help the other kids, and the horses would have broken. Wil and I had reached a compromise at the apartment. I wrapped them in sheets and towels, placed them and the platform that they twirled upon in the pillowcase, and hid them in the bedroom closet surrounded by pillows. Wil swore we would retrieve them as soon as we found a safe place to hide.

"You'll have your carousel horses by morning," he promised.

I wanted to believe everything he said.

*My family was on its way to the work camp and would be released soon.*

*The Allies won't let Hitler get away with this for long.*

*Marching into Austria was easy for the Nazis, since there are so many Germans here, but if Hitler tries to invade Poland, Britain and France won't stand for that.*

*And don't forget about the United States; they'll help too.*

Wil's talk of the USA, that fairyland that appeared in my dreams, the place where *Onkel* Ruby became rich and famous, the country where girls wore beautiful dresses and boys treated their girlfriends like princesses, made me wonder if Ruby knew what happened here in Vienna. Would he tell Madame Juliette to find me? Could he appeal to his politically connected friends and buy Mama and Papa's freedom from the work camp?

I jumped off a pile of rubble and into the side street next to my home and helped some of the other kids descend. A few blocks over, a gray plume of smoke snaked into the darkening sky.

"Where is it coming from?" Astrid, an eleven-year-old girl who had lived on the next block from me, asked. She was a slight girl, not even four and a half feet tall, but she was as tough as a gray wolf.

I knew where the smoke came from but didn't respond. We rounded a corner, walked two short blocks, turned left, and saw our smoldering temple in ruins. We stood, stiff. Wil held Johann. Astrid clung to my right arm; another child gripped my left.

The sight was almost as bad as witnessing Herr Kandel being shot in the head, almost as horrific as seeing Siegfried dead on the floor. Our temple destroyed, our people, our history, gone, and it had taken no time.

"What's going to happen to us?" Astrid asked.

"Yeah?" some of the other children echoed, their eyes wide, their voices hoarse.

We stood at the base of the temple stairs, charred remains of the front doors smoldered. Behind the broken frames, wood from the temple smoked, benches bent beyond recognition, the pulpit destroyed, the cabinet where the ark and the Torah were stored partially demolished. I pulled out the parchment from the front pocket of Papa's shirt. I unfolded it and read in Hebrew.

קְרֶצֶב לוֹדְג יֶנֶפ רַדְהֶת אֵלוֹ לְד יֶנֶפ אִשֵׁת אֵל טַפְּשְׁמִב לֵוֶע וֹשֵׂעַת אֵל .וֹט" רְהָימְעַ פְּשֵׂת"." You shall commit no injustice in judgment; you shall not favor a poor person or respect a great man; you shall judge your fellow with righteousness.

"Read it again." Seven-year-old Monika wrapped her

arms around my waist.

I read from the Torah again.

"One more time," Johann said from his perch in Wil's arms.

Standing in front of our burned-out temple and repeatedly reciting a passage from Leviticus felt hopeful.

"Once more." Astrid's grip on my arm tightened.

"Last time." The piece I had ripped from the Torah was coal black from my dirty hands. I folded it and stuffed it in the pocket of Papa's shirt. I had it memorized.

"*Halten.*"

Three Brownshirts faced us, guns in their hands. I recognized Werner and Udo but not the third one.

"*Juden sterben.*" Jews die, Werner said.

"*Keine.*" No. Wil put Johann down.

Johann ran to me and grabbed my leg.

Wil approached the Nazis, and spoke so low I couldn't hear. The Nazis scrutinized us as Wil explained something, animatedly using his hands. What was his point? Friend or foe? Rescuer or traitor? There seemed to be a meeting of the minds, heads nodded, handshakes exchanged, decisions made.

"*Kommen sie mit uns.*" Come with us, Udo said.

"No," Astrid yelled and bolted.

"Stop her, Lenz," Werner ordered.

The third Nazi, Lenz, cut off her path and pushed her to the ground. Several of the children cried. I seethed at Wil. It had been a setup. He had been assigned to gather us and bring us to the temple where the Nazis would capture us and take us to a work camp. I should have suspected. I should have listened to Papa, who told me not to trust anyone who wasn't a Jew.

"*Kommen*," Werner barked.

"Never." Astrid jumped up and ran again.

Udo leveled his rifle and fired. A loud boom, and a red blotch appeared in the center of her back. She fell forward, landed on the pavement, one spasm of her body and then nothing, splayed and motionless.

The older kids tried to act brave; the younger children cried. The Nazis poked us with the butts of their rifles, cursed, and called us dirty Jews and bastards. They ordered us to march in single file. The four Nazis, Wil included, commanded us where to go, waved their guns, cocked barrels, and laughed. Lenz led our forced parade while Werner, Udo, and Wil walked up and down the line. Werner and Udo passed a silver flask among them. Lenz accepted a sip, Wil declined.

The children whimpered, probably thought about Astrid dead in front of the temple and wondered what was going to happen to them. Johann held my right hand and did his best to keep up. Ida, a blond girl with knotted pigtails, grasped my left hand. Johann slipped, and I brought him to his feet.

Wil came up next to us, but I looked straight, determined not to make eye contact for fear that if I did I'd want to attack him as I had done in my bedroom. After he matched a few of my steps, he dropped back, out of my peripheral vision.

Johann tripped again. I bent and picked him up and rested him on my hip while I held Ida's hand.

"No," Werner screamed in German. "Put him down. He will walk on his own."

"He's just a boy."

Werner grabbed Johann and dropped him roughly on the pavement. Johann jumped up, took my hand, and jogged next to me, determined to stay in step.

"You're a brave boy," I whispered.

"Shut up." Udo pointed his rifle toward us.

"No." Wil ran our way, put his hand on the barrel of Udo's gun, and pushed it downward.

"As we thought," Udo snarled, "you're a *jude liebhaber.*" A Jew lover.

"I am no such thing. I hate the Jews." He spit on the ground. "We need her to help with the younger children."

"*Sie erschießen,*" Werner said dryly. Shoot them.

"No," Wil yelled. "They are needed in the camps. Hitler will be proud we delivered young and strong Jews who can work hard with little food or sleep."

"I suppose." Werner pointed at me. "But I know this one and she is trouble."

"I will keep her in line." Wil promised.

I didn't flinch and our eyes met. Was there something there, the sincerity I had thought I saw when he handed Johann to me out of the rubble cave and then again in the hallway of my apartment? *No, he's a Nazi. Don't trust him. Never trust a non-Jew.*

"‏םידחפמ לועפל‎." Act scared, he whispered in Hebrew.

I tilted my head, confused. Wil spoke Hebrew? Then I realized why he helped us. He was a Jew.

"*Juden,*" Udo yelled.

"*Jude spy muss sterben,*" Werner shouted. Jew spy must die.

Werner, Udo, and Lenz aimed their guns at Wil. Wil straightened his shoulders, looked at me, and then at his would-be assassins. Dressed in Siegfried's clothes, I thought of the similarities between Wil and Siegfried. It was more than their being the same size. They were young men, young Jews, dying, for what?

"On the count of three," Werner commanded.

"Wait!" I yelled.

Werner held up his hand. He chewed the inside of his mouth. I couldn't tell if he was angry or amused.

I spoke quickly in German. "You can't kill him."

"Oh? And why is that?"

*Think fast, Liana. Think fast.* "If you kill him, you will die too." I looked at Udo and Lenz. "And so will both of you."

I had no idea what I was saying. The Nazis laughed, amused by my heroic attempt, but I wasn't done. They couldn't kill all of us. I won't let them.

"Go!" I yelled. "Run!"

I pushed Johann and Ida away, toward a corner where they could duck behind a building and into an alleyway. We all knew this quarter of Vienna well, had explored it over and over on lazy Sundays. The Nazis looked at the scattering children and, in that moment, Wil charged and surprised Werner and Udo, knocked them to the ground. I ran into Lenz, the force took him and me to the pavement. He rolled on top of me, grabbed my hair, and jerked me to my feet. He wasn't holding his rifle, he must have lost his grip when I rammed into him. As I resisted, he tried to gain footing. I bit into the first body part I could find, his neck. A surge of warmth rushed into my mouth. He screamed and let go; I fell to the ground and spat. A few feet away, Wil wrestled with Werner and Udo, not besting them, but preventing them from going after the children. Their rifles lie on the ground.

Werner freed himself from Wil, while Udo and Wil continued to fight. Lenz tended to his neck, and I ran into Werner, wrapped my arms around his midsection, and rammed my head in his belly. He barely took a step back, grabbed me by the waist, and lifted me until I was almost doing a headstand. He tossed me away, and I landed hard, face down on the concrete.

Udo and Wil tumbled end over end, wrestled, grunted, and cursed. It was hard to tell one from the other. A few feet away, Lenz screamed as blood spurt from the wound in his neck.

I rolled onto my back and jumped up, about to run and help Wil, but I stopped. Werner was a few feet from me, his rifle directed at my face. I wished I could say good-bye to my family, but at least I would soon be with Siegfried. I tried to act brave, as Wil had, when a loud boom sounded. I waited for the pain to topple me, for blood to spill from my body, to lose consciousness, to stop breathing, but none of that happened. It was Werner who fell to his knees, a hole blown in his chest.

Lenz was immobile. Blood pooled around his neck where he lay on the concrete. Werner had been blown back several feet from the impact of the bullet in his chest. At the sound of the blast, Udo and Wil stopped fighting. They were sweaty, panting, and wide-eyed. Udo looked to his rifle on the pavement. I kicked it away.

I held out my hands and walked slowly toward Johann. "It's okay. Put the rifle down."

The boy pointed the gun at Udo.

"Don't do it," I said.

"He's a Nazi."

"Killing him isn't the answer."

Udo laughed. "Stupid Jew boy."

I looked at Johann, nodded. The explosion of the bullet fired from the rifle startled me, even though I knew it was coming.

Udo held his stomach and cursed as he fell to the ground.

"Let's go," I said. "Let's find the other kids."

Johann didn't move, and neither did Wil. Johann had the rifle pointed at Wil.

"He's one of us," I said.

"He's a Nazi."

"No, he's not." I scoured my own doubts about Wil. He had saved the children by hiding them in the rock cave, he had signed on with the Nazis to save his life, to save his family's life, and he had risked himself for us. "He's a Jew, like us."

"No." Johann's hands shook. Tears inundated his eyes.

"Put the rifle down." I walked toward him, and hoped I wasn't making the last mistake of my life.

Three steps from him, he lowered the rifle. I took it.

Wil ran to Johann, picked him up, and grabbed my hand. "Let's get out of here," Wil said.

"Where to?" I asked.

"We'll find a place to hide."

"We have to find the other kids first."

"How are we going to do that?"

"We can call for them."

"We've made enough noise already."

"Okay, then the temple, that's where I'd go." I let go of Wil's hand and ran, hoping he followed with Johan.

I stopped running when I was in front of the temple, bent over and put my hands on my knees to catch my breath. Wil and Johann came up behind me.

"Are they here?" Wil panted.

I looked and listened, saw and heard nothing. Tears came amid feelings of regret and despair. Despondent and desperate, how was it possible that one day ago I had my family, my home, the Jewish Quarter, and now I had nothing and no one?

I saw movement, and pointed. "Look."

"It could be Nazis."

I ignored Wil and ran into the temple, jumping over fallen beams and toppled benches. I stopped and looked around but didn't see anything. Had I imagined the movement? I then saw a remnant of the cabinet where the Torah had been kept, where I had hidden. I ran toward it, tossing debris out of the way.

When I got near, I called, "It's okay, come out."

Little faces showed from behind the ark. Ten-year-old Maxine, seven-year-old Dorothea and her twin brother, Konrad, Ida. More and more kids revealed themselves. All seemed to be present except for Astrid, of course.

Wil and Johann came up behind me.

"Let's go. I know where to hide." I ran and they all followed.

# CHAPTER THIRTY-NINE
## LIANA
### KRISTALLNACHT DAY THREE


HOFBURG PALACE WASN'T far from the Jewish quarter, ten minutes if we moved fast, which wasn't easy while so many of the kids sniffled and cried. Some were bruised and battered, all of us were hungry, cold, scared and exhausted.

Since I had made the trek to the palace many times, I knew the way, even with the street signs destroyed by the Nazis, even as it was past midnight, and even in the dark of the starless night.

I led the way with Wil and Johann behind me, and then Ida, Maxine, Dorothea and her twin, Konrad. Monika and Bettina followed. I tried to keep an extra eye on Bettina. As Rabbi Ehrenfeld watched over me, I watched over her.

"Where are we going?" Wil extended his stride to catch me.

"Some place to hide until it's light. Then we'll go to the train station and find Madame Juliette."

We turned into Josefsplatz, a public square, and stopped to rest in front of an equestrian statue of Emperor Joseph II dressed as a Roman conqueror.

"We're hiding out in the palace?" Wil pointed toward the Hofburg Palace, the official seat of the Austrian president.

"No. Come on." I jogged and the others followed. The bigger kids towed the smaller ones along or carried them. I crossed Josefsplatz and took a path toward another square, this one called

Michaelplatz. We then headed for a building that was not connected to the palace. Originally built as a residence, it had become the imperial stable. Also referred to as the Spanish Riding School, it housed the imperial stallions.

Ankle-deep in manure, Bettina and I shook and wept in the rear of a stall. A majestic stallion nuzzled us. The Lipizzaners were much bigger up close than when I've sneaked to watch them practice their classical dressage from a distance. In the first moment of stillness since my bedroom window was bombarded with rocks and bricks, my emotions bucked like a wild bronco.

Other kids cried in other stalls, amazed, I am sure, by how much changed so quickly. Two days earlier I was in my bed, dreaming of New York and riding the carousel horses high above the Statue of Liberty and along the Danube. If someone described all that was to transpire, I would have said, "Papa and Rabbi Ehrenfeld would never let that happen."

But they did and it had, and now I had no idea where my family was, except for Siegfried. I knew exactly where he was. My throat tightened and my stomach clenched like a vise. We had to be quiet but it was hard. I breathed heavily and sucked what air I could capture in and out, the noise like a braying mule. The horse whose stall Bettina and I occupied took a step back and scrutinized me as an intruder.

Bettina tried to comfort me. "Stop, Liana. The Nazis will find us."

I couldn't stop. My eyes wide, my mouth opened, my nostrils flared as I desperately fought for breath. My body quivered. I sweated, and cried.

"It's okay, it's okay." Bettina patted my arm.

I couldn't get my breathing under control. I couldn't release the pressure in my throat. Mama, Papa, and Renate were gone. Siegfried was dead. What was going to happen to us? I wanted Wil, he made me feel strong, maybe it was because he reminded me of Siegfried especially when he wore my brother's clothes.

I tried to say something but couldn't speak. My head spun. I was going to faint. Maybe then my panic attack would stop.

I heard shuffling and looked up at the front of the stall, where a tall figure swayed before me.

"Siegfried?" I smiled. My throat opened and the feeling of panic subsided. I blinked several times to chase away the tears, and I wiped spittle from my mouth.

Wil bent next to me in the stall. "Are you okay?"

"Siegfried. Where's Siegfried?"

"It's okay." He drew me into him.

The smell of Siegfried on the clothes Wil wore assailed me. "I want Siegfried. I want Siegfried. I want Siegfried," I yelled.

"Calm down, Liana."

"You're not my brother." My arms flailed.

Wil held me tighter, my head sideways against his chest. "It's okay." He stroked my hair.

Finally I managed to stop. I couldn't act like a child. I no longer was a little girl.

While I rested on his chest and listened to his heart pound, Wil put an arm around Bettina who cuddled into him.

"The sun is rising," he said. "The horses are getting antsy. It's probably close to feeding time. Someone will be here soon. We have to move to the train station to meet, what was her name?"

"Madame Juliette."

"Are you sure she'll be there? Are you sure she'll help all of us?"

I wanted to say I was sure of nothing. Instead, I nodded and pretended to have confidence.

"Then let's go." Wil helped Bettina and me to stand.

I wobbled at first, my legs weak from lack of oxygen, I guessed, but also from lack of food. I hadn't eaten since dinner two days before. The other kids were hungry too.

Weeping floated above the next stall, from four-year-old Johann and the seven-year-old twins, Konrad and Dorothea.

"I can't get them to stop," Wil said. "I've been trying all night."

"Let me try." I wiped my own tears away.

Wil followed me to the back of the barn where I tried several doors. Finally one opened, the feed room, as I had hoped. We ran our hands through bags of feed: uncooked corn, oats, and barley. The horses snorted and neighed.

"Think we can eat this?" he asked.

"I don't think it will kill us." I put a handful of oats into my mouth and chewed and chewed, finally able to swallow some of the mixture after it softened from my saliva. "It will have to do. We have to eat."

Wil ran out and returned with the others. I counted heads. There had been seventeen, before Astrid was killed, but I now counted fifteen. Recount. One, two, three... I looked to see who was missing. "Where's Monika?"

"I don't know. I haven't seen her since we got here."

No one else recalled the last time they had seen her. My stomach sank. Had the Nazis captured her?

"We'll look for her later," Wil said. "Food and water is our priority."

As hard as it was not to run out to find Monika at that moment, I knew he was right.

Bettina and I opened bags of feed. The kids ate first, shoving handfuls into their mouths. Wil ran out under the cover of the low-on-the-horizon moon and returned with a running hose. Everyone drank.

All fortified, I looked to Wil. "Can we search for Monika now?"

"*Ja*. As we head to the train station."

With the sun rising over Hofburg Palace, the streets and squares eerily quiet, our pockets filled with feed, we made our way toward Wien Sudbanhoff, Vienna's largest train station located in Favoriten in the southeast part of the city. Keeping eyes watchful for Monika but not seeing her, we hoped she ran away and was safe. She was seven years old and one of the quieter kids. I prayed she was okay.

We crossed a field where the stallions grazed, the grass wet and frigid against our ankles. Johann trekked on his own, not allowing Wil or me to carry him.

I walked with my gate tilted forward, my arms crossed to keep warm. I was determined to make it to the train station and Madame Juliette. What I didn't tell Wil or the others was that I intended to return home to retrieve the carousel horses before I boarded any train.

Bettina strode next to me. "I have a bad feeling, Liana."

"Everything's okay. I promise."

"It's too quiet out here. For two days the Nazis were everywhere, and today they're nowhere."

"Maybe they moved on."

"My father told me never to trust a Nazi." She looked toward Wil.

"He's not a Nazi."

"He was one."

"He pretended to be one."

"You have a crush on him."

"Don't be ridiculous."

"I can see the way you look at him."

"And what if I do?"

"My father said you cannot trust anyone who is not a Jew."

"My father said the same thing." I looked at Wil who was a few meters ahead and led the way through the field. "But Wil is a Jew."

"How do you know?"

"He speaks Hebrew and Yiddish."

"How come we never saw him in the neighborhood or during the High Holidays?"

"He must be from a different quarter."

"באזה ורהזיה," Bettina yelled. Watch out for the wolf.

The children scattered, but not Wil, who slowed and looked around, dazed.

"See?" Bettina said. "He doesn't understand Hebrew. He probably knows a few phrases."

"Everything's okay," I called. "False alarm. That was a test. Good job." I turned to Bettina. "Then why does he help us?"

"I don't know, but you need to find out."

Bettina fell in line next to Ida, the six-year-old whose blond pigtails had balled and knotted. Lulu and Max Wittgenstein walked beside them.

I hurried to catch up with Wil. "I haven't seen Monika. Have you?"

"No. Maybe she went home. Do you know where she lives?"

"A few streets from me, also in *Mazzes Insel*. How come you don't have side curls?"

"Huh?"

"My brother and his friends all have long side curls. You wear your hair short. How come?"

His hair was buzzed on the side, longer on top with a side part. "I used to have them, but I shaved them off when I joined the Hitler youth."

"Why did you join them again?"

Wil looked at me crossly, suspicious of my questions. I felt bad asking but Bettina had a point.

"I think I've proven myself to you and the others," he said.

"I guess."

He stopped, and placed his hands on my shoulders. "You guess? Don't you think Siegfried would be alive if he had pretended to be a Nazi?"

I didn't want to cry at the mention of Siegfried, but I couldn't stop the tears that trickled out my bottom lids and down my face. I shoved his hands off of me and darted away.

"Wait, Liana, I'm sorry. I shouldn't have said that." He ran after me. "Please stop. I'm sorry."

I didn't want to hear what he had to say, but several hundred meters away, I slowed. My actions were stupid. Where was I going to run? I didn't want to separate from the others.

I looked behind us and saw the line of kids, Johann, Ida, Maxine, Dorothea, Konrad, Lulu, Max, and Bettina, trudging through the wet grass.

"Hey," came a small voice.

I looked to the side of the pasture and squinted. Monika? The kids ran to her. As they neared, three Brownshirts rose from behind her and fired their rifles. The small bodies of my friends blew backwards. Blood and body parts flew into the air. Wil jumped on top of me and slammed my body to the ground. Gunfire raged.

# CHAPTER FORTY
## MICHAEL

I REACHED TO the side of the bed and to the table where I place a glass of water each night before I slide into bed. My hand hit something else, not the cup of water, and glass shattered as it smashed on the floor. One eye opened, I peered down, not the brown carpet of my bedroom but bleached wood. I'm not in my bed and I'm not alone.

I looked to the person beside me covered in a blue and green quilt.

*Sara?*

I used the moment to pretend the trial hadn't ended with a guilty verdict and that Sara and I had been waking in bed together every day since, but I knew it wasn't true. I also knew the only person who could be next to me in this strange bed was Elizabeth from the bar the night before.

I sat up naked and semi-erect. I moved the covers to look at my bedmate. She lay on her side, her back to me. Kinky dark hair and light brown freckled skin painted her shoulders. My erection grew.

I recalled too many beers at McCluskey's, seeing Mr. D'Antone my sixth-grade teacher, the most awesome flirting ever, and some hesitation when Elizabeth invited me home. The reluctance was because of her intentions. Did she like goofy, sneaker-loving, Mustang driving Michael Tucker, or was she interested in Michael Tucker, infamous trial lawyer? For the first time, I knew what it felt like to be a woman trying to decide if she should go home with a guy. Being a man invited home by a beautiful woman, I didn't hesitate for long.

She rolled over with a sleepy yawn and a stretch.

Our lips met in a soft caress, morning breath be damned. The fog from my brain cleared. The kiss a full-out mashed body-on-body embrace. Salt from her pores electrified my tongue.

Soft hues of orange and yellow morning light slipped through the blinds and our bodies tangled. She climbed on top of me and my hands wrapped around her slim waist. Her deep green eyes looked into mine. We rocked in syncopation.

Waking from a deep sleep, I looked at my iPhone and jumped up. "Shit!"

"What?" Elizabeth asked.

"Do you see the time?" I disentangled my legs from hers.

"It's early. Go back to sleep."

"It's after six at night. Have we been doing this all day?"

"Looks that way."

I sat up. "I have to go."

"You have a date?"

I couldn't tell if she was serious. You know that just-had-a-ton-of-sex feeling and you realize you don't know much about the person? That feeling swarmed me.

"I have a meeting."

She sat up. The quilt fell off her, exposing her breasts, her dark nipples. I leaned in and then stopped myself.

"Restraint, Tucker," I said.

She laughed, pulled the blanket to her shoulders, and rested on the pillow. "What does a high-powered attorney like you have to do that's so important on a Saturday evening?" Her smile quickly disappeared. "Oh no. You have a girlfriend, or a wife."

"No, no." I kissed her again. "Just work. I have to go see someone."

"What lawyer visits his client on a Saturday night? Unless the client's in jail."

"It's not a client. More like a witness."

"Is this for Sara's case?"

"Don't be so nosy." I kissed her on the nose, choosing to treat her inquiries as sleepy, light humor.

She sat up, more awake. "I'm curious, Michael, that's all. Let a boring real estate paralegal live vicariously through you. What's the harm?" Her fingers ran down my chest, to my belly. I stirred again.

It wasn't easy but I tenderly removed her hand off me.

"I have to go."

"Not until you tell me where you're going." She kissed my chest and then her lips traveled down my body.

She was near impossible to resist. I lifted her toward me, we kissed, and then I held her. Her body, perfect entwined with mine.

I whispered into her ear, "You sure you're not a reporter? Or worse, a blogger?"

She moved away, her eyes wide and solemn. "How can you suggest that? In my bed? After all we've done?"

"I'm sorry, Sara. I didn't mean—"

"My name's Elizabeth."

"I know your name."

"You called me Sara."

"Did not."

*Had I?*

She cast a stern look my way.

*Had I really called her Sara?*

She laughed and slapped me on the chest. "You are a serious one, aren't you? Do you want to see my certificate from paralegal school? Or my business card?"

"I didn't know paralegals had business cards."

"You need to learn to trust, Michael Tucker. Not every woman is going to break your heart."

I thought of Elaine, my law school professor and girlfriend who, when she ended our relationship, warned me that I was too much of a romantic. Hers would not be the only heartbreak I suffered.

"Forget it." She lay back. "You don't have to tell me about your meeting."

"It is about Sara's case. I'm going to talk to her uncle and brother." Regret hit my gut. Should I have said all that?

"Why are you meeting with them?"

I hesitated. "It's boring. You're not going to be interested."

"Tell me. I love this stuff." She threw the covers off of her and sat up in the bed, cross-legged. It was hard not to gawk at her breasts, at the muscles that framed her stomach, at the cropped mound between her legs.

*Relax, Tucker, not everybody is mal-intentioned.*

I caressed her knee. "Sara is suing me. She claims I messed up her defense and it's my fault she was convicted of murder."

"Do I look like some news junkie neophyte? Tell me something I don't know."

I sighed and moved my hand along her inner thigh.

"David, her brother, is going to help me defend against Sara's accusations."

She studied me; her green eyes steady, captivating. What was I feeling? Vulnerable; that was it. *Damn it.*

She leaned away from me. "Why would he do that? I mean, why would Sara's brother help you against her?"

"I shouldn't have said he's going to. I should have said I'm going to ask him to."

She lay in my arms again. The feeling of vulnerability passed as we snuggled.

*It's okay to trust, Tucker.*

We lay together for several minutes. I no longer cared about the clock. If heaven had a name it was Elizabeth.

"I don't want to sound dumb, but I don't get how Soldier Boy can help you against Sara."

I sat up. "What did you say?"

"I don't understand how he's going to help you."

"No, what did you call him?"

"David."

"You said Soldier Boy."

"Why would I say that?"

"It's his nickname."

"Whose nickname?"

"David's."

"Well, if I said it, I must have gotten it from you."

I shook my head. I had deliberately referred to him by his birth name. I knew the newspaper articles and the Internet referred to him as David the few times he was mentioned, and usually as a side note when their parents' murders were referenced.

She ran her fingers over my chest. "You're sex drunk. You're hearing things."

Maybe she was right. Maybe she hadn't said it, and maybe I hadn't called her Sara.

"So you think David will help you?" she asked.

"I don't know."

"Seems like there might be another reason you want to talk to David, and to his uncle."

"Like what?"

Her playful tone turned serious. "You're in love with Sara."

"No way," I protested. I hoped not too strong to be unbelievable.

Her eyes widened, as if she had solved a difficult math problem. "You want to prove her innocence. That's why you're meeting with them."

"No, no. I've already tried her case. I don't need to do it again."

"What did David tell you when you were Sara's attorney and you interviewed him?"

I unlatched from her. I wasn't about to share that I hadn't spoken with him because Sara wouldn't let me.

"You are curious," I deflected.

"Guilty as charged. Failed journalism major."

"More like relentless detective."

She exhaled in a strong sigh. "You're right. I'm sorry. I didn't mean to come on so strong. I love a good mystery. You should see my DVR. Loaded with reruns of *Law and Order*, *Criminal Minds*, and *Blue Bloods*."

I kissed her, forced myself out of bed, walked across the room, into the bathroom, and into the shower. While the hot water massaged my tense neck muscles, Elizabeth's words rang in my head. *You're in love with her. You want to prove her innocence.*

"No way," I said.

"What's that?" Elizabeth joined me.

Sprays of water hit her, and her skin glistened. She stood on her tiptoes and our lips joined in the sweetest of kisses.

*I am not in love with Sara; I am not trying to prove her innocence. I am only trying to help myself.* I repeated this mantra in my mind.

We soaped each other and rinsed. Outside the shower, towel dried, she grabbed my hand. "When you're done meeting with Sara's uncle and brother, will you come back?"

I didn't have to answer. We both knew I would.

# CHAPTER FORTY-ONE
## LIANA
## KRISTALLNACHT DAY THREE

WIEN SUDBANHOFF, VIENNA South Station, was the largest rail station in Vienna. Built in a classical architectural style, it was located in the southeastern part of the city and composed of two stations, one with tracks running south to Wiener Neustadt and the other with tracks running east to Gloggnitz. The stations shared the same depot. A house between the stations served as a restaurant.

I stood in the concourse, glad to be out of the cold and in shock over the murder of my friends. I don't know what happened to Monika but I would guess that the same Nazis that she helped hurt her too.

I looked in awe at the building that rose above me. I loved to hear Mama and Papa tell stories about the day they rode a train into the countryside and got in trouble with their parents because they were not yet married. I recalled being at this station before when my family had seen Uncle Ruby off on his adventure to America, never dreaming he wouldn't return. I had been nine years old when Uncle Ruby went to New York, and I remembered everything about the station and his departure. I longed to travel by train, to sit nose close to a window and watch fields and towns zip by and talk to the conductor who wore a handsome uniform and a square hat.

In the station, large bow windows let in streams of warm light that I longed to swallow and store within my grumbling belly. I could no longer eat the horse feed, as soon as I managed to swallow it, undigested portions rushed out of me at both ends.

People bustled around us, men in suits, women wearing tight skirts and dresses. All rushed toward a destination, work, home, or perhaps to visit a relative or to meet an arriving friend. To them, it was as if the past three days had not occurred. To us, it was too real. Losing our families, the burning of the temple, and the assassination of our friends, but to the *goyim* going about their regular business, the Nazis might as well have been street cleaners, barely noticed.

In the train station, I heard no Hebrew or Yiddish, only German. Two Brownshirts chatted underneath a large clock. It was ten o'clock in the morning, and no one seemed to notice the two Jewish children who stood in the middle of the concourse, our clothes ripped, our faces filthy, our bodies foul smelling, and our spirits broken.

"It's Friday, right, November 11th?" I asked Wil.

"*Ja, it's Freitag.* Do you see her?"

I looked around the station. Who could be Madame Juliette? She would be traveling alone, and would look like an actress, I thought.

Train whistles blew. Voices over intercoms announced departing and arriving trains. People crisscrossed in front of us, some bumped us as they rushed by.

I eyed a woman who stood alone. Tall and stately in appearance, she wore a brown wool coat with a mink-lined collar. Her stockings were black and matched her high-heeled boots.

I drifted toward her. "Good morning, Ma'am. Where is the bathroom?"

She pointed toward a door marked W.C. Water closet.

"Where?" I scrunched my eyes.

"Over there," she said impatiently.

Was that a German accent? Could it have been French? She hadn't spoken enough, and with the noise in the station, I couldn't pick it up.

"Are you Madame Juliette?" I asked directly.

She bent down, grabbed my arm and spoke in heavy German. "Listen to me little Jew girl, if you don't get away from me, I am going to call those Nazis over there." She nodded toward the big clock.

Wil grabbed my other arm. Tears clouded my eyes. I had been incorrect. The people running here and there and living their daily lives *did* know about the Nazis and what they had done to the Jews. I could stomach their ignorance but not their knowledge.

"I'm going to throw up."

"Not here." Wil lugged me to a corner and a garbage can.

Corn, oats, and barley splattered into the bin.

"We can't stay here." Wil's glance darted every which way.

"How can they act like nothing's happened?" I seethed at the fast-moving faces and bodies in the crowded terminal.

Wil's attention moved away from me and fixed near the clock. I followed his sight and saw the Nazis point at us.

"C'mon." Wil grabbed my hand.

"*Juden,*" one of the Nazis yelled.

We sprinted out of the station.

"Around here," Wil dragged me toward the back of the restaurant. I leaned against the building, out of breath. Wil bent, and put his hands on his knees.

"They'll find us here."

"Shh," he said.

I kept my back flat against the wall as if in front of a firing squad.

"Have you seen the dirty Jews?" A Nazi questioned.

"Where are the filthy Jew pigs?" asked the other.

"We need to get out of here," I whispered.

There was nowhere to run. We would have to head toward the Nazis to get away.

"I'm sorry, Liana," Wil said. "I thought we'd make it." He bent toward me and kissed me.

His kiss lingered on my lips. It was the moment I had waited for, every girl's dream. My first kiss.

I shook my head to ditch the momentary trance. "Don't say that. We're going to be fine." I put on a brave face, but we both knew we were about to die.

"Hey," came a loud whisper.

A door behind the restaurant ajar, a buxom woman bedecked in a white apron stained with an amalgam of foodstuffs and tied high on her waist waved us toward her.

"They must be close." The Nazi's voice was so near he had to have been right around the corner.

"*Ja,*" the other said. "I smell pigs."

I looked at Wil, and he nodded. I dashed first and ran up three short steps and into the kitchen of the restaurant, Wil on my heels.

"In here." The woman held open a large steel door.

We jumped in without question, and the door clanked shut. In the darkness and cold, I couldn't see Wil, not his outline, not his movement.

❧ ♦ ☙

I was tired of being cold, my fingers constantly numb, and my joints stiff and unyielding. I couldn't see where we were, but from the temperature, which was much colder than it had been outside, it was easy to guess.

"We're in a freezer," Wil said.

"Think it's a trap and she's going to turn us over to the Nazis?"

"I think if she was going to rat on us, she would have done it and not saved us."

I wrapped my arms tight across my chest. My limbs trembled.

"Can you see anything at all?" Wil asked.

"Nothing. You?"

"No."

"Think we'll be here long?" The question was stupid.

"I don't know. I hope not."

My teeth chattered. My fingertips tingled.

"Come here," Wil said, "we'll keep each other warm."

I reached for him, found his arm, and we huddled and shared what body heat we could generate.

It was hard to gauge how much time passed before the big-busted woman opened the freezer door, but it had been long enough that I felt as if my limbs were frozen in place. Wil and I had little but each other for warmth. I wore the pajamas Mama had made from the kitchen curtains, Papa's long-sleeved black shirt, and no shoes, only stockings, which had become filthy and worn. Wil wore the clothes I had grabbed for him from Siegfried's closet, nothing substantial, but at least he had shoes.

The fat lady stood in the doorway to the freezer, backlit by light from a hallway that made her appear as a shadow. *"Habe eine warme suppe."* Have some soup.

We exited the walk-in freezer and followed her to a back room, where two steaming bowls of *metzelsuppe*, a traditional German sausage soup from Bavaria, waited. Quickly and quietly, we ate.

"Slow down, *kinder.*" The woman said. "You'll get bellyaches."

I heard her words of caution but was so hungry I couldn't heed her advice. I hadn't eaten anything but horse feed for three days. My stomach grumbled and protested the blood and liver sausages, and the onion and lard, as it hit my intestines. Finally full and with feeling returning to my fingers and toes, I rested the spoon in the bowl.

*"Vielen dank."* Thank you very much, I said.

I took my first opportunity to study her. Large and jovial with a round face, jowls that hung and shook, and blond hair piled high on her head. Wisps of hair fell around her face, which she didn't adjust out of her eyes. Light from above encircled the top of her head. Her cheeks were red, as if laughter common in her life. She was the most beautiful person I had ever seen. She had saved our lives.

"What is your name?" I asked.

"Theresa."

"I'm Liana, and this is Wil."

Wil wiped his mouth with a napkin and moved to leave. "We will find a way to repay your kindness."

"You can't go," Theresa said. "There are Nazis all over. You," she pointed to Wil, "can pass for a German, but you, young lady, look like you have Jew written on your forehead."

"We're supposed to meet Madame Juliette at the train station." My stomach cramped, and I passed gas.

"*Tsu fartsn*" in Yiddish, my family would say and laugh. How I missed them, but I didn't want to cry or look sad for fear that Theresa would think I was ungrateful.

"Who is this Madame Juliette?" Theresa asked.

"She's to take us to Paris and then to America, where my uncle lives."

Theresa sighed. "I suppose that might have been the plan before the night of broken glass, but no more. I am sure your Madame is long gone, if she was ever here."

"Night of broken glass?" Wil asked.

"That's what they called the last few days, because there was so much shattered glass in the streets."

More protests sprang from my stomach, growls and grumbles, more cramping and stinky gas. Wil looked ill too, his eyes watered, his skin an odd and pale shade. I had learned not to be embarrassed from bodily functions when with my family, but I hoped Theresa and Wil weren't offended by the smell.

"You will stay here," Theresa said. "I will hide you until it is safe."

"Is there a bathroom?" I asked.

"Two. One over there and the other—"

We didn't wait for her to finish. Wil and I ran. I barely made it to mine.

I exited the bathroom weaker than when I stepped in, having emptied my bowels with a whoosh and at the same time regurgitated on the floor in front of the toilet. I did the best I could to clean up the mess and wash myself. I missed Mama.

"You're burning up." Theresa put a meaty hand on my forehead. "Come."

She led me to a small cot in a back storage room.

"Where's Wil?" Lightheaded, delirium knocked on my door.

"Sit." She guided me to a thin mattress. "Be right back."

The room spun as I waited. Cans of food, boxes of pasta and rice, crates of beer, and a box of potatoes circled in a cyclone over my head. Pots, pans, a pressure cooker, coffee and tea presses, cutlery and paper goods chattered for my attention.

I held my hands to my head. "Make it stop."

Theresa appeared in front of me, a stein in her hand. The liquid was thick and caramel colored. White foam sizzled on top. It smelled sweet like urine.

"Here." She handed the mug to me. "This is what my *mutter* gave me when I was death on slippers. I'd get a good sleep and wake up like new."

I closed my eyes and drank the lager, slowly at first, and then more quickly. It was heavy and bitter on my tongue and then light as it slipped down my throat and bounced into my stomach. I put the mug down and licked my lips, surprised that I had finished the entire drink. My head settled; the room no longer spun.

"Sleep now." She helped me lie back.

"Have you seen my mama and papa? Siegfried and Renate?" I asked.

"Shh, dear. You sleep."

I concentrated on the shelves of food that surrounded me and fought to keep my eyes open. The square spine of a book stood out among the circular cans. "Is that *Mein Kampf*? Where's Wil?" Fatigue the victor, I closed my eyes and drifted off as I boarded the carousel horses for another ride.

# CHAPTER FORTY-TWO
## LONDON, ENGLAND
## NOVEMBER 13, 1938

AS THE JOKE might go, a Jew and a Quaker walked into a bar. Rabbi Sol Lichtenberg and Horace Albright, members of The Central British Fund for German Jewry established five years earlier to support the needs of Jews in Austria and Germany, rested their elbows on the mahogany bar.

"Drinks are on me," the Quaker said.

"That is kind, sir." The rabbi summoned the bartender. "I'll have your house wine, please."

"No," the Quaker protested. "He'll have your finest champagne."

"That's too expensive," the rabbi said.

"Only the best for my friends. While I may not have many friends who are Jews, all Jews are my friends."

The bartender poured bubbly golden-hued liquid into two fine flutes while the religious leaders waited. They wrapped their fingers around the thin stems and toasted.

"*L'chaim*," the rabbi said.

"To life."

The rabbi sipped and placed the glass on the bar. He ran his fingers nervously through his long, gray beard. "It's happening as we speak."

"All over Austria, and in Germany too."

"The pogrom."

"What are we to do from here?"

Over a bottle of champagne that temporarily eased their worries but not their determination to help, they came up with a plan. *Kindertransport*, they called it. They would get as many Jewish children as they could out of Hitler's monstrous path. All they needed was Prime Minister Neville Chamberlain, the British Cabinet, and Parliament to agree.

## CHAPTER FORTY-THREE
## RUBY
## NEW YORK CITY
## DECEMBER 8, 1938

ALFONSO CARRARA WAS a likable Joe who communicated using his body more than his words: a look away with arms crossed expressed disappointment, a crooked grin showed amusement, flailing hands expressed a myriad of emotions from joy to anger.

He had an olive complexion and was handsome, short and stout with strong legs that bowed slightly at the knees. One year younger than Ruby, he walked with his fists clenched even when not looking for a fight, and his body bent forward as if wherever he were headed was of utmost importance. Ruby learned after knowing Al a few weeks that wherever he was headed was important to him, and he was determined to get there before anyone else.

"I want you to shadow Carrara," Meyer told Ruby after they broke up the German American Bund meeting.

"Why, sir?"

"You'll learn a lot."

"No, I mean, yes, sir. Of course I'll shadow him. What I'm asking is why are you helping me? Why do you want me to work for you?"

He recalled compassion in the gangster's eyes. "You're a Jew, and where this world is headed, we have to stick together. Besides, you do Charlie Chaplin better than the Little Tramp himself."

"Isn't Alfonso Sicilian?"

"You're going to be our liaison between the Jews and the Italians. You play your cards right, kid, and you'll never have to worry about your next meal again. You're a pleasant fellow. I have a good feeling about you, and I know you're not going to prove me wrong." He slapped Ruby affectionately twice on the side of his face. "Understand?" he asked in Hebrew.

"Yes, Mr. Lansky."

Years later, when Ruby visited Meyer in Miami Beach as they were lifelong friends, Meyer told him he had known the truth about what had happened to the Jews in Austria during *Kristallnacht* and felt sorry for him. "Best pity hire I ever made," he said.

Meyer reached into his jacket and handed Ruby a neatly folded piece of paper. "Here's where you can find a room. Tell them I sent you and send the bill to me. You got a girl?"

Ruby thought of Dixie and blushed. "Yes, sir."

He grabbed a wad of money and counted off four twenty-dollar bills. "Buy her something nice."

Ruby was thrilled. He had a place to live, a job, even if he wasn't sure what his job was, and money to help Dixie. He gave her half the dough and kept the other half for himself. It was enough cash for Dixie to take time off for her wounds to heal and for her to decide her next move, and it was plenty for Ruby to attain breathing space to search for his family members. He hadn't received any word of them since before *Kristallnacht,* one month ago. When he found them and knew they were okay, he and Dixie would put together an act that would make Sam Cohen and the Burlesque Theater regret letting him go. Once all was in place, he'd ask Dixie to marry him.

Ruby waited for Al Carrara each morning in front of the Sir Roger Dean Hotel on twenty-third and third in Manhattan. He followed him around the five-story walk-up hotel as Al whistled portions of Italian operas, cleaned rooms, acted as a bellhop, and was the concierge. The other employee of the Roger Dean was a middle-aged woman with pink rouge dabbed on her cheeks like a painter's palette and purple-red hair. She sat at the front desk, filed her nails, and waited for new guests. The Depression raged and hotel occupants were few.

Alfonso never complained that Ruby shadowed him, never asked for help, and offered little narrative as to his duties. Ruby wanted to ask on several occasions what Al thought Meyer wanted him to learn from him, but thought it best to obtain his education by watching and listening, rather than by asking questions.

Every Friday the owner of the hotel, an English fellow named Angus Smih, dropped in, looking more and more ragged. Al and the woman at the front desk asked their boss when they could expect their next paychecks, as they were always late, to which Smih offered inadequate and sometimes nonsensical explanations. One day, abruptly, the woman up and quit, saying she wasn't going to work for free any longer.

"Good luck finding another job," Smih spat, and then glared at Al. "You quitting on me too?"

He shook his head and pointed at Ruby.

"Fine," Smih said, "he can work the front desk."

As Smih walked away, seeming barely able to lift his tired feet, Al nodded toward the front desk. Ruby sat and his education continued. As far as he could tell, he was learning how to be good at hanging around and doing nothing. Ruby didn't understand why Al didn't quit since he wasn't being paid, but again did not ask questions.

After about three weeks of following his Sicilian mentor as he scrubbed toilets, mopped floors, and carried occasional luggage up the stairs, and another week sitting at the front desk trying to stay awake, Ruby learned the purpose of his master class, and why Big Al worked for free.

It was a cold morning on the eighth day of the last month of 1938 when Ruby exited his apartment house. Frustration and disappointment cast a shadow over his limber frame. He couldn't stomach another day seated at the front desk of the Sir Roger Dean with a silent phone and no guests. It had been three days since the last guest left without paying the bill and since the five-story brownstone hotel had been empty of all but Al and Ruby. Even Smih had skipped his weekly visit.

Ruby stepped onto the sidewalk in front of his apartment building on Fourteenth Street and Sixth Avenue. Meyer's familiar Buick idled in the street. Smoke seeped out of the tailpipe and dissipated as it rose into the frigid morning air. Snow fell, which made the down-on-its-luck city streets look hopeful.

"Get in," the driver told Ruby. "Hurry up. It's freezing." He rolled up his window.

Ruby opened the back door and was surprised to see the seat empty. There was only the driver this time, no Meyer in the back and no front passenger who rode shotgun.

"Where we going?"

"To the Sir Roger Dean."

"I can walk," Ruby said.

"Yeah, I know, but Mr. Lansky wanted me to give you this." He handed Ruby a thick envelope. "Give that to the Sicilian. Tell him it's from Mr. Lansky, and today's the day."

Ruby held the envelope. "What does that mean, today's the day?"

The driver didn't answer, drove to the hotel and parked out front. Ruby stepped out of the car, the envelope in his hand. The Buick drove off. Ruby ascended the four steps out front and pushed through the wood doors marked Hotel. It was early, so he sat behind the desk with the envelope in his lap and waited for Al to arrive. When he did, Ruby slapped the envelope onto the desktop and said, "This is from Mr. Lansky. Today is the day."

Al opened the flap enough for Ruby to see that it contained a hunk of cash. Al stuffed it inside his coat jacket. "I'll be back." He hurried out the door.

Ruby waited two hours and thirty-six minutes until his return. When he did, his shabby hotel uniform and tattered winter fleece was replaced with a brand new suit and coat.

"Nice," Ruby said.

"You have to look the part. Don't forget that."

"What part?"

"Hotel owner."

"You own the Sir Roger Dean?"

"I'm changing her name."

"To what?"

"Don't know, to something that sounds relaxing."

"Yeah, like a place where people can rest well in."

Big Al snapped his fingers. "That's the new name, the Rest Well Inn. What do you think?"

"I like it, but what makes you think you'll do better than Smih?"

"I won't, not as long as the Depression is going on, but it's going to end soon."

"How do you know?"

"Hitler violated the Versailles Treaty by taking over Austria. Mussolini is siding with him. The Nazis aren't going to stop with Austria. We'll be at war soon. War is the quickest way to boost an economy."

Ruby thought of his family. Dixie was trying to locate Madame Juliette, to no avail. Hitler denied reports of Jews being sent to work camps. And, Al Carrara found benefit in war?

"Nothing better for a bad economy than a good war," Alfonso said.

Ruby's face drooped. He hadn't told Al that he was an Austrian Jew or that his sister, brother-in-law, nieces, and nephew had been in Vienna during *Kristallnacht* and he hadn't heard from them since.

Al read the expression on Ruby's face. "Meyer told me you have family in Austria."

Ruby tried to smother tears from falling; a lump in his throat prevented him from speaking.

Alfonso continued, "I'm sure they're fine. Sorry if I came across as insensitive. I didn't mean it that way."

A kid, who wore a cap low over his eyes, stepped into the hotel.

He carried a well-polished leather suitcase. "Is there a Ruby Friedberg here?"

"Friedman," Ruby corrected.

"This here's for you. Mr. Lansky told me to give it to you." He put the bag down by the front desk and waited, palm up.

Ruby fished into his pocket and dropped change into the boy's hand. The messenger clamped the coins into his fist and ran off.

"What's this?" Ruby asked.

"Your clothes and personal belongings," Al said.

Ruby put the suitcase on the desk, opened it, and rummaged through it. "This is from my room."

"Mr. Lansky thought it'd be best if you didn't have to go back and pack. You're living here now."

"Here?"

"Yeah, at the Rest Well Inn."

"Why am I living here?"

"You're going to run it."

"I am?"

"Why'd you think you've been following me around like a puppy this last month? I hoped you were paying attention."

"I was, but I'm a song-and-dance man."

"Looks like you're the manager of a hotel too."

"If I'm going to manage it, what are you going to do?"

"I got business outside the hotel." Al handed him a business card. "Go see my tailor tomorrow. He'll fit you for a few suits. And here." He passed Ruby an envelope, the same kind the driver had given Ruby this morning, not as thick.

Ruby shoved the money into his pocket. "Okay, sure, what am I supposed to do until we get guests?"

"Wait. Mr. Lansky or I will be in touch."

Big Al strolled out of the hotel, disheveled when he had entered that morning, a man-about-town when he exited, with a fine felt hat on his head and elegant wood-carved cane in his hand.

Alone, Ruby opened the suitcase. He removed the bowler hat and walking stick and tumbled the hat up and down his arm. He walked up and down the foyer as Charlie Chaplin. At least while he waited for guests and wondered about the safety and location of his family, he wouldn't be alone.

# CHAPTER FORTY-FOUR
# LIANA
# DECEMBER 8, 1938

LIANA SAT ON a foldout cot. Although she was five-foot-one inches tall and down to eighty pounds, her weight was enough to make the thin and ragged mattress sag. Rusted springs from the flimsy bed cut into her thighs and hips, but she did not notice the pain. She was entranced with the carousel horses that she had set up on a small, upended carton.

She took a swig from a bottle of dark ale and pressed the lever again, and listened to Mozart's final requiem play while the four glass horses circled the platform. She thought about the man, Oskar, who had made them and all the stories she had created about him, tales she had shared with her father, who would laugh and tell her that each one had to be true.

Oskar was a giant, more than ten feet tall, with hands too large to fit into gloves, but he could handle the most delicate glass. His thick lips spoke the sweetest words, and his deep speaking voice came out as a beautiful alto when he sang.

At other times, Liana saw Oskar as an ogre who lived under a bridge along the Danube. When he emerged during the daylight, people gasped, and screamed, and ran. He made the carousel horses to prove he wasn't a bad ogre but a good one.

Sometimes, she figured the etched "Oskar Glasman Gloggnitz Austria 1791" on the underside of the revolving platform was there to fool her, as her father made the horses. He didn't want her to know the truth, since she would demand he make more.

Most recently as she slept, Oskar grabbed her with long tentacles and stuffed her into a small box. He laughed as Mozart's death march played in double time and dragged her to one of Hitler's work camps, where Liana desperately searched for her family.

Liana brought the lager to her lips and looked at her hand that clasped the bottle. Her skin was cut up, calloused, and dry. Those weren't her fingers swollen to twice their size, as if the scabs over the wounds on her hand and the bright red marks that oozed blood and pus on her knuckles weren't part of her body. She didn't know how she would scrub another floor or scour the insides of another cabinet or endure the cold of the freezer where she was repeatedly ordered to stand when Theresa deemed her cleaning skills insufficient.

Liana didn't mind as much when Theresa made her work in the kitchen or serve customers, because then she searched for people she knew who might have information on her family, or at least she tried to overhear talk of what was going on outside the four walls of the train restaurant. Liana and Wil hadn't been permitted outside since Theresa saved them from the Nazis about one month earlier, except for one time when Theresa allowed her to go alone to retrieve the carousel horses.

Liana thought more than once that maybe it would have been better to be captured, even killed, than to be the Bavarian woman's indentured servant.

Whenever she and Wil pilfered time alone, they plotted their escape. Liana wanted to run impulsively and find a place to hide, but Wil insisted they needed a plan, a definite place to go, plus food, warm clothes, and water to survive.

That morning she and Wil had talked about it.

"We've already run from the Nazis, and look what happened to…" Wil hadn't needed to say the rest. Liana easily filled in the blank. Look what happened to the other kids. Murdered, each and every one of them.

"I'd rather be dead than spend one more moment here," Liana said.

"You don't mean that."

"I don't?"

"That's the beer talking. You drink too much of that."

"Mind your own business. I want to go to the work camps and find my family."

"You're no good to them there. The best you can do for them is get out of Austria alive."

"Do you know something about my family, Wilhelm Goldenstein, that you are not telling me?"

He offered no response, no indication of his thoughts.

As the platform rotated and the requiem played, Liana held a beer bottle in one hand and with the other lifted one of the horses, the palomino, to her nose. She swore she could smell her family, her home.

Theresa walked into the supply closet that served as Liana's room. "What are you doing?" Her booming Bavarian voice, frightening.

Liana turned off the carousel. "Nothing."

"I knew letting you have those horses was a bad idea, but no, I had to have a soft heart. You're lazy. You'd learn about real work at a camp." She began to leave.

"No, wait." Liana reached for her. "I'm sorry, *Frau* Theresa. I've scrubbed the bathroom since early this morning, and I took only a short break."

"I'm going to call the Nazis." She headed toward the door.

Liana hesitated, and thought to let her go. Theresa kept them there by threatening to turn them in to the Nazis, and acted like she could pick up the phone and call Hitler himself.

What if she could?

"I'll work harder," Liana said. "I promise. Where is Wil?"

"Oh," she mocked in a sing-song voice, "are you missing your boyfriend? Don't worry, he's being productive."

Theresa forced them to work eighteen hours a day. She also fed them well, although Liana did not have much of an appetite for food and preferred to drink her meals. The frau gave them a place to sleep even if Liana's room was a closet and Wil slept on a blanket on the bathroom floor. Theresa informed them that Nazis patrolled Vienna day and night and looked for Jews to send to work camps. They continued to vandalize Jewish owned stores, homes, and temples, and they murdered Jews in the streets.

"You'd better work harder," Theresa told Liana. "Go, one of the waitresses did not show up today. I need you to serve the customers."

Liana gently pushed the crate and the carousel horses under her cot and tied an apron around her waist. She took a swig of beer and walked into the restaurant.

# CHAPTER FORTY-FIVE
# MICHAEL

I IDLED THE Mustang at the top of Sara's drive; Billy's black pickup was parked by the front door. I didn't see any lights on in the home. I checked my phone, no word from Major Higgins with information on Billy. I knew I needed to be fearful of him but this was the same kid I had helped as a child. Would he harm me?

The engine of the Mustang hummed. I called one of my Favorites, a lifeline.

"Michael, you okay?" Erica sounded concerned.

"Yeah, yeah, listen, sorry to call you on a Saturday night, but I'm sitting in my car in front of Sara's house."

"That's why you're calling me? It's true, lawyers suck as clients."

"If you want me to call you back—"

"Hey," Tish's voice carried from the background, "tell Tucker he's interrupting us trying to make a baby."

"Pause the movie," Erica called to her partner. "I'll be there in a sec. Okay, Michael, what's up?"

"I can call back."

"No, I was giving you a hard time, and you know Tish likes to tease you. How are you doing?"

"Okay." I thought of Elizabeth. "I mean, amazing. I met this woman in a bar last night—"

"Is this a joke?"

"No, why would it be?"

"Sounded like the start of a joke. A Jew and a Quaker walk into a bar…"

"No joke. Her name is Elizabeth, and she's super smart."

"Don't tell me. She's a news junkie."

I huffed. "That's not why she's interested in me,"

*Are you sure, Tucker?*

"Michael's met someone?" Tish's voice moved close to the phone.

"How interested is she in you?" Erica asked.

I thought of the hours we had spent making love but figured that information was better not shared. "Pretty interested."

"You slept with her."

"How did you know that?"

"You're a guy. Guys can't say no."

"Yes, we can."

"Okay, fine. I hope you used protection."

"Of course we did." *Note to self. Ask Elizabeth if she is on the pill.*

"Is that why you're calling?" Erica asked. "To tell me you got laid and you're over Sara? Because I would say that's a good call to make."

"I'm done with her."

Tish's voice drifted over the phone again. "C'mon, honey. I'm losing my hard on."

"If you have to go, I understand," I said.

"Ignore her. She's being a goofball. So, what's going on?"

"Like I said, I'm in front of Sara's house. I met with her uncle and brother yesterday, but it was Sabbath so I couldn't stay. I'm back to talk to them, to see if Soldier Boy can help us; I mean, me."

"You're rambling, Michael."

"I don't know what to say to him. I've already tried, and he told me no, almost kicked me out of the house. If it wasn't for Ruby, he might have gotten violent. Maybe I should give up this approach. What do you think?"

"I've never heard you sound so insecure. You sure you're okay?"

"Yeah. I guess. Maybe I'm losing it. There's also Billy O'Brien. He's threatened me to say I messed up Sara's defense and she's innocent. Some crazy stuff."

"Billy O'Brien from when you were growing up?"

"The same."

"He did time. Did you call the police?"

"I spoke with Major Higgins. He's supposed to check Billy out and get back to me."

"What's there to check out? The guy's bad. Stay away from him."

"Billy's here, at Sara's house."

"Then leave."

"Maybe we should offer a cash settlement, and she'll drop this."

"It's not cash she wants. She has plenty of that. She wants her freedom. I've read over the transcript of the trial. After living through it as the prosecuting attorney and then reading the transcript, I think their appeal is a dead end."

"Then why is Trautman pursuing it?"

"You know the answer as much as I do."

"Money," I said.

"Your money and Sara's money. Plus how do you tell someone who's sentenced to spend the rest of her life in prison that there is no hope of getting out? He had to come up with some plan."

"There is always the possibility the appellate court will see something in the transcript we don't see," I mused.

"You never know, but I doubt it."

I looked at Billy's truck. There was no sign of movement outside the house, no lights inside the house. What was going on?

"I get she has to try to get her conviction overturned," I said. "I would do the same thing, but suing me personally isn't going to get her out of prison."

"I've been thinking a lot about that. I don't know what their endgame is. Suing you isn't going to persuade the appellate court to give her a new trial."

"Maybe their angle is to fight it out in the court of public opinion," I opined.

"Yeah, I thought of that. But courts are not swayed by the public."

"At least they're not supposed to be."

"I don't see this as some sort of conspiracy, Mikey. There has to be a reason they're suing you we haven't thought of."

Tish's voice beamed in. "They're hoping Michael finds new evidence."

"What?" I asked.

Erica put the phone on speaker. "Say it again, Tish."

"If Michael has a lot to lose, maybe he'll do their dirty work and find new evidence."

"New evidence could get her conviction overturned." My statement was rhetorical, since as attorneys, Erica and Tish already understood. Even if Tish was a real estate attorney she knew her way around a criminal courtroom, since she began her legal career as a public defender.

"But why you?" Erica asked. "They can hire private investigators. They have cops in their pockets. What does Trautman think you can discover that their experts can't?"

Silence, and then a light bulb above my head flickered. "Solider Boy."

"Explain," Erica said.

"Yeah, explain," Tish added.

"Sara wouldn't let Soldier Boy participate in the trial, right? She's not suddenly going to change her mind. I mean, why protect him then but not now?"

"You're right. Brilliant," Erica said.

"I'm lost. Fill me in." Tish became fully integrated into our conversation.

"Sara will not let Trace question Soldier Boy or anyone else. No PI's can talk to him. Nobody." I continued slowly, figuring out the logistics as I spoke. "But if I get to him and discover evidence that might get her a new trial, they're betting I won't sit on it."

"Because you're in love with her," Tish said.

"Which I'm not."

"Which you clearly are," Erica added.

I thought of Elizabeth and the bed sheets a tangle from our acrobatics and sweat. "Whatever," I spat. A juvenile reaction, I knew, but I didn't care. I tried to redeem myself by saying something intelligent. "Even if there's some mystery we've yet to uncover, it won't necessarily stop Sara from going after my money, I mean Gram's money."

"It's your money now, Michael," Erica said. "You're right, it might not stop her. But if there's new evidence and her sentence is overturned, she won't care about your measly two million bucks."

"Hey."

"To her that's nothing."

"I'm with Erica," Tish said. "That's Trace's endgame. He wants you to do the work Sara won't let him do. Ingenious. The guy might be a royal asshole, but that's a brilliant move. This is much more fun than real estate closings."

Of course, Tish was a real estate attorney. "Hey Tish, do you know a paralegal named Elizabeth Innis?"

"Elizabeth Innis? Like the beer?"

"Yeah."

"Can't say I do. Did she say what firm she worked for?"

I thought of our conversations. "No, she didn't."

"I'll ask around. If she works for a real estate law firm in Nassau or Suffolk County, I'll find her."

A light went on inside Sara's house and over the front steps, and the front door opened. Soldier Boy and Billy stepped out.

"Michael, you there?" Erica asked.

"Yeah, I'm here. You won't guess who came out of Sara's house."

"Who?"

"Soldier Boy *and* Billy O'Brien."

"Who's Billy O'Brien?" Tish asked.

"Michael, leave, now," Erica said.

"No way," I said. "This is getting good."

I hung up, jumped out of my car and forgot to be scared.

# CHAPTER FORTY-SIX
## MICHAEL

I WALKED TOWARD Solider Boy and Billy, wondering what the hell I was doing, but I didn't stop. I had to take care of this. I had to get Billy to lay off of me. I wasn't going to live my life in fear of him, and I certainly wasn't going to give into his crazy demand about Sara. And, I had to get answers from Soldier Boy. Then, I needed to get back in bed with Elizabeth.

When they saw me, Soldier Boy and Billy halted in front of the big wooden front door. Billy reached behind his back, kept his hand there.

I got close. Billy wore a white tank top and cargo jeans. He stank like a brewery.

"I didn't know you and David were friends."

"It's none of your fucking business," Billy jerked toward me, to scare me I think.

I didn't step back, but Billy did. He retreated a step or two, almost walked into Soldier Boy.

I had a soft spot for that kid ever since we were young. I was four years his senior, and we grew up on the same street, in our younger years I felt like his big brother. One time I rescued him from a beer joint on the wrong side of town. I felt sorry for him, as he hadn't had the family support I had growing up. When he was arrested for being an accessory to murder what more could I do to help him?

I kept talking to Billy. "Remember when you were missing and everyone from the neighborhood looked for you? I found you at the dive bar and took you home."

"What about it?" Billy grumbled.

"I was thinking about that night, that's all," I said.

Soldier Boy stepped up. "We're looking for a landscaper, and Billy interviewed for the job. That's why he's here."

"Saturday night's a good time to interview," I smirked.

"I need the work, Michael, give me a break."

"Small world's all I'm saying." I said.

"Okay." Soldier Boy reached out his hand to Billy, who shook it. "We'll be in touch."

"Ah, yeah, right." Billy kept his eyes locked on mine as he walked by me.

I watched him head toward his pickup, his hand on the back of his jeans, on the handle of a gun, the entire time.

The tires screeched as he peeled off down the driveway. My breath hitched when he almost hit the Mustang.

I let out a big exhale, having survived that encounter with Billy. I knew I should be more afraid of him but I wasn't. I still couldn't fathom he would hurt me, not after how much I've helped him.

After Billy was gone, Soldier Boy glared at me. "What are you doing here?"

"I need your help. Sara needs your help."

"I'm not going to rat out my sister so you'll get off the hook for being a shitty attorney."

I thought about what Erica had said on the phone. *If there's new evidence and Sara's conviction is overturned, she won't care about your measly two million bucks.*

"I have an idea," I said. "Let me in, and I'll tell you about it."

I hoped to go inside and see Ruby, Ruby seemed a lot more logical and approachable than Soldier Boy. I needed Ruby to help me get through to him.

"Here's fine."

We stood on the front stoop. Soldier Boy's chest heaved. The Semper Fi tattoo on his bicep bulged.

"Okay, look," I figured this was my last shot to convince him to help me, to help Sara. *Think, Tucker. Say something smart.* I decided to go with the truth, or at least my new truth. "I know you're pissed I'm here, but if you have information about Uncle Charlie's murder, you need to let me know. That's the only way Sara's sentence will be overturned. If there's new evidence of who the real murderer is, the court could grant her a new trial. Or even better, if the evidence is conclusive she didn't kill him, the state could dismiss the charges."

"Sounds good, but you seem to be forgetting something."

"What's that?"

"You're not her attorney anymore."

"I know, but that doesn't mean I don't want to help."

"News flash, you're not her boyfriend either." He stepped close to me.

His breath reeked of beer, like Billy's had. Desperate, I had to think of something, some way to get him to cooperate.

"Please. Let's talk inside."

He put his hand around the front of my neck.

"Soldier Boy," I croaked. "Stop."

"Don't call me that."

His eyes bulged and he squeezed harder. I didn't know a man could have so much power in one hand. I grabbed his arm and tried to push him away, but he was too strong. The pressure on my windpipe grew, and then the pain. I had difficulty breathing, getting lightheaded. I kicked at him, swung my hands at his face. He pushed me backwards. I fell off the stoop and landed hard in bushes.

Mortified, I lay there. Hackles and bristles stabbed at me. I caught my breath. *Get up, Tucker, be a man.* I tried to get out of the bushes but I was off balance, wedged between shrubs with nothing to push off of, no leverage.

Uncle Ruby stepped out of the front door. "Help him up," he admonished Soldier Boy.

"He deserves to rot there."

"David." Ruby was stern.

"Fine." Soldier Boy extended a hand toward me.

My hands flew up to protect my face.

"He won't hurt you again," Ruby said. "Take his hand."

"No way. I'm calling the police. He's a maniac." I went to reach for my phone and realized I couldn't get to my pants pocket, and I left my phone in the Mustang.

"I'm not anymore of a maniac than you are," Soldier Boy snapped. "Why do you keep coming around here? What do you want?"

"Okay, enough." Ruby intervened again. "David, help him up. And Michael, let him. Enough with this macho bullshit."

I hesitated. I wanted nothing to do with that psycho.

"Now," Ruby ordered, his face hard.

Under the front stoop lighting, I caught a glimpse of the man who in his younger days ran with Meyer Lansky.

Soldier Boy and I locked hands to wrists, and he pulled me up. I brushed the stickers off my clothes and extracted several from my arms and face.

"Into the house," Ruby ordered.

I vacillated, part of me wanted to run for the Mustang; the other part wondered if Soldier Boy's attempted strangulation of me might be the ammunition I needed to get information out of him.

"Aren't you here for answers?" Ruby asked me. "Then go inside."

I couldn't argue with that fact and I was too embarrassed to do so anyway. I followed them into the house, sat on the couch in the living room, and accepted a tumbler from Ruby filled with whiskey on the rocks. I sipped quietly and waited for my nerves to calm.

After a few minutes, Ruby sat next to me. Soldier Boy eased into a chair across from us.

"You know," Ruby said, "we come from a family of survivors. Do you know the secret to overcoming adversity?"

I wasn't in the mood for a question and answer session. I sipped at the whiskey and didn't respond.

"The secret is getting along with your enemies, but to a point. When it's clear there is no escape, then you have to be willing to do things you'd never imagine yourself doing. It's either you or them. Like Soldier Boy when he was in the Marines, he did things and saw things you never imagined."

I looked at Soldier Boy, whose scowl told me he wished to have his hands around my neck again.

"I definitely did things I wasn't proud of as an immigrant in lower Manhattan in the thirties," Ruby continued. "Look at Sara and Soldier Boy's grandmother, Liana, my niece, and what she had to do to survive *Kristallnacht* and make it to America when the rest of her family, our family, was murdered in concentration camps."

I took a deep sip of the liquor. Soldier Boy walked behind the bar and emerged with a bottle of Coors Light. He sat back in the easy chair.

Ruby kept going. "It's in our blood to fight when something threatens our survival. We don't retreat. We fight when we have to, and when we do it's to win. We're not afraid to fight to the death. Do you understand, Michael?"

"I think so," I lied. I had no idea what he was saying.

"Good. David didn't mean anything out there. He felt threatened and acted like an animal when he shouldn't have. Right, David?"

"Sure, Uncle Ruby."

Soldier Boy sounded unconvincing.

"You accept his apology?" Ruby asked.

"I didn't hear an apology." I drained the glass.

Ruby pointed at Soldier Boy. "Say it."

"I'm sorry. Okay?"

Ruby looked at me "Well?"

"Yeah. I accept it. That's fine."

"Get him another drink," Ruby told Soldier Boy.

Soldier Boy took the glass from me and filled it with Pappy Van Winkle and ice.

I sipped and tried to recall the last time I ate, which had to have been at McCluskey's the night before. I didn't care. The whiskey tasted like gold. Who needed food?

"Family," Ruby's voice was soft and even, "comes first. That's why I took my life savings and paid it to Madame Juliet to get my nieces and nephew out of Vienna before they wouldn't be able to leave. I wanted my sister and brother-in-law out too, but I couldn't get the money together. Not then, anyway.

"We all knew Hitler wanted to segregate the Jews. I wanted my family out months earlier, when the Germans first marched into Austria. I could have gotten them all out at that time. The price wasn't too much then, but Amalie and Jacob said no. They never thought the Nazis would do what they did. I never should have listened to them. I should have been the man of the family, but who would have thought one maniac could orchestrate the murder of six million Jews? I never believed my family would be victims of a slaughter." Tears marred his cheeks. He wiped them with a blue-veined and shaking hand.

"So that's where we come from, David, Sara, and I. We're the last ones, the remaining bloodline of a family of fighters, the final lineage entitled to the Rest Well Inn fortune. And once I'm gone, which will be soon—"

"Don't talk like that, Uncle Ruby."

The old man held up his hand. "I'm ninety-seven years old. Even if I didn't have pancreatic cancer, I don't have long to live."

"What?" Soldier Boy and I reacted at the same time.

"Listen, boys, that's all you need to know right now. I refuse to die with my grand niece in prison for the rest of her life." His voice sounded stronger. "So David, it's time."

"Time for what?"

"Time to tell Michael the truth."

"Wait. Not so fast." Soldier Boy limped toward him. "Do you really have cancer?"

Ruby nodded.

Soldier Boy knelt in front of his great uncle, the lines of Soldier Boy's face filled with concern. "Are you sure?"

"Everybody dies, David. It's okay." Ruby's eyes were watery and kind.

He laid his head in his uncle's lap. Ruby stroked his hair. From next to Ruby on the couch, I felt like an intruder. I thought I'd finish my drink and slip out, but

Soldier Boy jumped up.

He paced in front of the couch. "We'll get you the best treatment, and research the best doctors. You'll do chemo and radiation, and if that doesn't work, there are experimental treatments and drug trials going on all over the world."

Ruby held up his hand. "Stop. I've refused all treatment. I've lived a long and full life, Davey. I haven't always made the best choices and I'm coming to terms with my regrets. I'm almost one hundred years old, for goodness sake. I've outlived Charlie Chaplin by ten years now, he died when he was eighty-eight."

"But we can afford the best doctors, *Onkel*. We'll find the best specialists."

"Enough. *Mit a lefl ken men dem yam nit oys'shepn.*"

Soldier Boy sat heavy in the chair he had occupied earlier. He must have read my confused expression. "It's Yiddish. You can't empty the ocean with a spoon," he translated what Ruby had said, and then looked to his uncle. "I have to do something. I can't watch you die."

I recalled the accident Soldier Boy had while in the Marines. Injured when a helicopter went down, it was the reason he walked with a limp. All the other soldiers in the training exercise were killed. The emotional pain was so great he had spent several months after his honorable discharge visiting the families of his fallen comrades.

"I have one request," Ruby said.

"Anything."

"We tell the truth. It's the way to help Sara."

"But that's not what she wants," Soldier Boy said.

"Almost eighty years ago I had the chance to save my family, but I didn't take control. I'm not letting that happen again. Do you understand?"

"Yes." David bowed his head like a child who had been disciplined.

"Good. Tell Michael everything."

I raised my eyebrows and hoped that was the only outward sign I showed of my euphoria. Finally I was going to learn the truth.

Soldier Boy looked at Ruby. "Where do we begin?"

Ruby's eyes clouded more. "It began with the Holocaust, but that's not what Michael wants to hear."

I started to protest but Ruby held up his hand and stopped me. He looked to Soldier Boy. "Start with what can most help Sara. Start with the story of your parents' deaths."

# CHAPTER FORTY-SEVEN
## STEPHEN GOLDSTEIN
## AUGUST 8, 1998

ON THE FIRST level of the Long Island mansion, Stephen Goldstein's long and elegant fingers lingered over the keys of the baby grand. Anxiety rolled through his body and into his hands.

*When was the last time I struck a piano key? Had to be when Sara and David were young.* He smiled. Such a sweet time when life held unlimited promises, when living was more than collecting Lionel trains, and when Cassandra's drinking seemed manageable and did not consume their home, their lives, and their souls. Sure, she had a problem when they first married, but she was never violent and seemed able to drive the kids to school on time, run errands, and take part in the Rest Well Inn business. It wasn't as if Stephen hadn't witnessed the same behavior before as a little boy with his mother, Liana Krochmal, and her abuse of alcohol.

He thought back to when his mother gave him the carousel horses. She had been drunk, as usual. She handed him the box and said, as her father had told her, "You must protect these horses always. When you are with them, I will be with you too." One month later, she was dead from alcohol poisoning.

He looked toward the winding staircase that led to the second floor of the opulent home. The horses and the trains were in a room he forbade the children to enter. The Forbidden Room, he had dubbed it, half as a guise to keep them out, half because the horses possessed the power of good and evil. He knew Sara and Davey would listen to his admonition not to enter that room, for awhile at least, but their disobedience was part of his plan, which is why he never put a lock on the door. One day they would enter the room to see what was inside, their curiosity overpowering, or perhaps to hide. As he had to do when his mother gave him the carousel horses when he was six years old, Sara and David too would learn the power of the horses on their own time.

He knew little of the horses' origin, only what his mother had told him and she was rarely a reliable reporter. Liana's father had purchased the glass horses mounted on a rotating platform at a market in Austria. According to the inscription on the undercarriage, the creator was a man named Oskar who had designed them in 1791 in Gloggnitz, Austria. When Liana escaped the Nazis, she had her clothes, a stuffed bear named Bloomie, the carousel, and oddly a copy of *Mein Kampf.* The bear had since been lost. Stephen had given Hitler's manifesto to Uncle Ruby. Stephen had no use for it. The sight of it made his stomach wretch. Ruby displayed it and explained it was his way never to forget.

The horses lived on through Stephen. They had always fascinated and frightened him, although he was never sure how they obtained their strength. Stephen had prayed the children could manage what the horses possessed, the power to seize good from evil, the ability to turn passion into power.

He looked at his watch. Charles would arrive soon. It had taken months of debate but Stephen had convinced Cassandra she needed to wrest control of the Rest Well Inn fortune from her uncle. Enough was enough. No more drinking, no more being taken advantage of by Uncle Charlie, no more attempts by Stephen to save Cassandra without professional help. Stephen realized his efforts to save his wife were his attempt to make up for not being able to prevent his mother from succumbing to the devil alcohol when he was a boy.

Through a lot of therapy, he had learned saving Cassandra would not assuage his guilt over his mother's death, and would not bring Liana back. Stephen, the adult, knew he could never have rescued his mother from the demons that drove her to drink, demons he could only imagine, as she refused to speak of her time in Austria and England. Stevie, the little boy inside the man, though, wished he had tried harder.

As he sat at the piano and debated whether or not to play, he thought of how Cassandra hadn't imbibed in eight days and had agreed to enter an inpatient alcohol treatment facility, as soon as she and Stephen had *the talk* with Charles. Maybe then, and only then, could their marriage be saved and their children live free of fear. No more hiding while their parents fought, no more cringing at the sounds of breaking glass. So many *no mores*. They could actually be kids.

Stephen was glad Sara and David had left to spend the afternoon and night with his sister, Claire, and her husband, Eddie. When the children returned the next day, he would explain mommy would be going away. He debated telling them the truth as to her absence, or some watered-down version as opposed to full out lying such as Mommy is on vacation, or Mommy is visiting a relative.

Sara and David were too smart for lies. It was no secret the way her alcoholism invaded their family and robbed them of happiness. It was no secret Cassandra needed professional health; all the family members needed help. Who could foresee the damage their mother's vice would have on them as adults? Yes, he would tell the children the truth, and then he would take them to Tiny Town where they would watch the toy trains go round and round, and then they'd get ice cream.

He took his hands from over the black and white keys and laid them in his lap. He would play the piano again. One day.

"Why wait?" he asked.

Fingers on the keyboard again, he recalled notes to Mozart's "Last Requiem in D Minor", an arrangement for the solo piano he had spent months learning as a teenager. Those were the notes that came out of the carousel when the platform rotated. It had been his obsession to learn them, so crisp and clean, heart wrenching and exhilarating, a composition bittersweet, chilling, and passionate; and an appropriate good riddance to all the wrong in their marriage and with their family. Once Cassandra was home and clean, he would play upbeat tunes with the four of them around the piano, singing.

Excited by thoughts of success, maybe this was the

beginning of something wonderful, he leaned into the piano, but could not make his fingers land on the keys. He shivered as the black-cloaked fiend of failure blew a cold draft down his back.

He slumped on the bench. "Maybe tomorrow."

"What about tomorrow?" Cassandra asked.

Stephen jumped up and knocked the bench over, feeling as though he were caught doing something wrong.

"Nothing."

She teetered toward him, his tall and thin frame a contrast to his wife's short and thick stature. He stayed next to the piano. As she neared, her bloodshot jade eyes widened. Her skin was blotched red, her nose covered with engrossed capillaries. She held a tumbler of bourbon in her left hand, her friend and his nemesis.

"No, Cassandra." He searched for words. "You didn't."

"Didn't what?"

Her cockeyed smile disgusted him. Her features when she was drunk had become more familiar to him than when she was sober: red eyes, unsteady gate, and slurred and nonsensical words. Next came anger. He was always doing something wrong, the children perpetually evil.

"Don't look at me that way." She threw the glass.

It hit the piano and shattered. He thought how to respond, he wanted to avoid a fight.

He fought to keep his voice calm and even. "Charles will be here any moment."

"I'm ready."

"No, you're not."

"What do you know about business?" she yelled. "I'm the businesswoman. I'm the heir to a fortune. What are you? A freeloader; that's what you are."

He had heard it before, Cassandra's deep-rooted and misguided resentment of him for everything wrong in her life.

"How about if I make coffee?"

"Fuck coffee." She reached for a glass vase, which she threw in his direction. This one came closer to him than the glass. It crashed against the baby grand.

She held something dark in the palm of her right hand. Her fingers clasped around it.

"Cassandra, what do you have? What are you doing?" His voice was shrill.

Never had their arguments gone to this level. She raised her arm and pointed the gun at him.

"I'm fucking sick and tired." She rocked on her heels.

Stephen thought to rush her, maybe dislodge the gun, but she regained her stance.

"What are you tired of, sweetheart?" He tried compassion to get out of his situation.

She looked at him blankly.

"You said you were sick and tired."

"Right, yeah." She waved the gun at him. "I'm tired of you controlling me, always telling me what to do. Don't drink. Be nicer to the kids. Go to therapy. Talk to Uncle Charlie. I don't want to fucking talk to Uncle Charlie. I want what's mine, and there's nothing to talk about. I am nice to the kids. You're the one who's mean."

He held up his hands. "Please. Put it down."

"Where are they?"

"Who?"

"Sara and David."

"Out. With Claire and Eddie."

"Too bad."

"What do you mean?"

"I want them to see this."

Her eyes glowed like an iron rod forged into a fire. She stepped toward him, shards of glass crunched under her shoes. She was angrier, more crazed than he's ever seen, as if it wasn't Cassandra but a devil that possessed her body, a demon worse than one he's witnessed before and he's seen his share of fiends with names like whiskey, bourbon and rye.

"Put the gun down, Cass."

"Don't call me that," she spat.

"What is going on?" Charles's voice echoed through the vast living room.

Stephen felt relief a buffer had arrived, and he relaxed a little. The boom that followed was odd, as if it came from another place, another time. What was even stranger was the sudden sharp pain in his chest. He looked down. A dark stain on his shirt grew. He put his hands over his heart. *Did she shoot me?*

Disbelief was his first reaction, followed by horror as she pointed the gun toward him again.

"No." His legs wobbled, his head unclear, dizzy. He lunged toward her, and collapsed. She stood over him. He crawled away, under the piano. Blood flowed down his shirt; it ran along his chin and cheek.

He looked up at her, and she down at him. A momentary pause was enough for Charles to grab the gun from her. Another shot, and Stephen waited for new pain, but none came. She crawled to him now, her hands groped for him, more blood spewed. From where, and whose, Stephen didn't know. He tried to rise, and then fell onto broken glass. Stephen's head spun. Nausea overtook him. Cassandra collapsed on top of him, under the baby grand, her breath rasping and gurgling as blood filled her throat.

He tried to hold his wife, to save her, to save them all: his mother, Sara, and Davey.

He wished he had played Mozart's final requiem one last time.

# CHAPTER FORTY-EIGHT
## SARA

ELIZABETH SAT ACROSS from me in the jailhouse visitor's room. What used to intrigue me about her, I despised: her curly hair, brown skin, pleasant smile, and congenial nature. Everything I saw in her when we were kids that had made me jealous disgusted me. She must have seen or sensed my contempt, her body language made it obvious. Arms folded across her chest, and forced, uneasy demeanor made me know she wasn't the same excited private investigator I had spoken with the day before.

Since she wasn't an attorney and hadn't brought Trace with her, we weren't permitted to meet in one of the rooms reserved for attorneys and their clients. It was just as well I wasn't alone with her, as my anger was palpable. Around us, other inmates met with their relatives, friends, or clergy, but I barely noticed. I was too busy seething.

"Sara, listen—"

I held up my hand and stopped her from speaking.

"Did you get anything out of him?" I said. What I wanted to ask was, did you fuck the man I am in love with, the man I will never be with again because I'm rotting in prison for a crime I didn't commit? But there was no point of confirming what I already believed to be true. Call it women's intuition; I didn't need her validation that she and Michael had slept together.

Her posture relaxed, perhaps because she thought I wasn't going to confront her about sleeping with my ex.

"Michael's meeting with Ruby and David today. He's hoping David will help him defend his case against you."

"Is that what he told you?"

She nodded.

Why would Michael think Soldier Boy would share information with him, I wondered, but asked, "What do you think Michael's hoping to learn?"

"If he obtains dirt against you, maybe he could use it to get you to drop the part of the lawsuit that could hold him personally liable."

"I'm already convicted of murder. What more dirt could he find that would make a difference?" I attempted to push images of her and Michael in bed together out of my head.

"Maybe he's looking for more evidence of your guilt."

"Even if I were guilty, which I am not, my brother would never rat on me."

"Then what else?"

"Maybe something to do with the Forbidden Room?" I immediately wished to swallow the words I spoke.

"What's that?"

I sighed. I didn't want to go into it. Not with her, that was for sure.

"Nothing."

She leaned toward me. "You said it. It has to be something."

I thought about where to start. With my grandmother, Liana? Or should I talk about how Soldier Boy and I used to ride the twelve-inch glass carousel horses? Or how Michael and I made love in the room, the same room where Uncle Charlie was murdered?

"Forget it." I spoke sternly and hoped my tone was enough to have her change the subject.

Elizabeth seemed to concede. "I have a theory about why Michael wants to speak with them and what he hopes to gain."

"And it is?" I slouched, tired of having to sit across from her and pretend I cared about what she had to say, when in actuality, I could not stop thinking about Michael and if he had sex with her.

"You sure you want to hear it?" Elizabeth asked. "You look distracted."

I sat up and focused. "No, go ahead."

"Michael doesn't want to speak with David to get his help. Michael is looking for new evidence."

"Why would he do that?"

"To exonerate you."

I digested this information. Was it possible Michael was in love with me, and trying to prove my innocence? If so, he never would have had sex with Elizabeth. My mood lightened.

"Is that what he told you?" I asked.

"No. He gave me the lame excuse of asking David to help defend against you."

"Why is that lame?"

"Serious, Sara?"

I waved her away. I knew it was stupid of me to ask. Michael had to know Soldier Boy would never betray me. "Why do you think he's trying to find new evidence to prove my innocence?"

"Because he's in love with you."

"How do you know that?"

"Women's intuition," she said.

"So you haven't slept with him." Euphoria encapsulated me for the first time since my incarceration.

Her posture sagged. "I didn't say that."

"Then you have?" My voice was staccato. I regretted venturing down that road.

"I didn't say that either."

I stood from my chair and raised my voice. "Then what, Elizabeth?"

A male guard chastised me. "Sit, Goldstein."

I regained composure and sat.

"Look," Elizabeth continued, her cadence awkward as her confidence sagged. "None of that matters. My job is to get information from him, right? In order to do that, there might be some things I need to do."

"Like sleep with my boyfriend?" I snapped.

"He's not your boyfriend," she shot back.

"Keep it down, ladies," a female guard cautioned.

I took a deep breath, using those seconds to determine where I wanted the conversation to go. "Why do you think he's in love with me? And don't give me that women's intuition crap."

She shrugged. "Maybe I'm wrong."

I sized her up. "You've fallen for him, haven't you?"

"That would be unprofessional. This is another job to me."

I nodded and determined my next move. It was hard to manipulate chess pieces from behind bars. "Tell Trace that Michael is off limits."

"Serious? How come?"

"Because I said so."

"You won't let us speak to David. You're not letting us find out what Michael is up to. The court record from the trial is clean. Trace is filing an appeal, but he doesn't have much faith in your conviction being reversed. Michael might be our only shot. What if he does uncover new evidence from your brother or your uncle?"

"Stay away from him."

"How are we supposed to help you if you keep tying our hands? Do you want to spend the rest of your life in prison?"

"I'm not the law firm making at least a half a million on this. Figure something out, but do it without involving David, and no more following Michael, or whatever it is you're doing with him."

Elizabeth's face reddened. "I swear, Sara, our relationship is purely professional."

She was irritated with this conversation, but not as much as I was. She was free to leave, to work off her frustrations at the gym or soothe her angst with a glass of Cabernet with friends at a restaurant. I had to return to my cell, to my unending negative thoughts, and to the nightmares.

"Visiting hours are over," the male guard announced.

Elizabeth stood, relieved, I'm sure. I stayed planted in my seat, positive my legs would give way if I tried to rise. I had acted like a fool, as if I had any control over my life, let alone Michael's. I wanted to trust her but all I could see was she and Michael coiled in bed.

"I'll talk to Trace," she said, "but I hope you'll reconsider."

"There's nothing for me to reconsider. In fact, tell Trace and your father that you're firm is fired."

She walked away. Both guards checked her out as she exited. I covered my eyes with my hands and cried.

# CHAPTER FORTY-NINE
## LIANA
### DECEMBER 8, 1938

LUNCHTIME IN VIENNA, the train station restaurant was packed. I scanned the crowd and saw no one I knew from Mazzes Insel, the Jewish Quarter in Vienna's Second District where I had lived with Mama, Papa, Siegfried, and Renate.

No Jews were dining. I never saw Jews. Wil and I had to be the last ones left in Vienna, from 200,000 down to two.

I began my shift and served *weiner schnitzel* and *spaetzle*, goulash and Allgau mountain cheese, and pretzels with sweet mustard. Mountain gentian spirit, beer, and wine flowed.

From table to table, people spoke without regard for the severity of what occurred. They talked of the weather. "Cold." Their jobs. "Happy to have more work now that the Jews were gone." How they had to maneuver around the Jewish district to get to work because of all the rubble in the street, angry at the increased time it took.

Their casual conversations infuriated me. I wanted to scream. What about my family? Siegfried was dead. Where were the rest of them? How about my friends who were killed? What about the other Jews who had been executed and those carted away with no rights? Don't you care?

My outburst would certainly give away my identity as a Jew so I busied myself with the work, sneaked sips of schnapps in the back, and concentrated on Wil's words. *We need a plan, and then we will escape*. Neither of us had been able to come up with a scenario that didn't end with bullets in our backs as we ran away.

With a nice light feeling in my head from the schnapps helping me forget, I took the order of a stocky woman who was dressed in her Sunday best, a relaxed-fit tweed wool skirt, jacket, and a smart, matching box hat, and I jotted on a pad the order of her companion, a thinner woman who was also in her late thirties or early forties.

When I served liver loaf to the stocky woman several minutes later, she smiled sweetly and said, *"Dank u."*

I looked a second time at her. Did I know her? No, she was no one I recognized. Her gaze lingered on mine. Was she a Nazi? Had she recognized me as a Jew? Uncomfortable, I was about to rush away when she spoke in Yiddish.

*"Hobn ir gearbet do lang?"* Have you worked here long?

*"Ye'."*

I scurried to pick up another order and felt the woman's stare on me. By the kitchen burners, I leaned over a counter, unable to catch my breath. The woman had addressed me in Yiddish and that was how I had responded. Even if my response was short, it was enough. She knew. She had to know. It had happened quickly. My heart pounded out of control. Sweat dripped from my pores. I had to find Wil. There was no time for a plan. We had to leave, now.

"Back to work," Theresa swatted my legs with a broom.

My knees buckled. I held myself up by the counter, steadied myself, and then grabbed another order. I needed time to think. I needed to find Wil. *Keep working*, I told myself. *Act like nothing was wrong.*

In the busy mess hall, I watched the women as best as I could while I served other patrons. The women seemed to be engaged in an everyday conversation, the weather, work. Perhaps I had imagined one had addressed me in Yiddish. I got close to their table, a risk, I knew. I strained to hear. This time, they spoke in German but I recognized by their accents they were not from Germany. Dutch, perhaps?

"I am hoping to meet with him today," said the stout one.

"Are you sure, Geertruida?" her friend responded. "You were told he'd meet with you yesterday and the day before, and both times were lies."

"I have hope."

Twenty minutes later, as the women enjoyed *windbeutel*, crème puffs, and *rumkugein*, rum balls, for dessert, two Nazis walked into the restaurant in full uniforms, rifles angled against their shoulders. The patrons froze, many mid-bite. I hid and looked for Wil.

The Nazis approached the women. One said, "Come."

The stout woman who had spoken to me in Yiddish wiped her mouth with a paper napkin, nodded to her friend, and said, "It's time."

# CHAPTER FIFTY
## AUNTIE TRUUS
## DECEMBER 8, 1938

GEERTRUIDA WIJSMULLER-MEIJER, known as Auntie Truus, was a Dutch crusader. About one month after *Kristallnacht*, she traveled to Vienna to meet personally with Adolf Eichmann, the Nazi SS-*Obersturmbannführer.* The meeting was held in a Nazi command post located in the only Viennese temple not desecrated during the Night of Broken Glass. Her intent was to convince Eichmann to allow the first *kindertransport*, the evacuation of Jewish children by train from Austria and Germany to Great Britain and other safe havens. The idea had been born by Rabbi Sol Lichtenberg and the Quaker Horace Albright in a bar in London, and agreed to by Prime Minister Neville Chamberlain, the British Cabinet, and Parliament.

Upon Auntie Truus's first request to meet with Eichmann, he refused, but she did not give up. Finally he agreed to give the stubborn woman five minutes of his time.

She entered the temple and noted remnants of Jewry had been removed or destroyed. The stained glass panels, no doubt with images of Jewish heroes, were smashed. The doors to the Ark were opened, the curtain ripped, the Torah scrolls gone. Piled in a corner were broken menorahs.

Eichmann stood near the *bimah* on a raised platform, the stage where the rabbi gave his *drash*. The Nazi commander looked massive elevated on the stage, but as Auntie Truus got closer she saw he was not physically intimidating: thin, balding, and dark-skinned, and his ears stuck out unnaturally from the sides of his head. Six Nazi SS guards protected him, three on either side, rifles cocked. Officers stood on either side of Auntie Truus too.

At barely five feet tall, buxom, and thick waisted, the Dutch woman tried not to show amusement at the firepower and brawn that protected Eichmann from her. She had been patted down three times by three different officers before being permitted a brief audience with the lieutenant colonel.

"You can have six hundred Jewish Viennese children,"

Eichmann growled from the stage.

She looked up at him. "When?"

"*Sofort.*" Immediately.

"How can I organize six hundred children quickly? They are hidden all over the city. You are making it impossible."

He dismissed her with a wave of his hand. The officers on either side of her grabbed her elbows and escorted her out.

Auntie Truus was not deterred, which is why she became known as one of the greatest saviors of the Jews during World War II.

The first *kindertransport* from Vienna left two days later on December 10, 1938, with six hundred children on board. Liana Krochmal and Wilhelm Goldenstein were on that train.

Liana shipped to the British port of Harwich, along with five hundred other children. For six weeks, she stayed at a camp at Dovercourt Bay until placed in a foster home with a Jewish family who lived in Staffordshire, located in the West Midlands of England. When she entered her new home, a two-bed cottage on Norton Lane in Norton Le Moors, in her possession were clothes and toiletries, issued to each child by The Central British Fund for German Jewry. She also had a copy of *Mein Kampf* and a stuffed bear hidden among her possessions, and she clutched a pillowcase she refused to let out of her sight. In the pillowcase, carefully wrapped and protected by towels, were four twelve-inch-high glass carousel horses that rotated on a platform as Mozart's "Requiem Mass in D Minor" played.

Wil, along with one hundred other children, began a new life in Holland.

# CHAPTER FIFTY-ONE
# MICHAEL

SOLDIER BOY AND I were in Ruby's room, the Forbidden Room. The old man had again fainted so we brought him to bed where he rested, eyes closed. He sagged on top of the blanket, his frame paper-thin. Dark blue veins and purple and black bruises crisscrossed his skin like an aerial view of highways and byways. His calves and feet swelled. Pill bottles were upended on his side table. The room smelled medicinal. A metal garbage pail was next to his bed.

I glowered at Soldier Boy. "What was Billy O'Brien doing here? And don't give me you're hiring-a-landscaper bullshit."

"Let's talk elsewhere." Soldier Boy shushed me and nodded toward Ruby.

"I'm not dead yet." Ruby opened his eyes. "Better stay here. You boys need a referee."

Soldier Boy sat heavily on the corner of Ruby's bed. The mattress sagged under his bulk. I leaned against the wall near the five-tiered glass case, viscerally aware of the carousel horses on the top shelf, the copy of *Mein Kampf* in the middle, and the bowler hat on the bottom.

"I've known Billy a long time," Soldier Boy began. "Since after my parents' deaths. We went to school together. How do you know him?"

"Same, sort of. We grew up a few houses down from each other. I looked out for him, that's what friends did for each other." I emphasized the last part and hoped Soldier Boy got the dig.

"You and I are not friends. Don't think we have any connection other than you were Sara's attorney, past tense. And that's it."

"I was her boyfriend too," I corrected, although I wished I could take it back since it sounded juvenile. I shifted my position against the wall. "I'm good with that, man. I know we're not friends." I hoped I sold my sudden too-cool-for-school exterior vibe, while inside I trembled, not from nerves, but from frustration. There were other places I preferred to be, like with Elizabeth. I thought of her body, her bed. *Soon, Tucker. You'll be with her soon.*

From my vantage, I assessed the escape routes out of the room. There was one window, but we were on the second floor. If I jumped, I'd be sure to break a leg, maybe both, from the fall. Otherwise, there was the door. If I needed to make a run for it, Ruby would be no issue. His eyes were heavy and he fought to stay awake, and he was almost a century in age. He was substantially weakened since I last saw him and would in no way have the gumption to stop me, but for me to escape the room I'd have to pass Soldier Boy. I thought to be concerned, maybe scared, but frankly I had enough of the game playing. I needed to know what he knew about Uncle Charlie's murder, what Ruby had told him to share with me, and then I needed to be done with this family, forever. I was over the Goldstein clan. Good riddance to them all.

I thought of Sara, of never seeing her again, never holding her in my arms. A twinge seized my heart.

*Don't think about Sara, Tucker. Get the info you need to get yourself out of this lawsuit, pass it on to Erica, and be done.*

"Tell him." Ruby's voice held none of the command of the man I met the day before. It was amazing how much had occurred in the last twenty-four hours.

"Tell him what?" Soldier Boy twisted his upper body toward his uncle.

"Tell him about Billy. Tell him the truth."

"Why, Uncle Ruby? Who is this guy? Why should we tell him anything?"

"He's going to help Sara."

Soldier Boy's voice raised. "No, he's not. He only wants to help himself."

I watched the door; maybe I would need that escape route. If I couldn't make it to the door, I could jump out the window. Broken legs were enviable over the result of Soldier Boy's wrath.

"He wants to do more than help himself," Ruby said of me.

I had enough of this conversation as if I weren't in the room.

"How do you know?" I snapped.

He gathered strength to explain. "You think you're here to ask David for his help to defend you against Sara, but you know as well as I do that's not true." Ruby's breathing labored.

Soldier Boy eyed him and appeared as confused as I was. "Are you okay?"

Ruby gasped, his face blue. "Why would Davey or I ever help you hurt Sara? Was that ever a reasonable assumption on your part?"

Soldier Boy jumped up, and I flinched, unsure if he was coming at me. He didn't.

He went to his uncle and tenderly lifted him. "You'll breath better sitting up." Soldier Boy propped him against a pillow.

Slowly Ruby raised his hand to his nephew's face and gently cupped his cheek. "You've always been a good boy."

"I love you too, *Feter.*"

A big smile graced the old man's face. I didn't know what *Feter* meant, or what language it was, but it had to be a term of endearment as it brought Ruby happiness.

Ruby took deep, slow breaths and normalcy returned to his skin tone. Soldier Boy helped him lie down and covered him with the blanket. Ruby closed his eyes and fell asleep.

Soldier Boy motioned me out of the room. I couldn't stand in the corner all night, so I followed, prepared to be side-cocked as I exited.

I followed him down the hallway where he paused at a door at the top of the stairs. He opened it, looked at me, and waited for my reaction.

I stated the obvious. "It's a linen closet."

"This is where Sara and I used to hide when we were kids and our parents fought."

I had heard the stories from Sara, including the one when they thought their mother was going to hurt them so they ran and, for the first time, entered the Forbidden Room and rode the horses.

The muscles on Soldier Boy's neck tensed. "You're a fucking idiot to think I'd help you with anything that could hurt my sister. She's protected me my entire life. Without her, I am nothing. Leave my family alone. You've done enough damage."

I thought again of Gram's saying, "It's not the mistake you make that's important but the choice you make after." I needed to make a good decision, and I needed Gram to be proud of me, even from the great beyond.

Soldier Boy stepped toward me, his fists balled. The Semper Fi tattoo on his bicep bulged. Red was the color of the fury in his eyes. "I'm going to tell you once. Leave now. You don't want to end up like Uncle Charlie, do you?"

The road forked in front of me. Go, or take advantage of this moment to discover the truth, what I've battled to learn since I first saw Sara on the Long Island Railroad, from the day we met and I gave her my sneakers.

Soldier Boy lunged toward me. He was fast. I closed my eyes and raised my arms to protect my face.

I had been in two fights before. The first occurred when I was in elementary school during a kickball game when the other guy, who was a grade ahead of me, got pissed when I called him out for cheating. Kid ended up with my two front teeth imbedded in his knuckles. The other time was a few years ago when I had a fistfight with Sara's ex-boyfriend. Somehow I ended up on the winning side of that fight and broke his nose. If I did that much damage with a single crack, I imagined one punch from Soldier Boy would put me in the hospital, unless he threw me down the stairs then I'd be in the morgue.

No jolt connected. Soldier Boy's breath blew heavy on my face. I opened my eyes. We were nose to nose. His breath smelled musky, the smell of rage if it had an odor.

I wiped sweat from my forehead and spoke as fast as I could while being comprehensible. "I never expected you to help defend me against Sara. It was idiotic to think you ever would." I didn't want to blather but that's exactly what I did.

He took a half step back. "Go on."

I craved distance between us. I stepped away. I didn't think, didn't plan my words. My confession came fast, thoughts I hadn't even known I suffered. "I didn't think Sara killed Uncle Charlie when we first met. I mean, she was beautiful and kind and I couldn't imagine her a murderer." The words tumbled out, end over end. "But then, as the trial approached, I had doubts about her innocence."

My legs felt weak. I sat on the top step. Soldier Boy loomed over me.

"By the end of the trial," I continued, "I thought she had done it for sure, she had killed Uncle Charlie. She was mysterious about everything. She wouldn't let me talk to you. She wouldn't let me force Blanca to prove she was at her sister's house the night he was killed. Sara was evasive. She tied my hands. I did all I could. Gram knew you were the key." I looked up at him. "I saw you coming out of Gram's hospital room before she died."

He sat next to me. I tensed, and then relaxed when I noticed tears in his eyes.

"Gertrude was a special lady," he said. "I knew her a short time, but wow."

"I know what you mean."

I thought of how gentle Soldier Boy was with Ruby and imagined him acting the same way with my grandmother.

"Thanks for taking such good care of Gram. I know you took her to the hospital." I added on a whim, "For a jarhead, you're good with the elderly."

Fear bulged within me. *Have I insulted him? Was that the totally wrong thing to say to a marine?*

A smile graced his lips. "I joined the Marines right after high school. Never went to college. I start Columbia next semester. I'm going to study nursing and specialize in geriatric care."

"You'll be a star, I'm sure. You're going to help a lot of people."

"Not if I'm in prison for murder."

I stiffened, unsure if that was his confession. Seated shoulder to shoulder with a potential murderer on the steps, nervousness overtook me again. *Did I want to hear his admission of guilt seated so close? What if he confessed and then decided to get rid of the evidence, me?* I squirmed.

He put a strong hand on my forearm. "I didn't do it. Neither did Sara."

"Why would she take the blame?"

"She thinks I killed him. She's protecting me like she's done since we were little."

"Did you tell her it wasn't you?"

"Of course I did. She told me to prove it. She told me to tell her who did it."

"Do you know—"?

"I can't tell her." He removed his grip on my arm and left behind white imprints of his fingers on my skin.

"Why not?"

"What's the use anyway? She wouldn't believe me. She's convinced I killed him to avenge our parents' deaths."

"And you didn't?"

"No, no, of course not."

"But somebody did. Who? We need to go to the police. We need to tell them so Sara can go free."

He looked at me hard. "You are still in love with her."

"No," I protested, "I'm seeing someone. As Sara's attorney, if she's not guilty I'd want to try and get her sentence reversed and, Soldier Boy…" His eyes widened with disapproval and I realized I crossed a boundary he didn't want traversed. I started again. "David, if you know who the murderer is and he's free while Sara is incarcerated for life, you have to tell the police."

He looked away and toward the open door to the linen closet. He probably imagined himself in that closet as a little boy hearing their parents fight, the shattering of glass, the threats, recalling Sara grabbing him and leading him to the Forbidden Room, and riding the horses.

I jumped up. "Come with me."

"Where?" he asked.

"You trusted my grandmother, right?"

"Implicitly."

"Then trust me."

I ran down the hall and hoped Soldier Boy followed.

# CHAPTER FIFTY-TWO
## MICHAEL

LIKE THE LOST boys of *Peter Pan*, we soared over Manhattan. It was a New York I barely recognized. The city I knew, with my law office building standing tall in midtown, where I tried Sara's case in the courthouse on Centre Street, where Gram died at Beth Israel Hospital on the lower east side, was there but not in the forms I knew them to be, and that's because this wasn't the present day. It was 1938, and below me everything rolled in black and white like an old newsreel.

I rode the white Arabian, Soldier Boy sat atop the palomino, and Uncle Ruby took flight on the chocolate bay. The spotted appaloosa flew behind us, Sara in saddle.

JM Barrie was wrong. There are lost girls, and Sara was their captain.

Ruby pointed downward toward a street on the upper eastside. "That's where I first became acquainted with Bugsy Siegel and Alfonso Carrara. Meyer Lansky introduced us. Five minutes later we were breaking heads of Brownshirts. I didn't know it then, but those were some of the worst days of my life, 'cause my family was in trouble in Vienna and I couldn't help them, but those days were also the best too. Hanging with gangsters was dangerous stuff, but they became family."

We flew north through Yorkville, along the Hudson River and over Gracie Mansion.

"Follow me," Ruby said.

We lined up behind Ruby, who dipped and soared through the clear blue sky. He looked to be the same centenarian who was mostly confined to his bed now, emaciated, bruised and weak, but his mind and spirit were of the young man he used to be. I happily got in line behind him, eager to find out where he headed. Soldier Boy and Sara followed too.

"There." He pointed.

The Arabian I was atop dove toward the street level until I was able to gander what Ruby wanted us to see. Tall and buxom, her legs were long and toned, her back straight, and her head held high.

"That's Dixie Lee." Ruby jumped off the bay and glided until he landed on the street next to the showgirl. He took her hand and walked proudly by her side. Dixie didn't notice, nor did any of the passersby.

The riderless bay hovered as we waited for Ruby to relish his moment. Below, hand-in-hand, Ruby and Dixie stopped at a cross street. Ruby kissed her on the cheek and watched her walk away. He rejoined us and mounted the bay with ease.

"After she was attacked, she didn't return to the stage. She started an agency that counseled abused women. She rejected my marriage proposals, she never married, but we were friends for life. She died of ovarian cancer in nineteen sixty. I was by her side." He wiped tears off his cheeks.

We rode silently, and then I looked at Sara. "Where would you like to go?"

"Can I change the past?" she inquired.

I shook my head. This was my dream, my rules. It was one thing to relive former days; it was another to awake and expect the present to be different. Despite what happened in my mind, when the day dawned, Ruby would be dying from cancer, Elizabeth would have used me, Soldier Boy would hate me, Sara would be imprisoned and I would seek ways to set her free.

And I would wish Gram were alive.

Framed by the azure sky, Sara hovered on the Appaloosa, her tears evident. "If I can't change the past, then I'll stay right here."

"Not an option," I said.

"How come?"

I hopped off the Arabian and sat behind her on the appaloosa's back. My arms encircled her waist. "Because this isn't real."

"Make it real," she pleaded.

❧ ◆ ☙

I gingerly held the carousel, the four glass horses atop the platform. Ruby snored.

"What?" Impatient, Soldier Boy stood by the door.

One by one I took the horses off the platform and laid them on their sides on the top shelf of the glass cabinet. I turned the base over and read, "Oskar Glasman Gloggnitz Austria 1791."

"Yeah. So?" He stepped into the room, his sour mood returned.

"As far as I can tell, we have two mysteries that need to be solved."

"Okay, Sherlock. I'm listening."

"Who is Oskar and what is it about the carousel horses that—"

"Make us loony?"

"What is it about them that make us free? And how'd they get that way?"

Soldier Boy joined me near the shelves, the glimmer of a little boy in his eyes. "When Sara and I rode the horses, no one could hurt us."

I knew the feeling, had experienced it several times with Sara, although in a different, sensual way. I thought best not to share that information with Soldier Boy, especially as he stood close to me.

"And the second mystery?"

I frowned. He knew it well.

He shook his head. "I know Ruby wants me to tell you everything, but I don't know if I should."

I took the Arabian from the shelf and held it out to him.

He hesitated and then opened his fingers.

I placed the glass figurine in his flat palm. "For Sara," I said. "For you, for Ruby, and for me. Set us free."

# CHAPTER FIFTY-THREE
## MICHAEL

"WHY DO YOU have a copy of *Mein Kampf*?" I asked.

Ruby sat up in bed. Soldier Boy had gone to the kitchen to fetch him a cup of chicken broth. Solider Boy was happy to have a break from me, I'm sure.

Ruby shook a crooked finger. "One must never forget what Hitler did. Liana stole the book from a Bavarian woman. When she gave it to me, that's what she said. Never forget."

"That's a hell of a reminder." I peered in at the worn, bound volume on the glass shelf. The book was the size of a paperback novel, about five by seven inches. On the cover, the sight of Hitler's menacing glower, comb-over hair, and small moustache nauseated me.

"A couple of years ago a signed original of the book sold at auction for almost sixty-five thousand dollars," Ruby said.

"How much is this one worth?" I asked.

"Financially, not much. It's not signed, and almost eight million copies were printed before his death."

"May I?" I reached toward the book.

"Sure."

I carefully took out the volume and inspected the blue linen cover and the dust cover. I examined the photo of one of the worst mass murderers in history. Questions abounded. How could one man lead the eradication of six million Jews and thousands of non-Jews based on his perverted logic to form an Aryan race? How did he organize the destruction of homes and land, of historical landmarks and invaluable art across Europe? Why hadn't the United States stepped in earlier to help?

Soldier Boy walked in and carried a steaming mug. He handed it to Ruby, who wrapped his twig-like fingers around the handle. The former Marine then eyed me like I had committed a war crime. Ruby concentrated on his meal and didn't notice the icicles that darted from Soldier Boy's stare. I realized Soldier Boy glared at the book, not at me.

Ruby inhaled the steam from the soup. "The first edition since Hitler's death was reprinted this year in Germany. Its copyright expired after seventy years. I read it's flying off the shelves in Germany, and they're going to print it in other languages, including English."

"What year is this one from?" I opened the front cover and answered my question. "Nineteen thirty-three."

"Give me that." Soldier Boy reached to take the book from me.

Instinctively I hauled it into my body like a basketball player who protected the ball.

"Be careful," Ruby warned.

Soldier Boy turned toward his uncle. "You need to get rid of that thing."

"Why?" I asked.

"Because of what it represents. We don't need negativity in our house. I've told him that for years."

"For years?" I questioned.

I didn't mention Uncle Charlie had been murdered in this room, and what could be more negative than that?

"I've told him to get rid of that stupid book since he first started living with us, like ten years ago."

I looked at Ruby quizzically. "You've lived here that long?"

Soldier Boy answered. "Sara and I weren't going to let him go to a nursing home."

"If he's been here that long…" I searched to organize my thoughts, and then looked at Ruby. "How come I didn't know you when I was Sara's attorney? That was only a few of years ago. I'd been to the house many times and never saw you. And this wasn't your room, it was the Forbidden Room."

I recalled how the room was back then, the carousel horses on a stand, a couch, the Lionel trains. I shook my head to eliminate the image of Sara and me making love in the room.

"This wasn't his room then." Soldier Boy's voice weakened as if he realized he had been caught.

"That explains the room, but not why we never met," I ventured, trying to contain the attorney in me. I badly wanted to go into cross-examination mode but decided to abide by the adage about attracting more bees with honey.

"Um," Soldier Boy said, "he was away then, visiting relatives."

"Like Blanca who supposedly was at her sister's house the night Uncle Charlie was killed?" I hoped my voice came out more sarcastic than I intended.

"Tell him the Goddamn truth already." Ruby yelled, his face red. His hands shook and broth splashed out of the mug.

I was stunned by his outburst and didn't spot Soldier Boy lunging toward me until he was upon me. He grabbed the book and then retreated across the room. Ruby's bed separated us.

"What the f…" I swallowed the profanity out of respect for Ruby.

"Fuck, fuck, fuck," Ruby screamed. "I've heard the fucking word before." He wheezed.

Soldier Boy opened the drawer of the table next to Ruby's bed, grabbed matches, lit one, and held it under *Mein Kampf.*

Ruby reached toward him. "Don't."

"This man murdered our family. This is not a collector's item."

Ruby put the mug down on the blanket. It toppled over, and the broth spilled out. "I don't have it to remember Hitler."

"Then what's it for?" I asked.

"To remember Liana. Other than the carousel horses, it's the only thing I have from her. When she came to America, I met her at Ellis Island."

"She had the book with her?" I asked.

"The book, the carousel horses, and the clothes on her back. She swiped the book before she and Wil escaped."

"Who's Wil?" It was a name I hadn't heard.

"Wilhelm Goldenstein," Ruby said.

"Goldenstein?" I asked.

"He changed it to Goldstein when he arrived in America."

I looked to Soldier Boy. "Your grandfather?"

He nodded. The match under the book extinguished.

"Was Wil with Liana when she arrived in America?" I asked.

Ruby shook his head. "Liana escaped Austria into London through the *Kindertransport*. Wil was rescued and taken to Holland. They didn't reunite until Wil came to America in nineteen fifty-five, seventeen years after *Kristallnacht*. They were married one year later. Stevie was born in fifty-eight, three months after Wil died." He looked at me. "Stevie was Sara and David's father."

I nodded. That much I knew.

"How did Wil die?"

"Car accident, he died instantly. Liana was pregnant with Stevie at the time, and it was hard." He shook his head. "Wil and Liana had a beautiful romance, reminded me of Dixie and me. I mean, if Dixie had fallen in love with me." He laughed at the ridiculousness of his statement. "Wil's death devastated Liana. I tried to be supportive, but I guess it was all too much, losing her family, and then losing Wil. Alcohol became her baby, even after Stevie's birth."

"You should incinerate the motherfucker." Soldier Boy tossed the book on to table. "Burning the book won't erase your memories of her."

Ruby took the paperback and shuffled through its yellowed pages. His eyes misted and then seemed to clear. He seized the matches, lit one, and put it under the paper.

The flame lapped and slowly digested the pages. White smoke curled into the air until the bottom half of the book was afire. The blaze grew dangerously close to Ruby's fingers. I grabbed the metal garbage pail and held it out. When Ruby's fingers began to singe from the heat, he dumped the book into the can.

*Mein Kampf* burned.

## CHAPTER FIFTY-FOUR
## MICHAEL

WHILE *MEIN KAMPF* smoldered I received a text from Elizabeth.

"Are you on your way? I had to run out. Be back soon. Key is in flowerpot by front door."

I wanted to see her. I needed her to get Sara out of my mind, to get Soldier Boy out of my head, and to be rid of the Goldstein family.

I looked at Ruby and tried not to sound impatient. "I'm ready."

"But I'm not." Soldier Boy walked to the window and glanced out.

I began to think Sara's jailhouse remarks three years before that Soldier Boy had murdered Uncle Charlie was about to be verified, and Soldier Boy was understandably conflicted by that truth coming out. He dug into his pocket, took out a twenty-dollar bill, and extended it toward me.

"What's that for?" I asked.

"I'm retaining you as our attorney."

I eyed the Jackson. "Whatever you tell me I can't reveal because of attorney-client privilege."

"Go on," Ruby encouraged. "Take it."

"It's the only way we're going to tell you anything," Soldier Boy said.

"But what about Sara? If she didn't murder Charlie—"

"Take the fucking bill," Ruby barked.

My hand shot out and my fingers wrapped around the twenty.

"Good." Ruby rested his head against a pillow on the bed. "Go ahead," Ruby urged Soldier Boy.

Finally. Soldier Boy moved his mouth to speak, but then looked to the glass shelves. I followed his gaze. The horses were there, along with old family photographs and the black bowler. Partially burned Shabbat candles occupied the shelf where *Mein Kampf* used to be. The history was no doubt significant, magical, and taunting. The horses Liana brought with her from Vienna held an unknown seductive and treacherous secret. The photos of her family and of Dixie Lee were ghosts of the past. The Charlie Chaplin hat represented Ruby's dreams to make it in vaudeville, only to have those aspirations pushed aside to become one of Meyer Lansky's most trusted advisors.

"The answer isn't in the horses," Ruby said, "or in the photographs or anywhere in the past. The answer is here, in this room."

"Sara didn't murder Charles," Soldier Boy said.

"Who did?" I asked.

"It was me," Soldier Boy said.

"He's lying," Ruby voiced. "Don't listen to him. I did it."

# CHAPTER FIFTY-FIVE
## MICHAEL

I PARKED GRAM'S Mustang in the lot of Elizabeth's condo and reeled from the account Ruby and Soldier Boy had told of Charles's murder. For several minutes, Ruby and Soldier Boy squabbled like schoolboys over the confession. As I watched, more bystander than participant, I was unsure why either would want to take credit. The story then unfolded. I was prepared to call Trace in the morning to let him know what I had learned. Ruby and Soldier Boy had given me permission; we all felt optimistic the new information would lead to Sara's release.

I looked up and was glad to see the light of Elizabeth's condo on. Wherever she had run, she was back. She buzzed me in, and I took the stairs two at a time. My heart pounded from excitement, confident Elizabeth and I had the start of a promising relationship. Sara might get out of prison, which meant she would drop her lawsuit against me. With Elizabeth's help I could move on from Sara.

Elizabeth greeted me at her apartment door with a wet kiss. She took my hand and led me to the living room couch.

"I have to tell you something."

*Oh no,* I thought. *Was I already getting the send-off?*

She sat, and pulled me down next to her.

"You might not want to see me again after you hear this," she said.

"This doesn't sound good." I removed my hand from hers.

"I'm not who you think I am."

"Who do I think you are?"

"What I meant was, I am not who I told you I am."

"You're not Elizabeth Innis, paralegal?" My eyebrows scrunched.

She shook her head. "I'm Elizabeth Trautman, private investigator."

It took a few seconds for those five words to sink in. When they did, I jumped up and headed for the door.

"Wait. Please."

I stopped, my hand short of the knob. I kept my back to her.

"I'm sorry," she said.

I reached to open the door. Sorry was definitely not going to be enough. Nothing she could say would. I breathed heavily; shock consumed me.

"I saw Sara tonight." She spoke quickly. "That's where I had to go."

"Your last name is Trautman?"

"Glen Trautman is my father. Trace is my half-brother."

I was about to leave, this time for real, but I thought of something important, something I had to know. "Did Sara approve of you sleeping with me to get information on her case?"

"Yes. I mean no. She reluctantly approved of the undercover assignment. But she never thought…"

Slowly, my realization of how I had been taken came together. "When I texted Soldier Boy to meet me at McCluskey's, he passed the information on to you. That's how you knew I was at the bar. When you said your last name was Innis, a brand of beer, I should have known. I'm an idiot."

Her silence validation, the full weight of what Elizabeth had done, what Sara agreed she could do, of how I had been foolish again, gnawed at my stomach. Sickened, my anger grew.

"Did Sara approve of the lengths you went to do your job?"

"Definitely not." She stepped toward me but I raised my hand to stop her.

She looked down, and then at me. "What you and I did wasn't about my job. I mean, it started as an assignment, but Michael, I care about you."

I didn't want to hear it. Nothing she said could be trusted. "You're good at your job, Ms. Trautman." I scoffed and turned to leave.

"Please. Don't go. We can work this out. I know we can."

"I hope you got the information you needed to help Sara. What else did she consent for you and your firm to do when you met with her this evening? Maybe follow my parents or put a GPS on my cat?"

"Sara fired us."

I let that sink in. "Good. One final question, did you go to Reinhard Elementary?"

"Newbridge Road School."

I slammed the door and seethed as I ran for the stairs.

# CHAPTER FIFTY-SIX
## MICHAEL

"DAMN IT." I slammed my fists on the steering wheel of the Mustang.

Elizabeth watched from her window, but I didn't care. As I fumed, I received a text from Erica.

"Tish couldn't find any paralegal named Elizabeth Innis."

I threw my phone on to the passenger seat. "Too fucking late."

I was done with women, just like I had promised Cardozo a few days ago in my apartment. I couldn't trust them, and I was finished being a lawyer too. What a horrible profession I was engaged in, where a firm would stoop so low to have me followed and where they would permit their P.I. to have sex with me to get information. I tried to recall what I had told Elizabeth about my investigation outside of what had been reported in the newspapers or on the Internet. Although my rage was clear and my thinking was fuzzy, I knew I had said too much, including my plans to meet Soldier Boy and Ruby and to ask Soldier Boy for help. What did it matter anyway? I was supposed to call Trace in the morning to tell him everything I had learned but with his firm fired who would I call? Should I go see Sara? How would I face her? Should I give the information to Erica and let her present it to the district attorney's office? Or should I do nothing, bury it? That was what Sara wanted anyway, to protect Soldier Boy. If I told what I knew, Soldier Boy could be implicated, although not in the way I had thought. He hadn't killed Uncle Charlie, and neither had Sara. The real murderer, according to what Ruby and Soldier Boy had told me, was out there, free. The information I had could free Sara, but could also bring Soldier Boy down. Was I okay with that?

I started the Mustang and drove. One o'clock in the morning, I didn't know where I would go and I didn't care. With the roar of the eight-cylinder engine, my arm out the driver's window, and the wind blowing on my face, everything came to me in flashes of euphoria and regret, seeing Sara on the train for the first time, the glory of trial preparation with Gram, Gram's death, the guilty verdict, and Sara's accusations against me.

The biggest memory of the carousel horses stuck in my head as I tooled along the winding roads, my foot heavy on the pedal.

"Idiot." I banged the steering wheel again.

The sharp horn blast startled me. I looked in the rearview mirror. Police lights whirred. I pulled over, and waited for the officer to approach my car. I wasn't in the mood for having to deal with a cop but I knew enough about criminal law that I couldn't act like I jerk; I had to do what he told me.

The officer shined his light, and I covered my eyes.

"Michael?" He shut the light off.

My eyes adjusted. "Major Higgins? What are you doing giving tickets?"

"I normally don't, but you were driving so fast I thought you'd hurt yourself or someone else."

"I'm sorry. It's been a rough few weeks."

"I was going to call you in the morning. Billy O'Brien is the suspect in several murders but no one has enough to bring him in."

I wasn't in the mood to mince words with him. "I know who murdered Charles Carrara."

# CHAPTER FIFTY-SEVEN
## RUBY
## CHARLES'S MURDER
## SEPTEMBER 1, 2012

THOSE STUPID KIDS didn't know what they were doing, especially David. He claimed it was his idea, but he never had the organic ruthlessness that flowed through Sara's blood, which was ironic since Davey was the Marine and Sara was the schoolteacher. You'd think he would have killer in his veins and not her.

David insisted on taking credit for the plan. I guess he felt less of a man, not having exacted revenge for the murder of his parents. We all knew Charles had done it. Sara said she saw him but never told the police, and we had no reason to doubt her. David even said he saw a man running out the back door. I attributed their not telling the police to their being young, scared, and in shock.

I've seen my share of murder, that guy on the subway grate during the Depression that I probably offed, the member of the American Bund that Meyer slammed his head into the sidewalk, and during that Brownshirt rally in Yorkville in thirty-eight when two Nazi sympathizers had their skulls crushed. I never had a hard time adjusting to the gore. Meyer must have sensed it, because it wasn't long after we met that he told me I was ready for my first assignment, a kid about my age who nosed around Meyer's territory.

I didn't kill that kid but I could have. I made him an offer he couldn't refuse and he was never heard from again. If he had reneged on our agreement, I would have put a bullet in his brain.

When I came to America from Austria, I was a vaudeville man, a song-and-dance man, but it didn't take long for me to become something else. The times required it. Those mafia guys were bright, especially Meyer. I was dedicated to Meyer, not only because he saved me at a time when I needed saving, but also because he became my surrogate family when my real family was shattered. Loyalty ran deep, as deep as family, and it came with a price.

Meyer eventually found an advantageous spot as the mobs' accountant, and I began to work for Alfonso Carrara in the hotel business. I was with Meyer on January 15, 1983, when he died in Miami. Three months later, I was by Alfonso's bedside when he passed in New York. During those first few months of 1983, I lost my best friends and ended my association with organized crime.

I never forgot the lesson of family first.

I was never a fan of Charles Carrara. I thought he was a *meshugener,* a crazy man. I knew a lot of smart, wild men in my lifetime, but Charles was the worst kind of crazy in that he wasn't bright. He was a *schmendrick,* stupid. He got by because Alfonso was his older brother and because he was too dumb to know when to be scared and back away. He became one of the wealthiest men in New York by pure luck, nothing more.

Alfonso never would have dreamed of all the events to take place after his death: Stephen and Cassandra's murders, Charles running Rest Well Inc. and shutting Sara and David out, and Charles's murder. Alfonso would have ordered Charles's murder from his grave, if he could have, so in my rationalization, I did what Alfonso would have done. I put family first. I shot Charles in the Forbidden Room.

I know Billy told Davey to do it in the woods, and he was right, but most of the time things don't go as planned. When Davey told me the how-to advice he had gotten from Billy, I was upset at first. I could have told him how it was done. I was an old man at the time, true, but I had my mind and the strength and dexterity to shoot a gun, but above all, I didn't like involving a non-family member. As it ended up, it was the best thing David could have done.

Let me tell you what I know. David and Charles were in the Forbidden Room, not yet my bedroom, when I walked in. David pointed a gun at Charles. The carousel horses and the Lionel train set were behind them.

"Where's Sara?" I asked.

"Not here."

I later learned Sara was at a Casablanca film festival.

"Tell him to put down the gun." Charles looked cocky, almost relaxed, as if he held the weapon.

"Put it down," I said. "This isn't the answer."

David's hand shook. "He has to pay."

"Pay for what?" Charles asked. I think a twinge of fear crept into his voice.

"You murdered my mother and father."

Charles let out a sardonic laugh. "I was cleared years ago."

"Consider this your judgment day," David said.

Charles looked to me. "Ruby, tell the boy to stop with this nonsense."

"Put it down," I said.

David's voice was weak. "What about my father? My mother?"

I thought of Stephen, my great nephew who was Liana and Wil's son. Memories of my sister Amalie, her husband Jacob, and their other children, Siegfried and Renate, flashed in my mind, along with images of *Kristallnacht*, Hitler, and the death camps. And then there was Cassandra, the daughter of Alfonso and his young, second wife, Sophia.

"Give me the gun," I ordered Davey.

Slowly, reluctantly, he handed it to me.

I pointed the gun at Charles. "You're not a killer, David, but I am."

The trigger pull was easy, like the old days.

That's what happened, from my mouth to God's ears, but that's not what David and I told Michael.

When I told David to tell Michael everything, I never thought he'd take the blame.

"Sara didn't murder Charles," Soldier Boy had said.

"Who did?" Michael asked.

"It was me," Soldier Boy said.

"He's lying," I voiced. "Don't listen to him. I did it."

I wasn't going to let Davey take the fall for me, but then I came up with a plan I was certain would work. All I had to do was make an offer that couldn't be refused.

## CHAPTER FIFTY-EIGHT
## BILLY O'BRIEN

DAVID AND I talked shortly before Sara's trial started. We were hanging out in the Village in Manhattan and it went something like this.

"What's it like to kill someone?" David asked.

"I don't know, man." At the time of this conversation, I told the truth. "You never killed anyone in the military?"

"No."

We walked toward Sixth Avenue. "I remember being in the car waiting for Slammer to get the cash so we could get out of there. I was only the driver, Dave. I swear I didn't know he had a gun. I looked through the window and watched him. I could see everything clear as day. It was dark outside but that store was lit up. When he took out a gun, I was shocked. I didn't do anything, though. I figured he knew what he was doing.

"And then I saw the flame from the gun and the smoke. It was like in slow motion. The man behind the counter looked surprised, like he hadn't gone to work expecting to get dead. He kind of crumpled, like a sack of shit, and he was a goner.

"Slammer got in the car and we drove off. I didn't say nothing about nothing because I knew he had the gun and there was nothing stopping him from using it on me. When the cop stopped us for the burned-out taillight, I knew it was all over."

"Think you could ever kill?" David asked. "I mean, actually point a gun at someone and fire?"

"I think about that store clerk all the time. I think what I could've done, but I guess it was fate. I mean, if I hadn't driven the car, another schmuck would've, but I helped end a man's life. He had kids. Unless your own life is threatened or there's good reason, no one has the right to kill anyone. It's like playing God."

Neither of us spoke about the murder of Charles Carrara.

Since that conversation with Davey, I murdered three men, all deserving crooks and creeps, but dead at my hand. The cops were wise to me and were trying to get me to become a confidential informant, which was a surefire way to a painful death if it came out I was a snitch. There was also a price on my head for a job I did. Some gang motherfuckers had ten large on the table for proof of my death. I was worth more dead than alive.

You know the other day when I was at David's house and Michael showed up? Do you remember? I wasn't there about a landscaping job. I was there because I was being shaken down, mafia style, by a pro. I was made an offer I couldn't refuse.

As I listened to Ruby explain most persuasively as to why I had to accept their generous offer, I considered I might spend the rest of my life in prison for a crime I hadn't committed, but I deserved doing time for ones I had. I knew I wasn't going to live much longer out on the streets anyway, not with the bounty on my head, and the cops were sure to corner me one day and force me into becoming a snitch. I was as good as dead.

I considered I could have my own gang in prison. I'm good at organizing people. I might not be a CEO on the outside, but I could be one on the inside.

Ruby promised to take care of my wife and daughter for the rest of their lives. No more roach-infested apartments or my wife giving head to the landlord. Say yes to a refrigerator filled with healthy food, fresh vegetables, and ripe fruits; say yes to dressers stacked and closets filled with clean clothes that fit; say yes to private school for my baby girl.

"If your little girl can get into Harvard, that's where she will go. Tuition fully paid," Ruby said.

As I've explained, and I hope you've listened, it was an offer I couldn't refuse.

# CHAPTER FIFTY-NINE
## MICHAEL

IN FRONT OF the Goldstein mansion, Major Kurt Higgins pushed Billy toward the patrol officer and car that waited. He threw him into the back seat and slammed the door, an exclamation point on Higgins' thirty-plus-year career with the Nassau County Police Department.

There was no celebration from Soldier Boy, Ruby, or me, although an upturn of the creased lines around Ruby's mouth suggested satisfaction. He held the Bowler hat, rolled it up and down his arm.

Higgins slapped the top of the patrol car, and walked to where we stood. He looked at me. "You won't have to worry about Billy anymore."

I was relieved, although I pitied the guy. I couldn't be certain but I had a feeling Billy hadn't killed Uncle Charlie. Like Sara, I wondered if Ruby and Soldier Boy were not reliable reporters, a quality that seemed to run in the family.

"Guess I can retire now," Major Higgins said.

I knew what he meant. In 1998 as a road patrol officer Higgins had been the first on the scene when Steven and Cassandra Goldstein were found murdered. In 2012, he was the lead detective investigating Uncle Charlie's murder. And now, four years later, he had arrested Uncle Charlie's true murderer, or he believed.

"If I never see another Goldstein again," Higgins said, "it won't be too long. This family has whipped my crime fighting ass." He looked at Soldier Boy. "No offense intended."

Soldier Boy glared, Higgins stared back.

I stepped forward. "A bad joke, David, that's all."

Soldier Boy walked into the house.

"What will happen with Sara?" Ruby asked.

I wanted to chime in. I was the lawyer, after all, and then I remembered I was a lawyer who no longer practiced law. I had completed my first week working at my dad's gas station, and even with the grease under my fingernails and the never-ending smell of oil on my skin; I'd loved every moment. Not just being close to Pops and getting to wear sneakers all the time, but also working with my hands. Concern over dirty spark plugs and temperamental radiators proved satisfying. I was glad to learn what Pops knew all along. You don't have to save the entire world all at once. One car and driver at a time would do.

I loved being in Dad's space, the mess of paperwork in his office, the photos of Mom and me crooked on the walls, along with his dusty civic awards and, recently added at Dad's insistence, my undergraduate and law school diplomas. When I agreed to partner with Dad in the gas station, I did so on the condition of one change: we'd computerize everything, from invoicing to maintaining an e-mail list of clients. After a slight amount of cajoling, Dad agreed; however, no matter what change I made, the office smelled like him, a combination of grease, oil, and Polo aftershave.

As I stood in front of Sara's house half listening to Higgins explain to Ruby how it was up to Sara's defense attorney to negotiate her release, I knew Gram would be proud of me. Maybe I wasn't made of the same stock as she was to be a successful lawyer, but at least I achieved what Gram wanted for me, to be happy.

"You arrested Charles's killer," Ruby wheezed. "Why isn't Sara being released right now? She didn't do it."

Higgins looked to me. "You want to explain?"

I could tell Ruby the state of New York would move slowly to release Sara to make sure it had everything covered. The state had to review the evidence against Billy and make sure it was satisfied Sara wasn't involved. Sara's new attorney would have to file a motion for Sara's release and for the charges to be dropped. Sara would get out, but not today and not tomorrow. I hoped soon.

I shook my head. No, I didn't want to explain. I liked my new, stress-free life.

Higgins reached out his hand to me, which I warmly took.

"You really retiring?" I asked.

He nodded. "You?"

"I'm taking over my dad's gas station."

"A long way from the courtroom."

"When you get tired of fishing every day, come see me about a job."

"I'll hold you to that."

He walked toward his unmarked car and drove away.

Ruby's grin outshone a forest of fireflies. "You're a good boy." He patted my cheek twice.

"Finish the story," I said.

"What story? I told you everything."

"You told me some of what happened to Liana, but what about the rest of your family?"

The skin on his face sagged, and his shoulders hunched. "The Germans kept impeccable records, that's how we're able to know so much. It wasn't Dixie's fault; she believed Madame Juliette was real. Turns out she didn't exist. A housewife in Brooklyn made her up.

"My brother-in-law Jacob and my nephew Siegfried died on the night of *Kristallnacht*. Amalie, my beautiful sister, was taken to Auschwitz and killed in the ovens in nineteen forty-three. Renate made it to an orphanage in Izieu, France, but the home was raided under the orders of Klaus Barbie in forty-four and the children were sent to Auschwitz, where they too were gassed."

The light in his eyes extinguished. His fingers clutched at the bowler.

"And Liana?" I asked gently.

A slight upturn graced his lips and a dim light shone in his eyes. "Liana was rescued by the Kindertransport and taken to Britain where she lived with a Jewish family and became a secretary. After the war she was able to secure transport to the States. The happiest day of my life was when she walked off that ship. It was late in forty-five and she was twenty years old, the most beautiful young woman I had ever seen, even more beautiful than my Dixie." He smiled sweetly. "When she got off that boat, she had the clothes she wore, *Mein Kampf,* and the horses.

"It was a miracle the horses made it. It's like they're not made only of glass. I don't think we'll ever know the full mystery of those horses, but they seemed to bring out the best and the worst in people. Liana was the one who told me that. I asked her why she didn't leave them behind or get rid of them. She said she couldn't. Her father had given them to her and it was the only keepsake she had of her family. She gave them to Steven, Sara and David's father, on his sixth birthday and told him the same thing Jacob had said to her, 'When you're with the horses, you're with me.'"

Ruby looked down, and then at me. His exhaustion was evident and he sat on the front stoop to the Long Island mansion. "Liana drank awfully hard. After Wil died, the stress was too much from all she had been through, and she was sad. I tried to help her.

"After Liana passed away," Ruby said, "I went home, to Vienna. It was the first time since I had left as a teen. Nothing was how I remembered. What was I expecting? Germany had bombed Vienna to pieces. It wasn't my home anymore. I didn't stay long. I couldn't. The memories, the losses, were horrific, so I went to Gloggnitz."

"Gloggnitz? Like the underside of the carousel?"

I recalled the inscription. Oskar Glasman Gloggnitz Austria 1791.

He nodded. "I wanted to find out the secret of the horses."

"And did you?"

He smiled. "I certainly did, but that's another story."

# CHAPTER SIXTY
## MICHAEL

I WAS ON Sara's jailhouse list as her attorney, an oversight or a deliberate move on her part, I didn't know. What I did know was, as I waited in the small room where attorneys and inmates convened, I was nervous. My foot tapped on the linoleum floor and my fingers drummed on the graffiti-scarred table.

*It's not like you're going on a first date, Tucker. Relax.*

I couldn't relax. I hadn't seen Sara in three years, although it was hard to believe so much time had passed when I've thought of her constantly. She stepped into the small, square room and my heart jumped like the first time I saw her on the Long Island Railroad.

In the room, she hesitated. Perhaps regrets filled her soul too, or maybe she simply despised me. Her actions against me suggested the latter, not love but loathing.

She sat across from me.

*Tell her you love her, Tucker.* I couldn't speak the words, and I couldn't look her in the eyes. She had murdered, not Uncle Charlie but she had killed a person, not any person, but her own mother. True Uncle Charlie fired the first shot that wounded Cassandra Goldstein, but fifteen-year-old Sara had finished the job when she realized her mother had shot her father.

There was no guarantee with what I'd collected to present to the district attorney, including Billy's arrest and confession for Uncle Charles's murder, that the state would dismiss the charges and set

Sara free. Doing so would require the prosecution to admit it had tried and jailed an innocent person, and had used taxpayers' money to do it. Of course I was the idiot who had been unable to get his guiltless client acquitted. That fact was sure to come out in the press and on the Internet once the charges were dismissed.

Thoughts bucked around my mind.

"Hi," she said.

I didn't speak; I looked down.

"Michael." She raised her voice enough to get my attention. "Look at me."

I did. My cheeks grew hot and I blushed, like a damn teenager. If Sara noticed, she didn't let on.

"You fired Trautman," I managed to say.

"I did."

"Are you dropping the lawsuit against me?"

"Yes."

"Have you hired a new attorney yet?"

She shook her head.

"I know the perfect lawyer to represent you."

She hesitated. "I don't think it's a good idea for you to represent me again."

I smiled. "I agree, one hundred percent. Anyway, I'm out of the law business."

"You are?"

I nodded.

"Then who do you think should be my attorney?"

"Erica," I said.

# CHAPTER SIXTY-ONE
# MICHAEL
# SIX MONTHS LATER

MOZART'S "REQUIEM MASS in D Minor" chimed and dread overcame me. I supposed this was Mozart's intent. The first chords were the melodious equivalent to *the end*. He had scored his own funeral march, dying before completion.

Like Mozart, Ruby had planned his funeral, not wanting Sara, Soldier Boy or me to be burdened by his demise. He never wanted to bother anyone while he was alive and did not want to be burdensome in death.

My cellphone vibrated and my hand shook as I accepted the call. Sara usually texted, but I knew what the call meant without hearing her words.

"He's gone." She either knew I would have no immediate response or she didn't need to hear it. She continued, "I'm waiting for you to get here before they move him. I want you to see how peaceful he is."

I knew Papa wouldn't mind if I took time off from the gas station to say my final good-bye to Ruby, so I told Sara I'd be there within thirty minutes, time enough for me to change out of my greasy coveralls and get to the house.

Driving Gram's Mustang, I was home within twenty-six minutes. I parked sideways in front of the mansion's double doors. A steel gray Hummer waited to the side of the driveway. Two men wearing black trousers, white shirts, and solemn looks stood nearby. My body hummed with vibrations of Ruby, ninety-seven years old; having left Vienna in time to avoid the horrors of the Holocaust; his attempts to get his family to America; all the stories about New York during the Depression, Meyer Lansky, and Bugsy Siegel; vaudeville; and the way he discovered what mattered in life, which was not being a famous song-and-dance man, but being the best uncle he could to Liana, and then the best great uncle to Sara, Soldier Boy, and yes, to me. I knew these past few months had been a gift to me and to Ruby. He had told me story after story about his life, his loves, and his losses.

Michael's Rule, to only represent innocent people, he told me, was *albern* in German, *narish* in Yiddish, *rubbish* in English.

"Life isn't black and white," he said. "It cannot be defined by good or evil, guilt or innocence. It's gray. That's Ruby's Rule. Revel in the gray."

I stepped out of the Mustang; the front door was ajar. I pushed my way in and headed toward Ruby's room, the Forbidden Room.

Sara met me under the doorjamb. The mezuzah sparkled above us.

"Look at him," she said. "Look at how peaceful he is."

Ruby lay on his side, his eyes three-quarters shut, his stiff body surrounded by the white sheets and bedspread Sara and I kept clean for him, sometimes doing up to seven loads of laundry a day. His face was relaxed. His mouth no longer opened in the silent, morphine-fueled scream that haunted him and us his final days.

"You're right. He looks amazing." I sat on the bed, rubbed his head, and kissed his forehead. I smiled through tears that welled and fell on my cheeks.

Sara sat next to me, her hand on my knee. "The nurse left about one hour ago. I think she knew. She bathed him, put him on his side, and sang to him the whole time. She even put a pillow between his legs the way he likes. I checked on him every few minutes. Last time I came in, he was gone." She choked up.

I rested my hand on hers.

"He didn't want me to be here when he died."

"Sounds like Ruby," I said. "Never a burden to anyone."

"I wish I could have convinced him he was no trouble at all. Look at all he's done for me, for us. I never would have known all about my family." She looked to his glass shelves. "I never would have been freed."

I followed her gaze to the twelve-inch glass carousel horses. Would we ever learn who Oskar was now Ruby was gone?

I looked at the engagement ring I had placed on Sara's finger two nights earlier, glad Ruby had been there to witness our engagement, glad he was now in his better place.

"Have you contacted Soldier Boy?" I asked.

"I left him a message and I texted him, but I don't know if he got it."

I wasn't surprised. Soldier Boy was known for his disappearing acts. He had been MIA since Billy's arrest for Uncle Charlie's murder.

"He'll be back." I intended for my words to soothe Sara, but we knew we might never see Soldier Boy again.

"Should I tell them it's time?" Sara looked at the body.

"Yes."

She left to get the undertakers.

I caressed Ruby's face again and Cardozo jumped onto my lap. I had spent so much time at Sara's house since her release from prison I had to bring my buddy over.

I kissed Ruby's cold forehead. "Meyer Lansky, Bugsy Siegel, and Alfonso Carrara never got the best of you. I'm not surprised Billy O'Brien didn't either. I know the truth, old man. As you always said, family comes before everything else."

I walked to the five-tiered shelf, took out the bowler hat and put it over his chest. I looked back to the glass cabinet where the carousel horses glistened, ready to take us on another ride.

THE END

# AUTHOR'S NOTE

*Forbidden Night*, book two of the Forbidden trilogy, is part murder mystery (a dead body + a crime to be solved = a murder mystery) and part historical fiction (a story told partially or wholly in the past that depicts real characters, events and settings mixed with fictional characters, events and settings). The historical part hopes to recreate the events of *Kristallnacht* in Vienna, as well as the atmosphere in New York and New Jersey around the same time. In doing so, I borrowed from real people, especially the Krochmal family. I wish to honor them in this novel and in this Author's Note.

The true story of the Krochmal family, to the best of my knowledge, is this:

Amalie and Jacob were born in Poland. They lived in Vienna with their three children, Siegfried, Renate and Liane. When the Germans took over Austria in 1938 the Krochmals escaped to France. Amalie and Jacob had an uncle in New York who was willing to guarantee the support of the family if the United States would permit them passage to America. Despite the uncle's promise, the United State's State Department refused the Krochmals permission.

French police arrested Amalie, Jacob, and Siegfried, who was eleven years old at the time, on September 16, 1942. The French turned them over to the Germans. Siegfried was shot and killed trying to escape and cross the Swiss border. Amalie and Jacob were murdered at Auschwitz.

Renate was seven years old and Liane was five when they were sent to live in Izieu, a children's home in France. On April 16, 1944, at the orders of Klaus Barbie, the girls were shipped to Auschwitz where they were sent to the gas chambers upon their arrivals.

The first Kindertransport (Children's transport) occurred on December 2, 1938 when approximately 200 children were brought from an orphanage in Berlin to Great Britain. The final rescue was

May 14, 1940 when children were transported from the Netherlands to Great Britain. In total, the rescue operation brought about 10,000 children from Germany, Austria, Czechoslovakia, and Poland to Great Britain, approximately 7,500 of these children were Jewish.

Auntie Truus was a real person who is credited with rescuing thousands of children from the Nazis.

I write of this in this Author's Note since Uncle Ruby was correct when he said, "we must never forget."

Joanne

# About the Author

Joanne Lewis is a writer and attorney living in Fort Lauderdale, Florida. She is the author of award-winning mystery and historical novels and novellas.

Please visit her website at www.joannelewiswrites.com and email her at jtawnylewis@gmail.com. She would love to hear from you.

If you enjoyed Forbidden Night, Book 2 of the Forbidden trilogy, please consider reading Joanne's other books:

Forbidden Room, Book 1 of the Forbidden trilogy

Forbidden Horses, Book 3 of the Forbidden trilogy

The Lantern, a Renaissance mystery

Make Your Own Luck, a Remy Summer Woods mystery

Wicked Good, co-written with Amy Lewis Faircloth

Michelangelo & Me Series:

Michelangelo & the Morgue (book 1 of 5),

Sleeping Cupid (book 2 of 5),

School of the World (book 3 of 5),

Space Between (book 4 of 5)

Michelangelo & Me (book 5 of 5)

I miss you, Pops.

www.ingramcontent.com/pod-product-compliance
Lightning Source LLC
Chambersburg PA
CBHW070843250626
47159CB00003B/904